Fragile Anthology

FRAGILE ANTHOLOGY

Edited by Michael Allen Rose

Cover design by Courtney Rader

Interior layout by Michael Allen Rose

Oak Park, IL

First Edition

ISBN: 979-8-8691-6875-7

Contents

Acknowledgements

Special thanks to Becky Spratford for her tireless promotional assistance and support, Amy Hofmockel for helping with the genesis and construction of the box and its contents, Sauda Namir for the loads of behind-the-scenes work she has done on this and many other publishing projects, Courtney Rader for her design work and assistance in all matters pertaining to creating this anthology, and everyone who supports independent literature.

Introduction

It all started with an unfinished story.

Something very unusual happened while I was working on my Patreon reward for the month of December 2023. Sometimes, when I'm deciding what to do for my patrons, I use something that already exists and lovingly create a new stand-alone edition of that work, whether it's a play, a short story, or a creative experiment. It's a fun way to share some of my previously published (or unpublished!) work with my fans and friends. Other times, I'll decide (as I did this time) to write something brand new for my patrons and that'll become a first draft. Sometimes that bears fruit later. Sometimes it's just a zine, standing on its own as a creative artifact. This time, it became something wholly other.

I had an idea for a short story about a guy working as an independent mover, carrying boxes into a client's home, alone at the end of the day, and one of the boxes… moves. He struggles with the ethical implications of opening it up, since that's against the mover's code, but his curiosity gets the best of him and finally he decides to open it, and things go haywire from there. This was the original idea for the story. As I was going through my options, I thought of a bunch of things that might be "in the box," but the more I thought about it, the less I wanted to decide and the more I wanted to turn it into an experimental piece. I was thinking of sending this out with 20 different "endings" that the reader could determine with the roll of a die. Maybe the protagonist would decide this ethical conundrum by flipping a coin. Or better yet, roll that very die in a meta-fictional stroke, to see whether he would open the box or not. Then I realized that would involve trying to write 20 different endings to a story, when coming up with one was hard enough.

Then I thought "hey, I wonder if the interest is there to do an anthology, just something fun to put out into the world and push with a bunch of my cool friends writing stories for it?" These could be more than one paragraph joke endings… this could be an amazing showcase of different styles tackling the same "opening/prompt." That seemed like a huge mountain to climb, but maybe, just *maybe*, I had built up enough cultural cachet to get a few authors interested in doing something with this. *Maybe* my long term strategy of "being a nice guy who is easy to work with" could pay dividends.

Cut to a few months later…

Get your D20 ready to roll and plunge in. I hope you find the reality you're looking for.

Love,

Michael Allen Rose – June 5, 2024

Prologue: Handle With Care

...and the die tumbles...

MICHAEL ALLEN ROSE

Something inside the box moved, which was impossible. It was impossible because, at the time, I had already set it down in the master bedroom, and was just pushing it into place beside the other boxes. It was just another moving box, a cardboard cube with a label in Sharpie that read "main bedroom" across the side, just under the "this side up" arrow. When I carried it in from the truck, it felt solid, packed so densely that nothing could slide or jostle. Probably a box stuffed full of thick comforters or blankets. So, I put it down with the rest, and just needed to bump it a couple of inches to make room for more boxes. But as I pushed it into place, something inside moved so suddenly that it pushed against the side of the box.

Freelancing as a house mover was usually backbreaking, but at least sometimes it was interesting. You get to see what people own, get some weird insight into their lives, it's a study of human nature as told through their possessions, what they choose to keep or discard. I'd started doing it during the last economic downturn, when a part time job wasn't enough to keep me afloat anymore, and I needed to find a new hustle to pay rent. I told myself it would be good exercise, get me outside, meeting people, good honest labor, set my own hours, all that good stuff. Most people were cool, and the work was straightforward, despite the occasional mattress stuck in a stairwell or a couch that pulled a back muscle.

Most of the time, the boxes, packed with any number of things, just stayed put, their contents inert. This one didn't. Whatever was inside it had moved under its own power. I thought about all the possibilities. It couldn't be a pet. There were no holes in the box, no slits, no noises, and besides, what kind of psychopath would put an animal in a cardboard box and leave it to the movers? Could be an electric toothbrush, or a sex toy accidentally come to life like an embarrassing Frankenstein. Maybe a kid's toy. Still, odd that it would choose that moment to turn on and flip out, especially without an accompanying light and sound show.

There was no need to expend any more thought or energy on a quirk of perception. I needed to save my energy for hauling boxes. Turning to leave the bedroom, I heard the shuffle of cardboard on wooden flooring and snapped back to look at the box. It had moved back to where I'd initially dropped it, gaslighting me out of my final efforts to nestle it beside its fellows.

Hour eight of an eight-hour moving day was always

tricky. Fueled by a thermos of black coffee and pockets full of granola bars, I was usually able to ignore the strain in my shoulders long enough to finish up, get tipped out, and arrive back home before collapsing into my couch. The mental strain wasn't usually a problem, but sometimes as the day wore on, the repetition put me in a zen state, a sort of unconscious momentum, where my body kept moving even as my mind took a vacation. Seeing boxes skitter across the floor was new; unusual at best, and somewhat troubling.

The contents of a client's boxes are none of my business. That's moving guy 101. Doesn't really matter what's packed or how, our job is just to move things from one room to another, get paid, and leave. People can pay extra to have us pack and secure their goods for them. Most don't. Most people want their privacy. Opening someone else's boxes without them present is the ultimate sin. You can get fired, blacklisted, sued, all sorts of things, if you trespass beyond that line of trust. So, I tamp down any burgeoning curiosity before it can take hold. None of my business. That's the mantra.

Something inside it shuffled like dry leaves. Only a second or two, a crackle, like something unfolding. That box. If there was an animal inside it, it probably wasn't happy. Maybe a rat had gotten in, but there were no holes chewed in the corners, and the tape was still perfectly sealed across the top flap. Whatever was moving had been placed inside and left there.

My partners had already taken off, so it was just me

finishing up the last few boxes, then I was responsible for taking the truck back to my place overnight. I'm a supervisor, so a lot of times I'll let the others head out and finish up a few last loads myself once we hit 8 hours. The company hates paying out overtime. I'm expected to gift them precious minutes of my life before and after that magic eight in exchange for a mediocre health plan and a desk. I have no problem with this arrangement, unless of course something strange happens and I need to consult my team. The clients were supposedly arriving tomorrow. They had pre-arranged a moving pod, and we were bonded and insured and trusted and all that jazz. So I couldn't even casually ask a household member what might be skittering around in there.

Turn the light off, leave the room, lock the door. Dump the last few boxes in the entryway. There was almost nothing left, ultimately it wouldn't matter if a few things were in the wrong rooms. Nothing was damaged. The clients would be happy. I needed to lock up, leave, and forget about this day, this place, and this box.

Scratches, like a small animal, like a kitten, gentle, small, barely noticeable, from inside the box, but inside the silence, it was impossible to ignore. Leave it to fate, then. I searched my pocket for a coin to flip, content to let the universe take the choice out of my hands. No luck. I would use the term "no dice," but that wouldn't be accurate, because there was a 20-sided die in my pocket from last night's game of D&D. Without really considering the parameters of my roll, evens or odds, highs or lows, or what any of it would mean, I flicked the die across the wooden floorboards.

And the die tumbles…

1

Because You're Mine

DAVID SCOTT HAY

I. Box

A natural 1.

Usually a disaster, but nothing was at stake here. Just the cat and its curiosity. (Remember: satisfaction brought it back.) I should have stopped there. I should have made a different decision. I should have accepted mystery. But this morning had inured me to critical thinking, the anathema of being a good cog.

The die don't lie.

I was in the garage now, hopefully hidden from any nanny-cams, as I sliced the twine-enforced tape on the short end of the box. The flaps tented a bit, freed from their shortened brethren, now just bound to their twin. I slit it open. Retracted the blade, set it down within easy reach, as if expecting Schrödinger's demon.

It was worse.

This motherfucking box was *empty.*

No ghost farts.

No trapped memories.

No priceless heirlooms.

No extortion material.

No Polaroids of ex-lovers.

No aborted suicide notes.

No Buffalo nickels.

There was nothing. There was nothing at all. Not even packing peanuts. Now don't get me wrong, I am prone to daydreaming, thinking of stories, songs, things that inspire me, to inspire someone else, to achieve a legacy (of some sort). Anything to make the day pass, though lately it had been a long cold winter of *what ifs.*

Especially with this morning's revelation.

What a kick in the Netherlands.

That being said, I checked other boxes on the truck, my box cutter as sharp as Excalibur. They too were empty. But they hadn't felt empty when I moved them. They hadn't felt as empty as myself when I started off my day at 7 a.m. to beat traffic. And my co-workers, how did they not notice? (At least, they hadn't mentioned the thing this morning. Maybe they sensed I needed my own space. For that I was grateful, but they'd taken off early. And were not returning texts at the moment.)

Ah, they're drinking already.

Box dust stuck to my contact lens, irritating my eyes. One popped out, but I was able to rescue it and clean it with a few tears.

Another bullshit day in the City of Big Shoulders.

The sad cry of a fiddle announced the arrival of Jack Spat. He crowed, "I slept with a one-legged woman last night…" His voice was a cross between a cough and a whisper without the sexiness of a cigarette or whiskey habit. I didn't look up, my eyes set on the original empty box, waiting for an ambush. As he finished the jig, a few loose strings floated from his bow, like streamers on old-school bicycle handles.

I hoped he wasn't going to bring up this morning, *the* song.

Jack eased himself onto the back edge of the box truck, leaving me plenty of easement. He cased his fiddle. You couldn't tell if he was a hipster, huckster, or trust-fund baby. But you couldn't hate him, even if his hair was as perfect as a werewolf's. Near the end of Happy Hour, he might claim to have more talent in his pinky than any opening act in town, but he wasn't weighed down like others, or myself.

"I fiddle, I fuck, I forgive, I forget, I fart." Pithy Jack.

He liked to hang out with us while we worked. *Watching the detectives,* he said. He lifted not boxes but our spirits with his playing. But today he thumbed through a glossy, rolled

magazine. *The Busy Worker's Handbook to the Apocalypse.*
"What's in that box?" Curious Jack.

"Nothing. But I think it just moved."

"Soul of a poet?"

I shrugged. My watch warned me about time management; I had another job (off the books) after this one. I had no idea how I was going to get that one done solo. I wanted to quit. Go home and stew in the darkness. But I was still paying off a PA system and a Strat (Hendrix model in Olympic White).

Why didn't I get the Les Paul…?

My body was beat, my head still pounding from this morning.

"Hey, Alexi…" Timid, searching, barely a whisper. "You catch *Fresh Catch?*"

Dammit.

"The Doormen sounded really good. They—"

I held up a hand to shut him up.

One, because I didn't want to hear that my old band killed on the hottest locally syndicated live music in-studio show. On our favorite station, WXRT.

With *that* song.

Two, there was a line attached to the box.

A long filament, like a fishing line, coming from the back corner of the box, now taut to the edge of the garage door. I thought back to when I used to fish with my dad. In the late afternoon light, it glowed like gossamer, a spider's signature. I felt like a rabbit sneaking up on an upturned box, balanced precariously on a twig with an offering of a moldy carrot. "Do spiders eat rabbits?"

"Probably in Australia," Jack said with a shudder.

The music for "Yesterday," one of the most covered songs in history, came to Paul McCartney in a dream.

The line twitched as if plucked. Like the high E string on my Strat.

I looked back inside the box and there was nothing. I reached down, hooking my pinky nail like it was a flamenco string, hitting the open E. A note resonated in my head. As if somebody held a tuning fork to my temple. I plucked the string again. The note was weaker, just an echo of the original. Not a melody, not a tune. Not a jingle.

Bob, I can name that tune in one note.

One note.

One song.

We used to say, Just need one hit song.

Fuck, even just a licensing deal.

Here's my horror story—the kind you read online now, used to be in zines, obscure music magazines, a footnote in somebody's history of music of a certain decade in a certain city in a certain scene: Donald, Jack and I were sitting outside a 4 a.m. bar at 5 a.m. We just started singing and riffing on lyrics. It felt good. It fit. I hadn't done anything creative since Carly left, taking closure with her. I looked at them and hoisted the last third of my beer that I had snuck out (one of the perks of being a regular and it being 5 a.m. and the bartender's already asleep).

"That was good," Donald said, already thumbing his Notes app.

"My parting gift," I said. "To you and the Doormen. May your music fill the spheres."

Donald was taking the band on the road, moving to a different cold weather city, and I had a litany of excuses not to make the jump. That was a year ago, after Carly, our band muse and guitar player, disappeared.

And now, just this morning, Donald and his new Doormen played their first single live on 'XRT hosted by a Brit tastemaker. A bucket list for local musicians. And national. The song wasn't exactly what we'd come up with outside that bar, but close enough a day in court would be 50/50. And no, I hadn't pulled out the calculator app to guesstimate future lost publishing royalties on a once-in-a-lifetime opportunity.

You wouldn't still be paying off that Strat…

That way lies madness. (Just ask Richard Ashcroft.)

But it was their *second* song. The one Carly and I created. The one where we fell in love. We bonded over our likes and philosophized over our differences (I was agnostic, she believed in a supreme being). Dredged up childhood pleasures (comic books, kites on the beach). Vulnerable lyrics revealing unspoken feelings. Now a dead end of grief. Being played for an audience of strangers, with neither of us involved. It felt like an invasion of privacy. Worse, someone signing their name to my heart and soul, and putting it on merch.

As if they owned me.

That song made me mad. That song killed a joint behind the moving truck. That song summoned this killer headache. Filled me with rage. I don't know how Donald got *our* song.

Lease the PA. Sell the Strat for a loss. Keep making payments.

"I'm never going to play again," I said to myself. The first time I'd said what I knew for the last year. *Fuck.*

Jack grunted. Empathetic Jack.

"Did you hear that sound?" Already my feet following the line. So odd that sound produced by a random fishing line (*or was it a flamenco nylon string*) grabbed my full attention. Nothing had for a long time. Not booze, not sex, not even masturbation. Books became paperweights; my Strat, an expensive wall decoration; my vinyl collection of first pressings, something to reorganize in silence. Other methods of self-care, i.e., self-medication. Buying expensive dust collectors. Grief, my friends, is a siren luring you onto the breakers of bad decisions.

But this sound… *what if…?*

The riff for "Satisfaction" came to Keith Richards in a dream.

The line stretched out of sight. "You see it, right—the string?"

"Yeah."

We followed.

A city block away, I plucked the string again and another note was added. The tune was almost familiar; had I heard it before? The buzzing caused an itching deep in my ears, my pinky useless to reach it. My temples and tongue tingled. I couldn't describe the musical notes in my head. Nothing you would call a jingle, a theme, nothing you would call ambient, or incidental music. Maybe a tone poem—a phrase I've hated since the '90s (thanks, Natalie Merchant), but now kinda understood. The notes rhymed. When they played, I felt lighter, my brain buzzed; it was an earworm and not an irritating earworm.

Was it a song I was chasing?

"Do you hear it?"

"I guess," Jack said. "Why don't we get tanked and jam later? Hoist one to Don and Carly." Jack kept trying to start a conversation. About this morning. About 'XRT. The Doormen. Carly.

No dice.

I followed the string, this thin line, this muse. It did not wrap around anything, but bent here and there, a fire hydrant, a tree, an illegally parked car, an abandoned car. A school.

II. Recess

It ran through a chain-link fence, into a schoolyard. Came out the other side. An app enthralled a security guard. I could have walked around but perhaps there was another note strung between those two fences, strung between the throngs of grade schoolers dancing and running and playing, the line passing just over their heads.

I would go around; perhaps I would miss a note or two, but it was more important that I listened to what else the string had to say.

"Well, that's that," Jack said. Pragmatic Jack. Quitter Jack.

A young girl squealed and screamed; a boy did the same. They had noticed the string running above their heads. They took turns jumping and trying to touch it. Finally, two boys gave the girl a boost, launching her up in the air like a cheerleader. The girl succeeded in swatting the string. Without precision, without knowledge. She fell to the ground, skinning a knee.

The children stopped moving and just stared at one another.

The girl stood up, was boosted again, and swatted the string again.

They heard something different. They all started crying.

One boy, snot-faced, booger-encrusted, reached into his friend's backpack and pulled out a pair of safety scissors. Plastic-handled, tips rounded.

Don't run with scissors.

He kept wiping his face, snot forming strings from hand to cheek. The boys moved to boost him. He was going to cut the string.

I screamed at them.

"Alexi, let's go." Cautious Jack.

The security guard finally looked up from his phone, saw me climbing up the fence.

The boy with the scissors looked as if he had been expecting me. I flipped over the fence, slipping through Jack's protestations. Legs flailing over arms, fingers clutched in the fence's chain links like I had done so many times at their age. During the maneuver, my foot connected with Jack's face.

Crunch.

After the band broke up (aka The Split), Jack took my side and we've been each other's best orbit since. Enough to see the local scene turn over more than once. Enough to slip from the footnotes of all but the savant of music critics. I'm not sure why he decided to stay. We may have talked about it, but we were a pitcher too deep into Goose Island to recall. It just was. And for that I was grateful, also because Jack alone would understand the devastation of hearing the *song.* While Carly's disappearance haunted me, the song, *our* song, gave her disappearance a spectral form, filling an empty spot with rusty nails of *what ifs.*

And yet…

How many more notes to this *song?*

The kids screamed at this wide-eyed man walking with a monster's gait in a jumpsuit worn by thousands of boogeymen in their collective dreams. Jack followed. Puppy Jack.

They ran in circles, not sure what to do, their fight-or-flight response short-circuiting any navigational gyroscopes they may have possessed. *Fight* did hit in a few of them and they came at me with scissors drawn. I did the only thing you could do in such a situation. I yelled *freeze tag* and they froze, including the security guard, who was still fumbling with his keys at the gate.

I couldn't reach the line. Was it higher than I'd imagined? "Jack, the bow!"

I boosted Jack, seeing his front covered in blood. I think I'd broken his nose, but faithful Jack was there. I lifted his thin frame and he bowed the line, the streamers catching the wind suddenly.

The sweetest note and vibration overcame me. Tears streamed down my face.

Oh Carlyle…

My body tingled. The same as when I'm on the verge of a creative breakthrough, when the sequence and phrasing of notes flips that switch in your brain and everything clicks.

Everything clicked with Carly.

The school bell sounded. A fire alarm knocking me back to the earth.

"*Let's go,*" Jack said, running for the far side of the playground.

A teacher came out to herd the children inside. Was that Ms. Bierce, my old music teacher? She was the only encouraging voice in my youth, the one that tried to explain the secret chord. Even when I was a brat. "You don't care for music, do ya?" I made to call out, but a janitor brushed past her with a couple of car batteries and jumper cables. He hooked them up to the fence. A cop pulled up and demanded he be allowed to retrieve his son. Chicago's finest shoved the security guard and the key snapped in the lock. The janitor shook his head and waved him off. Jack and I made it over the fence just as the hairs on our arms stood up, like someone had rubbed a party balloon over our bodies. The booger-faced kid tried to follow us, the big boys, up and over the fence. Whether with a *follow-the-leader* or a *let's cut this bitch* intention was unclear. What was clear is that electricity froze his hands to the chain link. His eyes rolled back and he vibrated.

Pick an emotional modifier to add to your d20 die roll.

- **– Kids are ugly and smell funny.**

If your roll (–3) > 10: You continue on.

- **– Your hero urge in front of Jack is strong.**

If your roll (+3) < 10: Save the kid. [1]

The cop shot the janitor and we fled. All the traffic lights flashed green. Around the school, across streets, parks, and boulevards, a cacophony of fender benders, horns, and tire screeching.

Unmarked gunships flew low through a valley of skyscrapers toward the lake.

Sirens followed as ill clouds gathered.

III. King

I hummed the melody in my head, trying to plant it deep, unforgettable, but it slipped a bit under an ocean of static. Was it the school fence? A transformer. As an insomniac, I recognized it as pink noise. It shifted to gray? Is that even a real thing? It was gray, in my head. I looked to Jack.

"I can still smell that kid cooking, Alexi. Burnt pork."

"Keep moving."

"That cop, Lord, that cop shot that guy. He shot him. We're witnesses."

Yes, we are. "Do you hear that?"

"I *don't*." Jack's melodious voice choked with blood.

I'd broken his nose. But I could tell he heard something. He looked like a kid in a haunted house. He fiddled a bit, trying to find a tune. A jig. Something to lift his spirits. "What was going on at that school?" Gone was the uniqueness to his voice. Adenoidal. Weak. And irritating. "What's going on with *you?*"

I wasn't going to let a bit of trespassing, or a shitty day job moving *empty* boxes make me turn tail. Not this time.

Was that it, my one shot? Was I a one-hit wonder for someone else?

"I have to resolve the song. I need closure, Jack."

A musician suffers more than his share of breakups. Band breakups, manager breakups, label breakups. Partner breakups. Muse breakups. Everything has a run, and if you don't make it to the next level, someone recognizes it and does the adult thing. If you're lucky, you recognize it at the same time and it's amicable. Like me and the Doormen. Okay, maybe it wasn't that amicable of a split. Most band splits aren't. The credit card purchases, the PA, the Strat, new computer and mic, were purchases of a frightened man. I had tried to make myself indispensable, valuable, with a Visa. Tried to bury the grief.

At each breakup you ask yourself, why am I torturing myself? Am I enjoying this pursuit? Those are sober thoughts. Then, late night: could I have done more?

Could I have worked harder? Could I have sacrificed any more?

(Later at night: *Why didn't I apologize to her?*)

What Donald and the Doormen really wanted was a change of scenery.

And with Carly gone, I'd lost my fire.

A vulgar sound, like a street festival or a protest march, caught our ears. Whatever the chant *du jour*, I couldn't make it out. It grew louder. We picked up our pace, me eyeing the string, trying to find the midpoint between two bridges so the note would be clearer. That's how it seemed to work.

The noise got louder, and I turned to see a mob of Lincoln Park assholes running in our direction.

They weren't looking back over their shoulders. They weren't running *from* something but running *to* something. And all I knew was there were way too many of them to try to dodge without being trampled. The string was high enough over their heads. It would be unscathed by the horde.

Light illuminated and danced off a slick alley wall next to a boarded-up storefront. The crackle of fire added to the static. I double-checked the line to make sure it was in sight, or didn't take a sudden turn trying to shake me, as if it was a living thing. Jack pushed me into an alleyway to let the mob run past us.

A man in a yellow rain slicker shook the hand of a business man. On fire. The man on fire withdrew his hand and walked on a few steps before collapsing.

"Curtain falls. Black out. End Act I," the man in yellow said, and then searched the alley for morsels to eat, spitting out pieces of his broken luck.

I greeted him even as my feet moved me towards him.

"Hey… don't," Jack said. Coward Jack. "You might, uh, catch on fire."

Stop, drop, and roll.

The closer I got, the louder the gray noise. He twirled around doing his own dance with his face to the sky, like a child trying to catch snowflakes on his tongue. And he did.

Snow?

Big flakes, the biggest I've ever seen, fell from the gray sky like camouflaged parachutists (behind enemy lines). WTF? Where's the sun? I wanted to push on. The line pulled at my heart now and to leave it would rip out whatever muscle I had left pumping the blood through my energy-less body.

"This is nothing," the man in yellow said, regarding the snow. "Just a warning."

I turned to the mob again. One, two, three, then four fell from the front of the phalanx and were trampled by the people behind me. No one stopped to help them. It painted a very clear picture as I heard their screams, and bones crunch under Crocs and Uggs. The man in the yellow rain slicker disappeared into a back-alley door. It slowly closed; slow-motion horror movie slow. Jack thrust me into the alley. The horde grew louder, their chants drowning out whatever pleas we could offer.

But the string…

Part of the horde turned down the alley like a river splitting along a secondary or tertiary route. I heard their words clearly: *"Ph'nglui mglw'nafh Cthulhu R'lyeh wgah'nagl fhtagn."* The bodies flowed, even as their feet stomped like SS storm troopers'. The body on fire crackled and my mind nearly snapped, only the notes in my head keeping me tethered.

"The door!"

My fingers caught in the door before it shut; I howled in pain. One was broken, I was sure. The pain: excruciating. Jack slipped his hand in the crack, those slender fiddle-playing hands of his like spiders.

With a satisfying *thunk,* it slammed shut. Us on the inside. Safe. The place reeked of stale beer and pot, familiar and comforting. I stood staring at the window watching an endless stream of earmuffs, hats, and scarves run by the window. Jack, Calm Jack, dropped the latches at the top and the bottom of the door, barring it. I couldn't hear him with the buzz in my head, but I could read lips. His said: what the fiddle fuck is going on?

The stage lights turned on, and the man in yellow stood

on stage, a homemade crown of zip ties upon his head. A lit cigarette on his lower lip defied gravity. Shoulders slouched as he looked over his script. He saw us. "You've almost missed your entrance," the King in Yellow said. "The second act is starting shortly. Bring your sword."

I was puzzled until I realized he was talking about the box cutter. "Jack," he said, "a little intermission music, please." And Jack obliged him. Showman Jack.

Something about his voice. Some folks are faces, some are names, I'm voices: the tone, the timbre, and here it was the grit. A pinched rumble of a stage whisper. "Is that Zeke?" I said to Jack. Zeke was the doorman at the Elbo Room. Bouncer, ID checker, sometimes working the bar. But he didn't like to talk to people all that much. He just liked the music.

Holy shit, we were at the Elbo Room. When had it closed?

When was it boarded up? Was he living here?

"Shame about you and Carlyle," he said. "Always thought you guys would make the big jump. Heard the song this morning. It's so good, so good. Yeah, it's a shame what happened to Car. It really had to rip your heart out, Alexi. She could shred, soul like Clapton, delicate like Gilmour, rage like Cobain, visions like Hendrix, eyes like Love."

"Purple Haze" came to Hendrix in a dream where he was walking under the sea.

Jack made a sound.

"You used to play here," Zeke said, scratching his louse-ridden beard; he went on to tell me who I had played with, naming Donald and Carly. Others. And even pointed at Jack. "That one." He talked of being proud of us, and that he always knew we'd make it.

I tried to tell him I wasn't in the band anymore, but he shook me off.

"You just need to sacrifice," he said. "Right, Alexi? Why don't we sacrifice a bit now, hmm?" He pointed to Jack. "Maybe a finger or two."

Jack WTF'ed the old man. Indignant Jack.

"How else are we going to paint the runes, open a channel, finish the song?"

"Let's go," Jack said.

"I'm only following the script, but it's true." He shrugged, greasy fingers smearing shabby clothes. "Think of it as an exchange. You gave him Carlyle."

"What?"

"And what did you get in return, an empty heart-shaped box?"

A metallic taste filled my mouth, silvery and slick. "Jack, what is he talking about?"

"If that's what you're willing to settle for, Alexi." King Zeke adjusted his crown. "But you know it takes more than talent to succeed. I've seen 'em rocket, and I've seen 'em OD. It takes commitment for the biggest song on the biggest stage. The *last* song requires sacrifice. Or…" A spotlight came up on stage, its halo giving an ethereal glow to a vintage Les Paul (tobacco sunburst).

The boards are ripped from the storefront. A crowd pressed their faces to the cracked window, its jagged edges drawing blood, unnoticed, while they chanted indiscernible words, but maybe, just maybe, my name threaded through the chant.

"Step up here and play. You know plenty of audience-pleasers, Alexi," the King said with a wink. He leaned into the mic, voice booming: "Let us turn UP THIS awakening to eleven."

Pick an emotional modifier to add to your d20 die roll.
– Put aside the alienation.
If your roll (–3) < 9: Take the stage, quitter. [2]
– Get on with the fascination.
If your roll (+3) > 9: Yes, sacrifice. Continue on.

A knotted handkerchief in his mouth doesn't stifle Jack's screams much, but it does catch the pain as it runs down his face. It takes work, and I think two fingers will do it, but King Zeke gives me the nod and I take a third finger (that talent-stuffed pinky) with the box cutter. The knuckles are tricky, but Jack is a trooper, and I am motivated. I've never had such a good friend.

The horde at the window has moved on. Show's over. Or maybe we were just the opening act. King Zeke draws runes with Jack's fingers on the stage. So much blood in that pinky.

"Let's go," I said, eager to find the line and finish my song.

"My hand hurts." His voice hitched with pain. Teary Jack. "It really hurts, Alexi."

"Hey, Jack, it wasn't easy to cut off those fingers, okay?" I poked his chest, like my dad used to do." It took work. You just stood there. Like you always do."

"I'm sorry." Repentant Jack.

IV. Lake

I followed the line past the Art Institute where I dreamt of seeing my own work hanging one day. What work that was, I couldn't say, I just liked reading the cards with the name of the work, the artist, and the medium. I just wanted to be preserved by history. A line of movers in red jumpsuits like mine moved framed artwork up and down the entrance stairs like ants bringing back a bounty.

The lake, the lake, the lake. I followed the line down past Lake Shore Drive through a pedestrian tunnel to the lakefront.

"I'm sorry, Alexi." Jack said, his face pale from blood loss. "I'm sorry about the song—"

The rest of his voice was lost in the thunder of fighter jets as they streaked overhead, banking sharply over the beach into the gray scrim across the lake. It's then I saw a box kite, fluttering erratically as if riding the lightning, at the end of the line.

During the end days of the Beatles, Paul McCartney's mother visited him in a dream and advised him to let it be.

Lake Michigan, for all intents and purposes, is an ocean. Spring is worshipped like a god. When the weather hits 55, citizens flock to the lakefront in T-shirts and shorts, laying out worshipping the sun, throwing plastic objects back and forth; while in California (real ocean), they are putting jackets on their labradoodles. Here, a throng of people stripped off their outerwear of North Face and Columbia gear and thrift-store gems, and kept filling the beach with naked bodies rippled with gooseflesh. They chanted to the sky even as their bodies became a carnal lollapalooza: *"Ph'nglui mglw'nafh Cthulhu R'lyeh wgah'nagl fhtagn!"*

I stand there. Jack says something, but my head is spinning. That tingling feeling, that jolt of electricity between the groin and the belly button, stands the hairs on my neck like a junkyard dog's. The line ran to her hand, and then bent skyward, terminating with the box kite. From here I could see her clothes—a bit tattered, a bit holey. Whether from wear or fashion, I couldn't say or dare guess. She was not among the naked chanters, who ignored her. I could not.

Under slim headphones, the woman's hair was short and chunky, as if she'd taken dull scissors to it herself. Again, fashion or distress, you couldn't tell these days.

However, there was something in the way she moved, the way she walked, the slight gait, the slight wobble on her left leg from a blown-out knee in high school soccer. When it would twinge, she would have to shake it to pop it back into place. Usually when she was tapping her guitar pedals. Kicking for overdrive, she used to say.

If it is her.

"Alexi…" Jack cried.

I got closer. Her hair was indeed chopped. Her skin appeared oily, as if she'd put on too much sunscreen, a greenish gray tint. But the headphones I thought she was wearing were her ears. They had shrunk, but the tops of them ran upwards, as if somebody had stretched them like taffy and pinned them to the side of her head. I thought of a bat.

Carlyle…?

She turned to me, and her big expressive eyes bulged, like bad anime, as if the contents of her skull required more room. Still, her smile; when she saw me, she smiled and my heart pranced a beat. A familiar queasy, lovesick feeling, only amplified since her disappearance, since our fight.

But now here she was, on the beach, the same beach where she had said she was going for a walk, when she disappeared. When she needed time to think. To consider us, the band, the plans to relocate. Something always drew her here. Her happy place.

Sting dreamt the chorus to "Every Breath You Take" and 30 minutes later at a piano he finished the song.

I realized now the box was a lure, containing all I ever wanted: to feel nothing, to empty my head, my heart out, to be a shell, to let whatever thoughts, whatever ideas might lie at the bottom of it, have a chance to breathe, to shape, to devour themselves. It was a lure. The box, the second-most empty thing I've ever experienced.

The first: she loved someone else. I knew.

"Car...?" I said.

"Lex, do you hear it?" she said. *"He is coming..."*

"Who...?"

The Great Lake roiled, whitecaps carpeting from horizon to horizon, those stupid Asian carp beaching themselves, creating jumping-off points for other fish, all sea life, not washing on the shore, but jumping for it, swimming for it, as if trying to get away. There was little difference in the shades of gray between the water breaking through the whitecaps, the sea, the sky, and the clouds. As if we were in a murky snow globe. Low-altitude clouds moved and circulated. I had seen those sick green tornado-spawning clouds in my youth in the summers in Oklahoma.

Sky or sea, something was coming.

Do you hear it? she said again. This time only I could hear her.

I tried to speak, but the wind and the mist blowing off the whitecaps stole my words. One contact lens blew away, the other rolled back into my head. I opened my mouth to say *what?* And Jack was yelling at me again. And I listened. And I thought I heard a vibration. A high-pitched barroom frequency murmur. I couldn't pin it. It was an itch scratching at the edge of my eardrum.

More chanters emerge from the city, the pedestrian tunnel.

Ten thousand people. Maybe more. *"Ph'nglui mglw'nafh Cthulhu R'lyeh wgah'nagl fhtagn!"*

Lexi… She points at the box cutter in my hand.

The beached fish hiccup black and yellow spiders.

There's so much we can't hear.

People rending clothes, fighting and fucking, rage and lust, chanting as the spiders skitter and snow falls. All this a blur. I tried to blink my one lens back into place.

"What the motherfuck?" Terrified Jack.

Kill him so we can finish the song.

The voice reverberates in my head, but Jack heard it, too.

"I'm sorry, Car. Your song was so beautiful. And Alexi wasn't going to do anything with it."

I look at Jack. Pop the blade on the box cutter. Spiders circle him.

"I didn't kill her, I swear. I just played the song for Don. As a remembrance for her." To Carlyle: "You're supposed to be dead."

Our new song requires sacrifice, Lexi.

"You couldn't have done it without me, Alexi." He screams at me, frozen in place as spiders swirl at his feet. "I played that note. In the schoolyard. *I did that!*"

I slash Jack's neck. He flinches as if stung. His brain has not let him know he is a dead man. This box is not empty. His shrieks, warbling, vibrato, like a woodwind section to a symphony of destruction. He is on all fours, his hands in a puddle of himself. Bleeding Out Jack.

A wiry spider creeps up Jack's arm into the cut in his

neck, fighting against the flow of blood, this itsy-bitsy spider, and then another. As the blood settles, more spiders crawl over their sickened and suffocating ilk and burrow into Jack's neck. Others take the long way, pouring into his mouth. They make quick work, eating him from the inside out, his body dissolving until there is nothing but his head and a set of lungs, black-spotted.

Jack's eyes bend down and take in his new form, and a keening scream escapes his mouth. Jack's head moves on the treads of spiders, as if they were carrying a king, or a trophy.

His eyes looking around, still screaming with drying lungs.

One lung filling impossibly, while the other empties, like tandem bellows, his scream does not stop, joining in the cacophony.

It is almost done.

She points knowingly to the sky. An immense entity beyond the clouds, a living moon the color of dried blood. Unfathomable, singing its song. A transmitter of the one true song. *You are the receiver.* She holds my hand with the knife and uses it to cut the line. The kite spins off into the clouds, a geometry of dancers in tidal lock. My hand slides smoothly up her back to her neck. My grip slides around and I hold her out, box cutter in hand, my other hand on her throat. Do I even feel her pulse in my palm? I can't tell. Everything is thundering and vibrating so loud. We start to sink into the sand. The vibrations are so much.

She's screaming, *look at me, look at me, do it.*

But all I want to do is look at him, the ancient one, the Elder God.

I want to see it.

I want to know it all.

I don't want to be surprised again.

I just want to be empty.

Knowledge untethers me.

She loved someone else. Someone else had been calling her. It's the same beach. She had heard the beginning of the song, and now I had been fished from the land to finish this song…

They can't do it without me.

…the final song, the song of Cthulhu.

Moving your feet, it wasn't a choice. It was inevitable and matter-of-fact, like the weather. An impending sense, not of doom, but of the natural order of things, before we went on factory time, spreadsheets, and gunpowder. I'm drawn to it, with pull of dark gravity toward an event horizon.

"Ph'nglui mglw'nafh Cthulhu R'lyeh wgah'nagl fhtagn."

No dice needed now; this choice is yours alone.

The end of sleepless nights, searching for that tune, that puzzle of musical notes that would calm your brain, the litany of failed relationships, halfhearted creative efforts, and abandoned projects is no longer left up to chance. This is you, this is now your choice. Your choice to end the cycle of bills. AI news items. Bots. Auto-Tune. The daily struggle of survival. For every critic that damned you with faint praise, for every manager that ghosted you, for every time your dad had a better idea. For every time this city ate its young. Maybe it's time the city got eaten. Just an *amuse-bouche*.

Carly Cosa reaches for your hand.

– Take it? It's right there.

– Reject it? Next page, please.

TAKE IT.

I don't want to leave her now.

She takes your hand as if you're a child. Brings your hand and the knife up to her throat. Floating spiders swirl around your knees. The wind-whipped mist off the lake plasters your hair to your face. Her wet clothes cling, revealing odd shapes (eggs?). Entire galaxies reflect in her eyes. So much to explore, so much unexplored.

Her fingers caress your face, so soothing you forget about the burnt child. The fingers worm through your hair, over your ears, in your ears. But you feel her hands on your waist. The fingers are small tentacles, writhing from her face like Medusa's curse.

Alexi… do it. She screams, unearthly and high-pitched, opera-soprano strength; it cuts through the rumble and thunder, a slash of color across a canvas of gray, just like your knife to her throat. Your scream joins hers.

And you hear the final note.

Untethered despair.

Ghroth.

The Music of the Spheres.

Lost in an ocean of waves crashing over you, pulling you

under, every break of the surface only leads to being pulled further under. Your hands begin to curl and your arms raise. The gate is open and you cry out full throttle. Another shadow. A skyline. A city rises. Water retreats from the edge, revealing bent-over shapes. Humanoids. Water pouring from their scaled bodies. They stand and wade into the horde of chanters. Half the scream in agony, half in ecstasy. The beach becomes a pungent pea salad of molted cocks and tits.

Jack's head squawks behind you:

He comes!

He comes!

Explosions flash, the light illuminating clouds and colossal shapes, before the rumble reaches the shore and rattles skulls. It is the planes or their ordnance or both. More explosions, like a string of firecrackers. The strobing outlines, backlights, paints the batwings of a titan. Shredded metal pieces with painted call signs fall from the sky like angelic tombstones. Embers of white-hot metal do not fall, instead becoming eyes of the Ancient One.

The mountainous shape blocks out the sky as it advances, *kaiju* slow, each step sending out a small tsunami; impossibly long tentacles dangle from its mouth, sometimes swaying with each step, sometimes whipping through, each a giant serpent testing the new air. Colossal wings unfurl and flap once or twice, a post-slumber stretch. The ensuing wind and water wreck the beachfront, chants become louder, encouraged, encouraging the humanoids to till fertile fields, even as the worshippers are washed into the depths.

The dreamer has awoken to your song.

WGN AM 720: This is the Emergency Broadcast System…
Please Shelter in Place… This is the

Your journey begins here.

REJECT IT.

Fuck this.

Who gives a shit about a song in the face of madness? What kind of choice is this anyway? A cog in the corporate capitalist world, or a smaller cog in a bigger machine, a mote in an ancient god's eye? You turn your back on this dumpster fire. Carlyle screams at you, but the wind blows her influence towards Michigan. Man, her ears and eyes were fucked up.

You find a half-full (not empty) forty. 50/50 it's piss. A smell test is worthless. You shrug and take a swig. It's not. It's beer.

That's right.

You sit and drink the rest of it.

The Ancient One comes close to shore, hesitates expectantly, as if listening for the next note. The final note.

A whisper caresses your mind, as you avert your gaze. Already, your mind expands past your skull, the biosphere.

Sing.

Its gaze will destroy you, this you know. You pinch off your contact and toss it to the wind. The whole apocalypse is a blur now. Should have come with vision and dental.

Sing.

You pop the blade and with a final cut sever your tongue

and throw it towards the Elder God. A middle-finger salute follows as beer washes down your blood.

Not today, fucko.

The Outer God above the earth ceases its singing and will not receive an ovation today. Silence, silence, silence.

Jack's head circles your tongue on its spider carriers, screaming: *Alexi is not afraid!* Cheerleader Jack.

The Elder God in the lake roars, though maybe it comes from the Planet Fitness orgy on the beach. Your ribs vibrate harder than any Marshall stack. A cloud of ink squirts from the Elder God's cephalopod head, floating in the air as if in water, suspended by its power alone. Its mouth tentacles sweep through the cloud, a behemoth fingerpainting an obsidian sky. The chanting stops. The city of R'lyeh sinks, submersible slow, back to its bed, and the lake rushes in Archimedes-style, drowning the chanters. Several are pulled under by the humanoids. Carly's voice fades from your head as she is carried away. The fish start jumping, flopping their way back into the relative warmth of Lake Michigan.

Now the Elder God is shadow within a shadow.

Then a shadow,

and then gone,

back into the depths,

back to slumber.

And you feel fine.

WGN AM 720: A Lincoln Square man was arrested for the murder of Carlyle Cosa. Her body found on the beach a year to the day she went missing, last sighted in the same area. Also: weird lake-effect snow, Tom up next to explain. Your journey ends here. Toss the d20 into the lake.

Notes

1. The boogers on the kid's face boil and bubble away. His hair starts to smoke. You grab Jack's violin and poke the kid through the chain link, but he only dances on the end of it like a harpooned tuna. You kick the fence, trying to loosen his grip. With your sleeves pulled long as makeshift gloves, you try to pry the kid's fingers loose. You make contact flesh to flesh. Electricity completes another circuit, sending your heart a countermand. Jack screams: I'm sorry, I'm sorry. For a moment there is pain and then a blissful empty. WGN AM 720: Police involved school shooting. Local hero dies trying to save the police chief's son. Your journey ends here. The Doormen play at your wake. Roll d20 to reopen the box.

2. The light, the light, the blessed spotlight, the Les Paul, maybe this is all you ever wanted, the spotlight by yourself, people listening, captive audience. A broken finger can't stop you. Tommy Iommi played with a missing finger. Jack plays along assuming (as always) his accompaniment is welcome, nay required, in all matters of F (fiddle, fuck, fight, forget, forgive). Strap on the Les Paul feedback Hendrix-style squeals from somewhere maybe it's in your head the king in yellow begins to sing you think of Carly your mind starts to shrink a small seed of doubt wish now that you'd cut up those fucking fingers of Jack's. The song would've given you peace. The feedback continues in your head. You scream. It sounds just like the scream of the chanters outside the window. The King in Yellow howls and you crank up the volume. It's your version of the Song. Eardrums be damned. Your skull splits, your heart beats in rhythm with your rage. Until it stops. Even at the end of the world, you're an opening act. And now as your heart slows, a sweet oblivion welcomes you. Rest now in the music of the spheres. WGN AM 720: Fire at the Elbo Room. Homeless suspected. Next in Sports, same old Cubbies?

Your journey ends here. Roll d20 to reopen the box.

2

Here's Looking At You

GARRETT COOK

Not quite a critical fail. Could have done worse. This is something I think every wannabe rockstar who ends up working at a moving company with their college buddies tells themselves. I could be a predatory bridge troll with an acoustic Yamaha and the best Molly in town finding my groupies at kink events, I could be in a dad band unleashing unholy Guns N' Roses covers onto people who just want to burn out their eyeballs playing video poker and eat General Tso's chicken that has nothing going for it but the fact that it will generally not give you salmonella. I could be a lot of things worse than what I am, though maybe, like that Brando character, I could have been a contender, though, maybe, like that Brando character, a bum was also what I am. A two. While yet to eviscerate myself with my own halberd, I wasn't hittin' shit.

I wanted to go home. I didn't want to go home. The paperwork I had to do before closing up shop was an annoyance. The paperwork I had to do before closing up shop was a godsend. The box was rustling. Perhaps this was a sign the box was rustling. More likely this was a sign I was getting tired, more likely, this was a sign I needed something, anything, to break up the monotony of boxes and cleaning and emptying out and porting peoples' lives from one place to another with no end in sight. More likely that, than for the box, apropos of nothing, to be rustling.

This could have kept me from slumping vanquished over the desk and letting sleep get the better of me, but that wasn't going to happen. I had paperwork to keep me up, and paperwork was a whole lot more likely to put me back to sleep. So I ended up doing just that, which should have led me to waking up at 3 am and finishing up that paperwork before going home, squeezing one out, and then sleeping in because those motherfuckers owed me a day of sleeping in and they knew it and they wouldn't begrudge me that. There are some perks to your friends finding you fucking pathetic.

My eyes close. They perk open, blink a moment, finding the walls in front of me adorned with thousands more eyes of different colors and shapes, all staring at me, watching me. Hypnagogia. Hopefully not sleep paralysis, I could blink back to sleep and things would be just fine. A nightmare.

So too is the tall, black haired beauty in a red dress, whose green eyes are every bit as piercing as any of the gazing orbs on the wall, who has appeared from nowhere to haunt me. I don't know whether to let my eyes open or close to let this dream continue. The woman speaks and my decision becomes pretty clear.

"If you close your eyes again, they will be taken. The box has a way."

I let my eyes open, in my groggy state, not protesting the reality of the situation but the justice of it. A better argument would be that eyes do not appear on walls, and that you are all a nightmare or hallucination. That's not the argument I make. Something about the eyes and the feeling of having them on me makes it clearer than one would think that this is a real thing that's happening to me right now and has real consequences, possibly losing my eyes it seems.

"It's not my box. This belongs to a customer."

The woman's expression is stern.

"You're good enough, close enough. You aren't untouched."

She clearly wasn't referring to my love life. It's been months since I had been on a date. I don't know why my mind went right there but her curves and lithe but powerful legs were distracting, even in a room with eyes on me. Maybe it was the eyes that made me think about her that way so quickly. I'm not a pervert, I'm big on consent and I don't pick up random women who manifest in our office in the dead of night. My body is tingling now, a little buzz of static from face down to stomach and crotch.

"I suppose," says the strange, green-eyed lady, approaching and reaching for my zipper, "yes, I could do that."

Her touch makes me spring to life. It's light, measured, and talented. I don't often think in terms of these other adjectives when there's fingers on my cock but she's noteworthy, she's good. I feel the little thrill this used to give me when I was a college freshman who had gotten lucky in such a way that you would definitely have to call it lucky. I feel like I've gotten lucky, as weird and fucked up and insane as the situation was. I let myself meet the thousands of eyes that have appeared on my wall. I don't go soft, I don't get nauseous, I don't get scared. There's something about the eyes and the hands together that makes me think of the dream.

It's the good gig. This is the good gig. This is the room that gets me, that's calling out and whooping and happy to have me there and each applause I can feel maybe I'm that much closer to squeezing out another couple of celebratory drink tickets. Fuck. I'm some kind of pervert. I knew I was some kind of pervert but I'm full of full of… pride? Is it pride? Is it excitement, validation, triumph? Maybe this was how it was supposed to be, even with the bizarre ghost eyes floating on my wall, opening, closing, shifting back and forth, some shyly looking away, some hungry, predatory and envious. Yeah, envious. They want this. They want to be me right now. I want to be me right now. FUCK.

She opens her mouth, flicks her tongue over the head of my cock, over the slit, teeth grazing as she opens up and she starts to suck and this, this is the shit. This is the performance I want. Did I pick up a guitar just because I wanted this? Did everyone who ever picked up a guitar do it for this? Is this the whole ass dream of human civilization, the very project of personhood? Fuck. She's so good, so weird, so nowhere, so ghostly, so other, so off and there are so many eyes upon me, so many complicated inner worlds converging upon mine as I sit here in this office where I'm supposed to be filling out paperwork, and instead being fellated by a ghost from a mysterious box full of ghostly eyeballs.

In one eye, I see reflected the image of a blackened silhouette, painted in eternal fire upon the wall of a tiny house. I know what this means, I know what this is and my eyes almost close to look away from it, and almost get overwhelmed by the tears, yet still I am engaged by the mouth upon me and the lust and excitement it elicits, still even in the wake of the deepest human suffering, I am experiencing ecstasy. Why do I get this relief? Why does my body still respond? I am trying not to hate myself for all of this, I am not trying not to judge myself and damn myself. Her tongue should not be the sum of this.

I don't feel comfortable and I would like for her to stop. I would not like for her to stop. I would like to like for her to stop, I would like to just experience the dread of the ghostly eyes and the sadness of the tragedy they reflect and the knowledge that I am considered distantly or directly or whatever an accomplice in the pain I am observing, enough that I should be punished with reflected sorrows and threats upon my eyeballs. Then suddenly, she pulls my cock from her mouth.

"If you want me to stop, I'll stop, but I don't think you want me to. You have so many eyes upon you, seeing this. Haven't you always wanted all these eyes upon you?"

In one of the eyes, I see the face and twisted form of a towering, muscular giant. Its skin is blue and there are horns upon its head. Its eyes set deep in its sockets blaze with an unearthly fire that threatens to consume the onlooker. The creature by its nature promises violence, to snap in two those who do it offense and I know that I've done it offense. I could blink or close my eyes and make it gone but I know that I absolutely mustn't, or the wall of eyes will keep its promise and take from me my own.

"If you want me to stop," she repeats, "I'll stop."

Yes, I want her to stop, yes, I want this to be over and to be freed from the company of demons and I want morning and sense and the rules of consensus reality to arrive. I want to know that I can resist the arms of the unnatural and I have the decency to resist being a spectacle. I want her to stop. I want to feel like someone I can like and trust and wouldn't judge from a distance. But I want her to go on and I want her to finish and I want to be the focus of all those eyes. Please let me be seen, I feel so invisible so much. Will you look at me? Fuck. No, no, no, this isn't the way.

So what do I say? I say nothing. What do I do? I do

nothing. I let her mouth take me someplace better, I keep my eyes upon the eyes that watch me, the thousands of onlookers, whoever and whatever they are, I look and they look back. Some are hooded with disgust, some wide with thirst and envy, some flaring with contempt and somehow I understand and read each expression, each of the possible reactions to what I'm doing right now and who I am because I am doing it. I might just cum in her mouth, and when I do my eyes might roll back and FUCK NOT YET NO NOT YET I want her to stop I want her to stop I need her to go on I need I need–

She is swift and unceremonious as she pulls away a moment, leaving my hard-on exposed to the scrutiny of all of the disembodied onlookers. She is swift and unceremonious as she pulls off her dress, and her body is the interplay of firm and sleek, unmarred, unlined, mannequin smooth save rosy labia, the kind of body that these thousands of onlookers watching this porn play out demand, and that I would have chosen, and perhaps somehow in my subconscious, I have chosen something pinup unreal, something sculpted to entertain, and built to please. I am looking at her in a way like an object, and she's looking at me like an object, and with a beckoning finger, she lies down on the floor and I undress, follow her to the floor and I get on top and I give in to grip and surrender and promise and I go on in.

If what went on before was somehow anything but right (which it was), then what's happening now is certainly wrong (which it is). Bareback in this unknowable echo of spankbank and complicated feelings that I have no desire to get to know or understand. If disgust can push me off, it will fail to do so. I am held tight, the grip, the fingers she drives maybe too deep into my back, her nails are sharp and yet the pain only spurs me on to thrust faster and deeper and to give that wall of disembodied eyes something to look at. My mind has fled from notions of absurdity and threat and is now taken over by the drive to put on the show.

"If you close your eyes," she reminds me, "then you will lose them."

And so as I go on, I keep meeting the gazes of the eyes and one should give me pause. The eye is grey and miserable and full of disappointment in me. It's familiar and it takes it second and it should be able to make me soft and drive me out and ruin the whole experience that's already ruined by the grotesquerie and madness of it all. The eye is the eye of my great grandfather who I had seen on many weekends, who fished prodigiously and loved the land and water where he lived. The eye is the eye of a humble, gentle man who carried with him the burden of doing his work in the worst of circumstances.

My great grandfather was a fisherman, called up during World War 2 to drag bodies from the ocean, among them some of the dead of Hiroshima. He lived knowing that the skills that he made his life with, and the act that was his passion, was put to this disgusting end and that if he had not loved what he did so much, that he would not have witnessed horrors that he'd witnessed, horrors he carried in that big, gentle heart until finally it gave way, and now I looked at that eye and I was under his scrutiny. And this, this should have driven me away from the act that I was literally entangled in just now.

I am sorry, I am so very sorry to so very many people and I haven't lived a life of particular offense to anyone. I haven't done too wrong, even in my younger days when I didn't know how to be a good boyfriend or a half decent man. I never failed as hard as I could, even when I could have. I rolled a 2. I am by no means a success but I am not the worst failure, the worst monster, the biggest disappointment I can be. I rolled a 2, and that's so much of what I am, except right now that under this gaze and in these circumstances, I feel like a guy balls deep in the hottest woman I've seen being watched by thousands of eager and voyeuristic eyes. I am sorry, I'm not sorry, I am sorry. I am awesome.

And they all have to watch me as I suck on her neck and grab her breasts and put my hips into meeting her building tempo so that I can be what part of me wants them to think I am. I am hard and I am happy, even if I'm unhappy, and I am eager even if I'm ashamed, and I am glorious even if I'm the fucking worst man I could be in this situation. I could not let my eyes close if I tried, I treasure every gaze, even those that I know I wish weren't watching, and I have power even if I'm being led to something I will never comprehend at all. And they all have to watch as I don't even ask before unloading into her body.

She practically shoves me off as I finish. She smiles and her eyes, though green, grow greener, and her pale body shrinks down to a small, dark shape that could not be what I think it is. In seconds, a beautiful woman who I had just filled up with a large load of semen has transformed into a two tailed, green eyed cat that smiles at me as if eating the proverbial canary.

"That was fun," the cat says, "but now you have to go home."

"Why do I have to go home?"

"Because the rest of us are waiting, we're not done with you yet."

"But…"

I try to protest but the office has faded from view and I am alone outside, naked. I could flee from this, I could but I know that things have changed and yes, I must go home because something waits there.

3

Head

BRIAN KEENE

The die came to rest against a stack of other boxes. I stepped forward and bent over to look at it, ignoring the pain in my knees and lower back.

It had landed on 3.

The box fell silent again, as if whatever was inside was waiting to see what I'd do next. I had to admit, I was curious about that myself. Like I said, I hadn't really given any deep thought to the rules or parameters of rolling that die. I'd just acted. It occurred to me that this was probably some sort of psychological response. I'd been confronted with something strange and unexpected, and my first reaction had been to retreat to something familiar and known. Now, I was faced with the results of that casual roll, and still had no clear plan of action.

The box rustled again, and the scratching sounds returned, more insistent this time.

I took a deep breath, closed my eyes, and stood with my fists balled at my sides. If there was an animal in there—and that seemed the most likely explanation, since a toy, be it a child's action figure or an adult's vibrating butt plug, wouldn't randomly click on and off—then I could not, in good conscience, leave it trapped inside. If it was indeed a pet then these asshole clients didn't deserve to own it. If it was a rat, or some other critter that had chewed its way inside, then it wouldn't do for the clients to find it in there later.

I opened my eyes, exhaled, and then turned away, intent on retrieving my box cutter from the truck. By the time I'd reached the front door, the sounds of the box were inaudible. I again considered just leaving. It wasn't any of my business. I should just return the truck, go home, and relax. Maybe cook myself some dinner if I still had the energy. Maybe microwave a few Hot Pockets if I didn't. Probably fall asleep on the couch again. Or maybe I'd treat myself tonight. Maybe I'd run a hot bath, and pour in a double dose of Epsom salt, and just soak my aches and pains away.

The weather outside was gorgeous, and still quite warm, despite the sun's steady descent. That only solidified my desire to forget about all of this. I passed by the back of the truck and eyed the few remaining boxes piled at the bumper. Once again, I considered just hustling them over to the entryway and calling it a day. But then I remembered those scratching noises—their quiet, frantic insistence—and I relented. I opened the driver's door, grabbed my box cutter, and slammed the door.

"Yo."

Startled, I barely suppressed a shout. I turned to see Jorge, one of my fellow freelancers, standing just a few feet away. He held up his hands in mock surrender.

"Sorry, ese. Didn't mean to scare you."

"That's okay," I said. I took several quick breaths, waiting for my heart rate to return to normal. "Just some weird stuff going on. What are you still doing here? I thought you'd left."

He muttered a string of curses in Spanish, and cocked a thumb at his beat-up Saturn parked along the curb nearby. The dark green paint was faded from years of sunlight, and the tires were as bald as Vin Diesel. I tried to remember the last time I'd even seen a Saturn outside of a salvage yard and couldn't.

"My car won't start. Need to catch a ride back with you, if that's cool?"

I shrugged. "Okay by me. I've got to deal with something first, though."

"Yeah, I'll give you a hand unloading."

"No, not that. It's…"

I glanced at the house and then back to him. Jorge followed my gaze. Then, he noticed the box cutter in my hand.

"What's going on?"

"I… I think there's a cat or a gerbil or something in one of the boxes."

"What, you mean like dead and shit?"

"No." I shook my head. "Something is scrabbling around inside. Come on. I'll show you."

I led Jorge back into the house and down the hall. The noise was noticeably louder now and had taken on a frantic urgency. We entered the master bedroom and I was surprised to see that the box was now some five or six feet from where I'd left it. As we watched, whatever was inside slammed against the cardboard, moving its prison another inch across the carpet.

"Yo," Jorge wheezed. "What the fuck?"

"Help me," I yelled. "You hold the box while I open it."

Eyes wide, he ran over to it and knelt, seizing the box in both hands. The cardboard crumpled and bulged beneath his palms and fingers. Whatever was inside unleashed a volley of high-pitched angry chittering, like a cricket or a locust on helium. Jorge looked up at me. Flecks of spittle flew from his lips.

"Well, don't just stand there, bro! Open the fucking thing."

Nodding, I tentatively approached the box. Jorge strained, obviously having trouble keeping his grip. It shook violently, and the thing inside shrieked.

Kneeling, I depressed the button on the knife, extending the blade. I tried to press it against the seam, but my hand shook so badly that the tip of the blade glanced off the side of the box, gouging the cardboard, but not piercing it. The occupant reacted, heaving itself against the interior, and the box rolled out of Jorge's hand and skittered across the floor. We both watched, gaping, as something punched through the cut I'd made. I couldn't tell what it was, exactly. It looked insectile, but far too large for any sort of bug here on earth. The appendage was segmented and greenish brown in color, tapering off to a rusty red at the tip, which was sharp and pointed. Tiny, coarse hairs grew along its length. Before we could react, the appendage withdrew back inside.

"What the fuck," Jorge repeated. "The fuck did you do, cabrone?"

"Me?" I scowled, incredulous. "I didn't do shit, man. I was just—"

I was interrupted by a loud tearing noise. Two identical appendages had now punched their way through the cardboard. They flexed, ripping a hole, and the occupant shoved its way through like some blasphemous mockery of a birth ritual. It was a human head, covered in a fine, soft drift of silver hair. The face was that of an old man, but the eyeballs were empty sockets and the mouth nothing more than a desiccated hole. Six insectile legs jutted from the head—one out of each ear, and four from the stump of the neck. Two smaller appendages dangled from the nostrils—greenish tendrils the thickness of a pencil.

Jorge screamed in Spanglish, and I fell on my ass, scrambling backward as the thing wholly emerged. It righted itself on those spindly legs and whipped around to face us. Deep inside those empty eye sockets, I glimpsed a different pair of eyes staring out at us—black and shiny. Then, with a speed that belied its size, the creature scrambled forward, clambered up onto Jorge's leg, and climbed atop his face. It squatted there, legs bending, and then another protuberance burst from the neck stump—a grey, slimy tube, swollen and thick and shining in the bedroom's light. With a chittering squeal, the monster stabbed all six legs into the sides of Jorge's head, holding him in place. The two pink tendrils flitted forward and seized his lips, forcing his mouth open. Then, before I could react, the beast thrust that new appendage into his mouth. Jorge choked and squabbled, arms and legs floundering. He clawed at the hardwood floor, and raised both feet in the air, bringing them down hard, but the attacker held him in place. The grey appendage pulsed and throbbed, and the creature made an insectile moan, shuddering with pleasure.

Moaning, I crab-walked backward out of the room, then jumped to my feet and fled the house. I didn't stop until I was inside the cab of the truck. I locked the doors and rolled up the windows and fumbled my phone from my pocket. It slipped from my hands and fell onto the floor. After retrieving it, I tried dialing 911 but it took me three attempts because my hands felt numb and I couldn't make my fingers work correctly.

Shock, I thought. *I'm in shock.*

And why wouldn't I be? I'd just watched a human head with some kind of bug monster living inside of it hatch out of a cardboard fucking box and fuck one of my coworkers in the mouth. Witnessing something like that was what shock was invented for.

Stammering, I gave the emergency dispatcher my name and the address. When she asked for the nature of my emergency, I told her that an animal was attacking my friend. She informed me that a unit had been dispatched and asked me to stay on the line, but I hung up, barely managing to put the phone on the dashboard before bending forward and vomiting on my boots. I sat there, shaking, until the police arrived.

Emerging from the truck all wild-eyed and stinking of puke, I explained to them what had happened. They stared at me, their expressions full of disbelief and suspicion, and then told me they were going to detain me. When I balked, one of them took hold of me, explaining sternly that I wasn't under arrest. I wept as they cuffed my hands behind my back and placed me in the back of the police car. Then, they cautiously approached the house. After a moment, they disappeared inside the open front door.

I waited. I don't know for how long. The radio inside the car squawked with snatches of conversation and static as arcane police codes were given, and units were dispatched to various destinations. If either of the cops who'd detained me said anything, I didn't hear it.

Eventually, there was movement at the door. I glanced up and saw the creature trundle outside. It stopped on the front stoop, basking in the sunset. A moment later, Jorge's head waddled out to stand beside it. Then both of the police officer's heads. I glimpsed more movement behind them, there in the shadows, and wondered just how many boxes were hatching.

Soon, as they skittered across the lawn and spread out into the yard, I got my answer.

4

Dingy

LAURA LEE BAHR

Human cruelty has its own calculus, but I always sucked at higher math. I don't understand it.

No air holes. I mentioned that about the box, right?

And who knows how long the poor thing has been in there. Luckily, it's still alive. Whatever it is. Shining gold eyes stare up at me, as it tries to make itself small in the corner of the box. It's not one of those four-flap top boxes, that plebs seal this over that, over this, over that, like a cardboard square braid, it's one of those law-firm type boxes with a lift off lid.

"Hey, hey, I'm not gonna hurt you," I say, soft. Poor thing is shaking.

The underneath of the lid is gadget-ified, so I am telling

myself not to jump to conclusions. Maybe this is some newfangled but low-fi animal carrier, and there's something in this cylindrical liquid wired to a hexagon filter that allows this guy to breathe just fine in here, because who knows how long it's been in this box. But my whole body is tense with the type of rage that has got me into more than one fight defending someone against a bully.

What kind of asshole does this with a live animal?

There's a label on the underside of the box. A name, and what looks like a return address in a nightmare. But when I look a little more closely, I can see it's not an address at all, it's an equation, because there's an equals sign. But I don't recognize any of the symbols. The name is foreign. Maybe German, because there's that weird two dots above the *o*. It doesn't take a genius to realize if it's German, good chance it's something fucked up.

A yowl and the thing—it's not a thing, it's a *cat*, clearly a cat, I just couldn't see before—jumps out of the box and streaks in a gray blur under that couch we'd moved in this morning.

Also, clearly a *cat* because my nose is starting to twitch. I'm super allergic.

I crouch down so I can see beneath the couch. Eyes glow at me in a gray fur face. Poor thing is shaking in fear and makes this small, sweet "mew" sound that breaks my heart.

"Hey," I whisper. "Hey, you're all right."

My septum is riding up into my skull and I don't want to sneeze at it. I sneeze like an earthquake.

I move as fast I can, as far as I can, as four big sneezes rock my head.

I search my pockets for a tissue or something, I don't want to use my sleeve—so gross.

Three more sneezes and snot sprays. Shit, okay, I'll use my sleeve.

I am not going to be able to save this cat myself. I need to call someone else in. Call in the reinforcements here, to help. I think of this woman I saw a couple of times who was really great, but her cat was the deal-breaker. I mean, I could never stay over there and she was obsessed with her cat, which was a major turn off to me. I can't remember her name… but I sure remember her cat's name: Pickles. And it looked like a Pickles, too, with this smushed-in scowly face, and Pickles was an old cat, with like that kind-of-matted, long, orange fur. Ugh. Pickles.

Yeah, I couldn't get past Pickles. But then, to add further insult to injury, this woman was also into *saving* cats, like as a whole species. She volunteered to trap strays and she fostered cats, so there were cats *everywhere* when I was at her place. On the dating app it had said she just had one cat, and I thought, okay. I can handle dating someone with one cat. But turns out she only had one permanent cat, and a constant crisis of mew-nami waves of temporary cats in need of rescue.

But now I need her to save this cat. Shit, what was her name?

◆◆◆

Rachel Heliotrope. I don't know how I'd ever forgotten a

name like that. It took her less than twelve minutes to arrive. I told her that there was a cat in the box, and a German name on the box with a weird equation, no air holes, and about the little cylinder, and she declared it a CEEP—Cat Emergency of Epic Proportions.

"Some crazy fucker is trying to prove a thought experiment. And be careful… that box could be an atomic detonator."

It was a long twelve long minutes.

In that time, I did a lot of thinking. First, I thought about everything I knew about whoever was moving in here. That took less than a minute. I don't know much. What I do know, I'm starting to doubt I actually know anything true.

I thought about whether or not something radioactive had already leaked on me. That thought made me fall into a wormhole of time that spread from the beginning to the end of my life. I started thinking maybe I already had cancer, and how much having cancer was going to suck. What kind of health insurance I have, whether that would cover anything, or help anything anyway. How if I die, what is going to happen to my parents, who are getting older and counting on me to finally figure my shit out and justify why they had me—to be able to take care of them. I am so far from being someone who could take care of their parents. I take care of one person only— myself. And even that, just kind of.

I thought about girlfriends I've had, and dates I've had, and friends I've had, and why everything in my life seems so random, and like nothing's ever really settled into what I thought would be my real life. So far it just seems like me deciding the things that suck way too bad to accept, and trying to get by *not* doing those things. But how long can I ride that? How long if I suddenly got cancer because I opened a box?

A series of small "mews" came from under the couch.

Keeping my shirt over my nose, I got down again and started really talking to it. It made me feel better, talking to the cat instead of just thinking to myself, staring into its glowing, gold eyes. I started to think about what it would be like to be a cat. To be small like that in a world of giant smelly apes and beast-like dogs. To hear mice in the walls, and hear every noise like I do, but times a million. To see in the dark.

"Mew, mew, meo-w," the cat said, moving toward me. And I started to tear up, which let's say is due to allergies but felt like because me and the cat were on the same wavelength. In the same boat, or the same box, would be a better metaphor, this cat and me, with the random radiation that could end us. Actually, poor thing was probably more scared than me. At least I knew where I was, and I wasn't stuck in a box for who knows how long, where I didn't know if I was going to ever get out alive.

"Aww… we'll be okay, buddy. We'll be okay." And the sweet gray face came a little closer and rubbed its little gray head against my hand. Allergies or not, I felt something warm in my chest that I knew was as undeniable as it was true—love. Strong. Like, strong and true.

Shit.

"Aww, Dingy. Do you like that name? Should I call you Dingy?" The cat put her head in my palm and started purring.

Time stood still. And it was all right.

◆◆◆

"Where's the cat?" Rachel Heliotrope bursts into the place, and suddenly time starts again. Rachel knows what to do in a CEEP. And she's cute as hell—all short, feisty, with a curly hair halo. She's dressed like a burglar.

Crazy cat lady or not, I'm an idiot for ghosting her. She's bending over, trying to get the cat from underneath the couch and her hoodie rides up, showing the skin of her back. I remember my hand rubbing her there as we lay in bed together, my fingers touching the little knobs of her spine.

"You're okay, you're okay," Rachel's saying as she pulls the cat out, holding it by the scruff. It's limp in her arms and she has it zipped up in a little backpack carrier so quick I barely realize what's happening.

"Okay, let's get out of here," she says. "Make it look like nothing happened."

I put the lid back on the box and place it back where I'd first moved it, before I'd rolled a die and decided to violate the Sacred Law of Box Movers Everywhere (SLOBME).

"I took the train and then booked it so no one can track me back here," she says, a storm of a thousand conspiracies beginning with this whisper. "Let's leave in your van. *Schnell*!"

◆◆◆

"*Cogito ergo sum*, but only if you *cogito* the way that Descartes recognizes *cogito*, that fucking speciest," Rachel says in a baby voice to Dingy. She rides next to me in the front cab of the moving van. I don't remember how to get to her place, but she barks directions at me in between sweet nothings to Dingy, and a long string of sinister assumptions about mathematicians, philosophers, and scientists.

"I don't know if you were meant to be the observer, in which case maybe there was some two way mirror or hidden camera, in which case we're fucked," she says to me. "No, don't go straight, get in the left turn only lane, you want to get on the freeway— or more likely, the box was awaiting some other soon-to-come-along observer, maybe even the people who are moving in. Either way, the sick fuck is someone who doesn't understand quantum mechanics but is trying to make some sort of sick statement about it. And this cat was just in the wrong place at the wrong time, until you came along." She has her hand inside the zipper of the carrier, and is rubbing Dingy's chin.

"I named it Dingy," I say.

"Dingy? Oh, that's cute!" Rachel says. "But Dingy's not an *it*. She's a female spayed domestic shorthair, and is as capable of thought and feeling as you or me. And she has her own purpose in life apart from whatever we humans think is our business to impose in our human determinism on her."

"Okay," I say quickly. "Sorry. I didn't mean to be imposing human determinism on *her*."

Rachel looks at me with that little lip curl I'd forgotten.

"But we can call her Dingy. I think she likes it. I mean, it's cute."

"Do you think it's —I mean, do you think *she's*— okay?"

"We'll find out. I need to get her to a vet. Can I trust my vet? Do we think these speciest scientists have her chipped?"

Speciest, by the way, is like racist or sexist but it's the belief that your species (in this case, *homo sapiens*) is the best and most important species, and meant to dominate and rule over other species. In our two dates, I did learn a lot from Rachel Heliotrope, even if I temporarily forgot her name.

"I don't get it. Why would anyone put Dingy in a box that could kill her?"

"Okay, take this next exit. No, sorry, 12B not 12A. Stay left. Now, right. Good job. You know something about the thought experiment called Schrödinger's cat, right?"

I don't. "Yeah, that sounds familiar," I lie. We had two pretty good dates and good sex and then I ghosted her because of her cat situation, so I'm the asshole in her story. I don't want to look like the *stupid* asshole.

"Great, so you know it's not, like, supposed to actually be representational of real-life. It's an in-joke between Einstein and Schrödinger. About how other, dumber, scientists understand quantum mechanics. They know that's not really how it works. But most people don't get it. People use things all the time without getting how they really work. I mean, like cell phones. Do most people understand why their cell phone works? I mean, it might as well be magic."

Now that she says it, I actually don't have any idea why

my cell phone works. Is it because of quantum mechanics? I can't ask because then she will know I was lying about being familiar with a thought experiment between Einstein and the guy who was addressed on Dingy's box. And Rachel hasn't slowed down enough for me to jump in with a question.

"And the people who do understand it get so far off the mark with their heads up their own asses they start to make up all sorts of bonkers explanations, and what's in front of their faces, they ignore. They think: oh, no, really, there ARE these different realities depending on whether or not I see it. Like, they see the world like they are some Boltzmann's *brain* floating in space that can *observe* something without participating in it. They just don't understand the nature of the universe is *not* observation and isolation. Okay, it's this next building. Just put on your hazards and double-park." Rachel takes her hand out of the carrier and zips it all the way up. "Almost home, Dingy."

Rachel Heliotrope is about to jump out of my moving van with Dingy before telling me the secret of life. I hope I don't sound desperate, but I have to ask. "So what is the nature of the universe?"

Rachel turns a million dollar smile at me. "Relationship. The nature of the universe is relationship."

Right on cue, Dingy gives a mew. And I sneeze all over the steering wheel. Even though Rachel Heliotrope is familiar with my bodily fluids, there's nothing sexy about sneezing.

"Sorry," I say, trying to wipe up droplets. "I'm super allergic to cats."

"And to relationships," she says.

Ouch.

"No, I'm not." I protest.

"Well, then come up for a minute. Find a place to park and come up. Or don't. I'll take care of Dingy from here."

She gives me a quick peck on the cheek and jumps out.

"Good job saving the cat, either way."

I don't know about thought experiments and quantum mechanics. I do know about the moving van, idling, that requires two plus parking spaces to fit in on a part of the street zoned for residential, and the trouble of finding a space that will not get me a ticket, that is not ten miles away, that I will have to walk while re-thinking and regretting the decision to go ahead and go up to Rachel Heliotrope's place.

I do know about being tired and congested, and Rachel Heliotrope's place is going to be covered in cat fur, and I am going to regret ever coming up there and ever calling her again, and ever opening the box and saving Dingy.

No. Scratch that. I will never regret saving Dingy. Even if I didn't call Rachel, I would've taken Dingy. I could have never left it—*her*—to maybe die in a box. Even if my eyes swelled shut and I broke a lung sneezing. Even if I do get a weird, crazy cancer and never find out what my real life really is, well, I do know I couldn't live with myself if I'd left her there.

And well, here's a parking space with extra room in front, all the way to the next curb. And here I am, exercising my super power of being able to parallel park a giant van as easily as most people do a compact.

And here I am, walking up the street toward Rachel Heliotrope's, a name I forgot, even though how could I have ever forgotten her name, especially her last name— it's a type of flower but not a common name, or a common flower. At least not where I'm from. And I'm pushing the buzzer, and I hear Rachel's spunky little voice saying, "Yay! Come up!" before I suddenly remember that of course it wasn't the relationship to *her* I was allergic to. It's cats. And that's to ALL cats. Especially… Pickles.

Ugh. Fucking Pickles. And who knows how many fosters or sad strays are lurking in corners… but then I think of poor Dingy who doesn't know any of the other cats, and probably doesn't like any of the other cats, either.

Cat hair hits my nose the second Rachel opens the door to her place. But damn, she is so cute. And she hands me a box of allergy meds. Even though it's the type that makes me sleepy.

◆◆◆

What is a choice? Is there actually destiny, and no matter that I ghosted her, some way or another, I would've found my way back to Rachel Heliotrope's bed?

I rolled a die. I opened a box. What was inside the box was Dingy. She could have been alive or dead—but I never would've known unless I'd opened it. But what if Schrödinger's thought experiment was all wrong? What if it wasn't about Dingy being alive or dead, but other possibilities? As many as the number on the die I rolled? What if there was something *else* in the box that created a whole different world the moment I opened it? I didn't know, and so it could have been anything, right? In the box could have been a dog, or a rabbit, or a raccoon… or maybe something else entirely. Maybe I could have opened the box and opened a portal to another world… Other worlds… All of them just as real as this one.

But no. I mean, that's ridiculous.

And anyway, my relationship is to *this* world, where I am waking up with my eyes like I have pink-eye—crusted partly shut—barely able to breathe, next to a gorgeous woman, with a gray gold-eyed cat sleeping on my chest.

Dingy is purring, and my heart purrs with her. It's the best of all possible worlds.

If only I weren't totally allergic.

5

Filler

BRIAN PINKERTON

The die didn't lie. It told me to open the box.

I knew I had to do it. Otherwise, the suspense would nag at me all night long, and I didn't need that. I needed deep and true sleep when I hit the pillow.

"Let's be quick," I muttered to myself. I pulled my handy box cutter from my jeans pocket. I popped the blade.

Looking at the top of the box, there was a clear path to cut between two top-side flaps, held down by a stretch of packing tape. I could slice a clean line, open up the box for a look-see, then grab a roll of packing tape from the truck to reseal everything back the way it was. The client would never know.

I pressed the blade into the tape, perforating the top of the box carefully, without stabbing whatever was inside. Then I dragged the blade with a steady hand in a straight cut, edge to edge.

My heartbeat began to accelerate. What if there really was something alive inside? And it was coiled to jump out at me with sharp little fangs, freed to attack, riled up from being held captive and jostled for hours of bumpy transit in complete darkness?

I kept the blade extended, just in case. With my other hand, I reached down, slowly separated, and lifted the flaps.

I exposed the interior of the box.

And faced a sea of Styrofoam packing peanuts.

I stared at it for a long moment, then sighed.

"Okay, then." I gently inserted my hand to recirculate the spongy white material, digging, searching for a glimpse of something beneath. All I found was layer after layer of packing peanuts. Frustrated, I dug harder. I put aside the box cutter so I could use both hands, submersing them, scooping, obsessed now with revealing the hidden contents.

My fingers reached the bottom of the box.

"So, an entire box of packing peanuts with nothing else in it?"

Perhaps someone had forgotten to include whatever they were packaging? In the rush to get the boxes prepared for transit, an object was overlooked. That part was logical.

But why had the box shuddered? And what were those noises?

It could have been an illusion brought on by fatigue. Seeing things, hearing things. It had been a long, grueling day. Maybe it was a lingering hallucination from the magic mushrooms I had consumed the prior weekend with my buddy Kip. A random flashback, teasing my brain. I chuckled at the thought. Maybe the box would grow legs and a face and make a mad dash for the door, like a cartoon.

I gave the box an impatient shake. That offered no clues. Then I reached deep inside one last time, more aggressively, clawing at every corner, hoping to brush up against something that wasn't a packing peanut.

Nothing. Nada.

Fuck it. I was done with this distraction. It was time to reseal the box, finish up, and get out. It would be dark soon. I wanted to go home.

I withdrew my hands. Now they were covered with crappy little white Styrofoam crumbs, clinging to my skin with static. I brushed them off as best I could, directly over the box, but they were stubborn bastards, remaining in place. I wiped my hands on my pants. It barely had any effect. The little white dots continued to stick to my skin.

It was really bugging me.

I stood up. I wanted to get to a sink and wash my hands, cleaning this crap off once and for all. Then I would reseal this stupid box of nothing, lug in the last few boxes, lock up and leave.

There was a small bathroom connected to the master bedroom, and I made that my destination, maneuvering around the other boxes on the floor. I coughed out loud, lungs irritated. The house had been vacant for many months, so the air was ugly and stale. You could see glistening, floating dust particles in the dying sunlight from the window. As I headed toward the bathroom, I felt my eyes itch and, without thinking, I reached up and rubbed them vigorously.

"Ow, Jesus!" My eyes immediately burned from the contact. I jerked my head back and scowled. It must have been a reaction to the damn packing peanut chemicals. They were probably created out of some cheap, environmentally unsound substances from a faraway foreign factory for maximum cheapness. Not the kind of thing you wanted rubbed in your eyes.

I headed for the bathroom sink, feeling my eyes redden and the eyelids puff up, like a bad allergic reaction. My hands were tingling. Pissed off, I grabbed the faucet knobs, left and right, and twisted them hard.

A fast, strong spray of water hit the sink basin and splashed up all over my face and shirt. I thrust my hands into the flow.

Then I screamed.

The pain was insane. As soon as the water struck my hands, I felt an instant, fiery burning. I looked down to see a horrible, bubbling foam, eating at my skin. The water was interacting with the packing particles, creating some kind of raging acidic reaction. I pulled back from the sink, howling, waving my hands as if they were on fire.

The pain was so intense that tears flowed from my eyes. Not good.

As soon as the moisture from the tears mingled with the packaging residue I had rubbed into my eyes, I was overtaken by a new stratosphere of agony.

I could feel the simmering, sizzling foam overtake my eyeballs in a thick, slimy coat. My vision faded down a long tunnel until vanishing entirely, replaced by solid black.

In a wild panic, I impulsively reached up to my burning eyes—with my burning hands—which further spread the flesh-eating fire across my face.

My screaming reached new heights.

I staggered from the bathroom, blinded, calling for help. My cell phone was useless without the ability to see the screen or coordinate my numb, corroding fingers. I needed to get outside where someone could hear me and see me and call an ambulance. I was badly fucked up.

I had a fairly good memory of the layout of the bedroom and the general direction of the door, but I didn't make it very far. I tripped over one of the boxes on the floor and fell...

... directly on top of the box I had opened.

Styrofoam peanuts were everywhere, clinging to me like hungry leeches. New pain erupted wherever they found moisture from the sink spray on my face, hands, and shirt. It felt like little volcanoes of lava searing inward. It ate through the fabric of my clothes.

I struggled to get to my feet. I tried to brush the horrible packing residue from my body, but only succeeded in spreading it around further.

Taking careful steps, I managed to escape the bedroom, my hands outstretched, entirely blind.

I advanced through the house, doing my best to remember the path to the front door. I was gasping, too hoarse to continue screaming, and afraid that if I opened my mouth real wide, a packing peanut might hop inside and attack the moisture of my throat.

I bumped into the wall and felt around for a door. I finally found a knob, barely recognizing its shape under the increased numbness of my burning fingers.

I twisted the knob. The latch disengaged, and I threw the door wide open. I thrust myself forward, ready to dash into the open street like a wild man to draw attention in hopes someone would call 911.

Unfortunately, I had not opened the front door. It was the door to the basement.

I began a long, painful tumble down the stairs, absorbing large, blunt blows of hard pain to accompany the burning coating much of my face, hands, and chest.

When I finally landed at the bottom of the steps, I knew I had accumulated an assembly of broken bones. Most notably, my right leg and left ankle. I lay on my back, breathing hard, unable to move, unable to see, growing more numb, losing various senses but still equipped with the ability to hear.

What I heard was not comforting. I could hear the popping of packing peanuts melting into my skin, sizzling my flesh, feeding on me like a hungry, living organism.

There was nothing to do but pray for unconsciousness and death.

Sadly, that never happened.

Many hours passed. It was difficult to know how many. My reality shifted in tiny increments. I gradually felt weightless and small, scattered, rather than whole, and strangely spongy. I was relinquished of all pain, but still sightless and immobile. It was a weird, detached sensation.

It must have been the following morning when I heard my coworker Harold come down the basement steps. I couldn't call out to him, but I could perceive his words. He did not see a fallen man, even though I was right there in front of him. He saw something else.

"What the hell," he said. "Somebody spilled a big pile of packing peanuts down here."

"What?" said another voice, upstairs, instantly recognizable as another one of my colleagues, Hector.

"Get a box," called up Harold. "Let's scoop this shit up. It's everywhere. Marty left a mess."

I realized that a cardboard box would be my destination, my resting place, like a thin, square coffin. But I was not completely dead. I was only idle. And thirsty.

I could use a little water.

6

Paul Is Surprised

MATTHEW HENSHAW

Paul looked into the box open before him and saw a variety of small, cardboard chads. The variety of colors was vast, and Paul bent to look more closely at them. He felt a pull, not just psychically, to the myriad hues, but physically as well—a tug not just on his shirt, but on his entire body. The tug became sustained, lifting him off the ground and into the box. Paul's face breached the surface of the cardboard chads; he was shocked at how freezing cold they felt, like stinging sleet. His whole head was now under the surface of the cardboard blizzard, and he still felt a pulling, down and down, further into the box, which seemed impossible given its size.

Paul spun for what felt like hours, his body battered and

bruised by the excoriating chads. His clothing was shredded off and lost to the storm. Eventually, he landed on solid ground. Looking up, he was stunned to see the storm of cardboard roiling above him like a multicolored ocean. Seeping from the cardboard cloud was a luminosity which lit the barren landscape where Paul found himself, naked, cold, and alone. He made his way to his feet, sensing a gravity stronger than he was used to. Paul took a step, then another, and made his way across the field to what appeared to be the horizon.

The glowing clouds above moved slowly across the sky. Occasionally, a black aperture would bloom from the heavens. When this happened, a certain energy animated Paul, pressing him to continue walking. The ground had a fine layer of sandy dirt but felt hard and stony beneath. There were times as Paul went along where he clearly took no steps but continued to move. When he became aware of this involuntary motion, his sense of movement ceased, and he felt vertigo until he started moving again. The sensation was not unlike moving on a tilted carousel; like he was about to tip over or be flung off into a void.

Eventually, Paul reached a decline leading into a valley. The light from above cast unusual shadows from misshapen, lumpy formations. He approached one of these and reached out. The lumps were some kind of ossuaries, covered by sheets of slick black tarpaulin. There was a slight smell of rot, but Paul gathered the tarp together and covered his nakedness. In the dim light, Paul could make out the bones within, ranging in size from a couple of millimeters to almost half a meter. They were interred in no real order, and they spilled over from the container, lending them the random shapes he had noted.

Still, Paul made his way through the valley of bones, toward another dune up ahead. He had no idea how much time had passed. In spite of trying to count between the openings of the heavenly void, he'd inevitably lose count and come to in the midst of his automatic movements. He was curious about those bins of bones, and that he had thus far encountered no life that might account for them.

Eventually, Paul crested the zenith of the dune and stared in awe. Far off in the distance there was a conglomeration of buildings, some stretching far into the sky. The word "city" came to Paul's mind, but what was striking was that the group of buildings seemed to expand and contract in a biological way that made him think of a beating heart. Flowing out from the city were a series of tributaries, black streaked, with milky rivulets. He could hear, even from this distance, a vast sucking sound. Paul walked for what seemed like an eternity, eventually coming to the Stygian shores. A fetid smell assaulted his nose, and he gagged involuntarily. The whitish streaks, which were more the color of aged ivory up close, were bubbling and popping, the source of the foul stench. Paul was turning away when he saw a disturbance near the edge of the black liquid. Emerging from the channel was something Paul had no words for. His mind said "lobster" and "jellyfish", and in spite of what otherwise might have been a whimsical child's idea of a cartoon creature, it could not capture the alien beastliness and horror of the thing. It was about five feet long and the size of a large cat. Trailing behind it were dozens of thin tentacles, like pasta. The body was round and segmented into four sections. The second and third had a series of irregular stalks, acting as legs. Out of the bottom of the fourth section emerged two thicker stalks, terminating in sharp pincers with thin hairs growing from them. Atop that section was a head, mandible dripping with the black liquid of the stream, and three eyes bearing an uncanny resemblance to human eyes. One rolled madly, never stopping, while the other two stared at Paul with slyness and balefulness. The top of the head expelled some liquid in a gray mist with a terrible hiss. The creature's color was an iridescent blue, and it would shift at times into greens and reds. It made Paul feel that sense of unbalance, yet he couldn't tear his eyes from it, being the first true form of life he encountered.

"Your presence here is a mistake," bloomed in Paul's mind, "you should not have come." The creature was communicating telepathically, and the voice carried a tone of malice. Paul felt panic and deep confusion. Somehow this beast received this thought, and replied "Do not try to speak, for you have no mouth." Alarmed, Paul tried to speak but only anxious noises came out. Reaching up, he felt his face and noted with fear that indeed, his mouth had vanished, even though he could still sense his tongue and teeth within his head. "The atmosphere here sufficiently provides for your human appetite, and your nostrils allow for the necessary respiratory elements to enter your system. You are not the first of your kind to arrive at this place," here the monster made some unidentifiable sounds in Paul's mind, "but you should not be here. I will lead you to the Council, who will determine your fate." The "lobster-jellyfish-thing" began to make its way, compelling Paul to follow. As though under hypnosis, Paul followed. The creature trailed a mercury-like substance that glowed for a few moments before coalescing into small, hard puddles the size of a quarter.

While Paul had dozens of questions during the trek, he got no answers from the creature. They moved closer to the city, the sky lending a multicolored hue to their path. Paul could not determine how much time had passed, and he occasionally lost consciousness, regaining it while in motion. The city was now within a few kilometers, to Paul's estimation, and he perceived a thin industrial sound in the air. The air took on a sulfurous and mechanical smell, which overtook the rotten stench of the river. Across the bank of the now distant river, he spotted gargantuan creatures even less familiar to any concepts of animals Paul possessed.

Soon they arrived at the first buildings of the city. The structures bore signs of both being biological and technological. Paul almost thought "man-made" but dismissed it, given how they appeared up close. They were scored with thin lines converging in dizzying patterns. The glyphs appeared to be writing of some kind, though Paul could not hope to translate them. Rhomboid portals appeared at various intervals near the base of the buildings, some glowing with a purplish light. At their top, orange flames licked out along with obsidian smoke. The mechanical smell was stronger near these buildings, and he wondered whether these were manufacturing complexes of some kind.

Paul continued to make his way through the cityscape, led by the creature through alleyways that were narrow but allowed just enough room for Paul. The sizes, shapes, and colors of the buildings varied, some reminding him of experimental Eastern European architectures featured on programs about eccentric designers. There was a brutality to their appearance that made him shiver and feel danger in the pit of his stomach.

Soon, the two arrived at a superstructure which seemed administrative. Two entities cloaked in red robes emerged from oversized portals. Their heads were obscured by hoods, but Paul sensed that he was being examined and evaluated. They gesticulated with their limbs, and the lobster-jellyfish-thing scurried away, while Paul was lifted off the ground and turned. The two things made clicking and popping sounds at one another, conversing in their strange language, as they drew Paul to them. Sweat pricked at Paul's brow as he noted how tall these figures were, at least three or four meters in height. They, unlike his guide, appeared to be humanoid, though the robes and hoods obscured any features that he could readily identify. Their gibbering communications continued as Paul floated mere meters from them. One turned to the other, who made a motion toward Paul. Paul's body fell to the ground as though a wire he was suspended from was snipped, and he hit the stony ground headfirst, losing consciousness.

He awakened in a cavernous chamber, dimly lit by a series of sputtering torches. He was lying down on a flat, stone altar. While he was not bound, he couldn't move his legs, and his arms could move only enough to feel around his head. His mouth was still absent, and on the back of his head he felt a lump, presumably from the fall. He groaned and tried to gather his bearings. He couldn't make out details, but it seemed he was in the center of a hall, with portals spaced out at regular intervals. This was, so far, the most terrestrial seeming of the environs he had been in for God knows how long. The smell of the air was different here, almost spicy, and the sounds he had heard outside were almost entirely dampened.

Time passed as he drifted in and out of consciousness. Periodically, he would try to move but his situation hadn't changed. From the shadows came a dozen or so figures, all wearing the same formless robes as those who examined him outside. He could see some held tablets in front of them. Three taller figures came within a meter of the slab, forming a triangle. In Paul's brain, a cacophony of noise burst forth – if Paul had a mouth, he would have screamed for it to stop. From the stochastic burble, some semblance of order took hold, like a radio station tuning in. The only external sounds were clicks and pops, but in Paul's mind questions formed – "why are you here", "how did you arrive", "what are you".

To all of these, Paul's thoughts answered with confused and terrified exclamations of ignorance. He trembled in abject fear as the alien presences approached him. From within one of their robes emerged a square-like "hand," resembling a box. Six tri-segmented stick-like things ("fingers," thought Paul) grew out of them, and they held a thin rod which was passed over Paul's body, starting at his feet. The rod brought with it a wave of electric current, aggravating every nerve in his body. He felt as though warm water was being poured through him, and he struggled to move away from the source of the agony. He simultaneously felt like his legs were fusing while also being filleted into thin strips.

Further up the rod moved, and Paul could feel himself changing. His knees flattened and became disjointed. His hips and groin turned gelatinous, his genitalia shrinking into his yielding core. He now felt numb from the waist down. Paul's mind completely lost its grasp on reality as the rod made its way over his torso. He felt his navel invert and disappear with a distinctive, wet pop. His arms now grew longer, so long he felt his hands touch the cold stone floor below. Paul's hands gripped into tight fists, then changed completely into something he couldn't identify. They itched madly.

Now, the rod passed over his head, and Paul felt his beard fall away, bare skin remaining. His nostrils flared and his eyes crossed, doubling his vision. Finally, the rest of his hair fell out as the rod completed its circuit. He felt reborn, naked, into an entirely different life than the one he had lived up until now. A cough wracked his lungs and throat, but without a mouth, he could not clear it. The chamber became more illuminated, as though the very air itself was brightening up, and soon Paul found the light becoming harsher, obscuring the details of his surroundings in a sea of light. It felt like a sea he was drowning in, the light filling and clogging his nostrils. He tried expelling it but it was no use, the light now filling him, and surrounding him. It pressed down with an enormous weight that had Paul feeling his very bones would break under it. His eyes lost focus and purpose; his ears roared with sound like crashing waves.

Another period of unconsciousness passed.

When he came to, the assembly stood before him in a semi-circle. The impulse to move, to get away, led Paul to lift his elongated arms. He stared in terror at what he saw at the terminus of each. The same box-like limbs, six stick-like fingers writhing, were now his hands. His broken mind was now an incoherent babble of unanswerable questions and entreaties to perish. One of the figures shook its head, as though saying to Paul, "No, not yet." The itching on his left side was unbearable, and he managed to scratch at it with his right "hand". The flesh peeled away as though his skin was the rind of a citrus fruit. A rotten odor was unleashed, and Paul felt nauseous. He saw that his box-like right "hand" was pulsing, as though something within wanted to come out. He involuntarily picked at the hand with his left, eventually worrying open a scab. The scab became a seam, which his finger-sticks followed along searching for egress. He pulled, and his hand opened, not unlike a box. Spilling from inside, hitting the ground with wet splats, a series of one-eyed worms emerged, and Paul's mind reached new levels of insanity. The worms resembled oversized spermatozoa, cascading down and wriggling away. Paul looked down at his torso, and saw where he had two legs before, these had fused and now ended in tentacles like those of the lobster-jellyfish-thing that had led him here. Tears stung his eyes and ran down his bare cheeks. Above, a bell or gong tolled hundreds of times, the clash vibrating his entire wrecked body.

As the worms continued to spawn, the figures reached up and the hoods fell away from their heads. He couldn't understand—could never understand—that the faces of the figures were all his own. All of them had no mouths, flared nostrils, and mad, insane eyes fixed on him. Paul shook with terror, with hopelessness, with weakness. The will to live vanished from him entirely, and he wanted nothing more than to cease to be. Above him, the ceiling of the building shifted and spun, revealing the endless blackness of space, along with the void, which continued to pulse. His mind, in the throes of irrevocable madness, took in the sight with awful wonder. Paul realized there was no returning to his life before opening that damned box. His curiosity had cursed him to this fate. Still the worms came, still they fell, still they slithered away. Still, the tears came from his eyes, still his limbs itched, still Paul found himself surprised by the agonies that wracked his body and his spirit, and wished he could retreat from them into the cool cavern of unconsciousness.

Moments grew like a fungal infection, rotting away, only to bloom into moments ever madder. The surprise Paul felt, the only emotion besides the Vantablack despair and doom, could not be relied upon to judge the passing of time. Such were the unexpected nature of his changes, and the place he found himself in. He even found himself forgetting what had just happened to him, subsumed by the torrent of torture he was swept into and under. Still the agonies came, and visited for a time, and departed, making way for new agonies. The assembly bore witness to Paul's eternity, occasionally transmitting signals that Paul couldn't begin to understand. Eons stretched out, Paul's body becoming undone, reworked, broken down, built up, repeating but unrepeatable. The witnessing of the assembly coalesced into one voice which expressed a single, terrible, and mocking thought. This echoed in Paul's mad mind, the only semblance of rationality that nonetheless fed his hungry, fathomless insanity.

"We are all Paul, and We are all surprised."

7

Goopy

BRIDGET D. BRAVE

That scritch-scratching came from the unlabeled box standing on the coffee table. The box wasn't taped like the others. It was resting closed, not sealed, not even one of those faux-fancy fold-over jobs people use to close boxes without adhesive (usually succeeding only in destroying the box and preventing re-use). It was both a different color and a different style than all the other company-issue packaging filling the truck, generally indicating a last-minute addition by the client. Since I wasn't quite sure which room it belonged to, or what might be haphazardly shoved inside, I had placed it in the center of the low teakwood table to deal with after I'd unpacked the rest of the condo. The scratching started again, the sound of tiny fingernails probing the inside edges of the package. I reached for the yardstick I'd left resting against the entertainment center and used it to cautiously open one flap.

There was a strange scent, like stale bergamot, a waft of cedar dotted with mildew, crushed and desiccated rose petals, undercut with a strong, musky tang of copper. I imagined what horror might lie inside: some musty plant full of spiders, leftover skincare products long gone sour, a rats' nest wrapped in perfumed sachets.

I gingerly lifted the other flap of the box with the yardstick, half expecting some kind of rabid vermin to emerge and attack. Instead, there was no movement, only a breath that sounded like an irritated sigh.

I grimaced and peeked inside. Blonde hair, slightly matted, definitely in disarray. Then I caught a glimpse of something rust-brown and crusted. Scabby.

I'm not paid enough for this.

Backing away, I let the cardboard fold back to its closed position. The yardstick clattered to the floor. From within the container, there was a rustle followed by another loud sigh.

Then, the worst possible thing happened.

"Uh, hello?"

I felt like an idiot for immediately checking behind me, a futile act of futile hope. The voice wasn't coming from some unknown visitor, someone who managed to slip in without my notice. Not the homeowner, arriving two full days early to surprise me. Not one of my fellow packer-movers who discovered they'd left behind a favorite pair of gloves, or their phone. Not even the faintest hope of a delivery person with a housewarming gift for the occupant.

Of course. It was coming from the fucking box.

Now, I'm not one of those everyday rubes who just haplessly walks into the dark basement, wanders into the forest alone, or goes for night swims in the ocean. I had seen my share of scary movies. Would I shoot a friend right in the face if he had a zombie bite? Absolutely. I didn't get this far in life by being an idiot. I *know* that when you find yourself in a horror movie scenario, confronting the terror of the impossible unknown, the absofuckinglutely *last* thing you want to do is shout out "hello?" like someone looking to get got.

I know this.

Despite this, I pinch my eyes closed, take a deep breath, and respond, "Hello?" like a total fucking idiot.

I already regret this.

From the box, there is another quiet scratch and a noise of frustration, then an exasperated huff.

I try to clear my throat, but my mouth has gone so dry it only results in a strange, strangled sound.

There is a pause that feels almost contemplative, before the box responds. "I can hear you, you know."

My heart is threatening to evacuate my ribcage, yet I find myself stepping closer to the table. "Is someone there?"

I want to punch myself in the fucking face. Am I only

capable of using the most trope-heavy, tired scripts? Am I trying to die?

"Clearly someone is here." The voice had an irritated air about it, nasally and self-important in a way that struck me as familiar, down to the vocal fry that set my teeth on edge.

"Where?"

Another loud puff of air sounded from the coffee table. "Well, it *looks* like a cardboard box and smells like a cardboard box so…"

"Is this some kind of prank?" I look behind me again, wishing for my coworkers to pop through the front door and laugh at me.

The box shifts slightly on the table. "This conversation would be much more effective if we could speak face-to-face. Help me. I'm not able to get out of here on my own."

Not wanting to touch whatever the hell is inside, yet driven by an insane *need to know* that overrides my common sense, I use the edge of my boot sole and try to flip the box over. I mostly manage to achieve rustling it up a fair bit, which earns me additional annoyed noises from whatever is inside. There are several loud gasps and one whispered "*for fucks sake*" from the box before I am able to kick it onto its side.

Something roughly the size of a bowling ball, wrapped in golden blonde hair streaked with maroon gore rolls onto the table's surface. Unable to control my sick fascination, I slowly creep around the table to get a better view. The red, stringy substance globbing onto the hair is now also congealing on the coffee table's surface, leaking from a ragged stump. I can hear myself breathing loudly through my nose as I continue my path, stopping when I finally see a pair of cloudy blue eyes peering out through the mess.

Lying on the polished wood surface of the table is a woman's severed head.

Worse yet, she's glaring at me.

She blinks and my lunch—a Reuben from the place just down the block—immediately and violently exits my body through my nose and mouth.

The head reacts as anyone would if a dude like me were to start yakking rye bread and pastrami all over the engineered hardwood right in front of them. I've never seen a severed head change its expression, not in real life. Something about watching the way it curls its cracked lips into a sneer causes another eruption of vomit.

I fall heavily onto my ass, narrowly missing the pile of puke.

This has to be a hallucination. Too much acid that summer I spent with my cousins at the lake. Flashbacks, right? That's a very real thing. People see all sorts of shit, yeah?

Meanwhile the head is back to glaring at me.

"If you're done with that overly dramatic display, would you mind moving me? I've had a really bad energy around me all week and I'd rather not lie here smelling your leftover processed food sick."

The airy, almost bored voice combined with the weirdly archaic word she used for vomit sparked recognition. My eyes narrow, taking in her features as best I can through the hair and clotted blood. The blue eyes, covered in a milky haze, are dotted with pinpricks of bruising. A petite, sculpted nose that she was likely not born with. High cheekbones, the skin smooth despite the beginnings of pallor. Before I can think better of it, I lift the section of hair covering the lower part of her face, kerning my head to match her horizontal posture.

"Holy shit," I whisper, letting the hair fall back into place. "You're that actress, aren't you? You were in a movie I watched on late night cable, when I was stoned."

She frowns deeply and rolls her eyes. "Oh terrific. A *fan*. Tell me, was it the nudity in the Dickens' adaptation catching your interest? Or the charming, quirky one where I fuck my brother?"

Despite the vitriol in her tone giving every indication she doesn't want a serious answer, I find myself saying, "The one where you wore that fat suit. The kids do video essays about how problematic it is now. The guy from Tenacious D was in it."

I can tell this answer does not at all amuse her.

"What happened to you?" I ask.

The haughty expression falls slightly. "I hardly think that my personal affairs are any of your business. I would appreciate you not inquiring into the details of my life. Now, could you please remove me from this table and this humiliating position? I would love to at least be upright while you're interrogating me like this.

I grimace, but put on my work gloves before gripping the head by the hair at the crown of the scalp. Holding it out in front of me like an executioner of Ye Olde Lore, I carry an Oscar winning actress' severed head into the kitchen.

"This is so weird. You know what this reminds me of?"

She cuts me off instantly. "If you say it, I will bite you."

Once I've managed to prop her up on the counter with the assistance of some crumpled packing paper, a cookbook labeled "Easy Weeknight Dinners for One," and a heavy flour canister, she looks around the room with an appraising eyebrow raised.

"You've started unpacking in here? Is this your home?"

"Uh." I pull my gloves off and toss them in the corner. "No. Not mine. I work for the moving company."

"You're a mover."

I nod.

"And you're unpacking for the owner."

I nod again.

"Are you some kind of interior designer?"

To that, I shake my head.

"Do you have some sort of specialized training in home organization? Feng shui? Wabi-sabi? Vastu? Wu wei?"

"Lady, I don't even know what half of that means."

She sighs heavily. When she speaks again, it's slowly, as if speaking to a child. "How do you know where to put things?"

"Oh," I reach into my back pocket and produce a folded spreadsheet. "They leave me a list with instructions and there are details on each box. It's a whole color-coded system so we match the client's needs." I stop. "Wait. Why is *this* your primary concern right now?"

"Why wouldn't it be?"

I sort of wince and shrug, and her lips purse into a tight frown.

She rolls her eyes and fixes another glare on me. "You *clearly* know who I am. So you should know that I'm not just an actress, singer, producer, writer, and sometimes director. I also happen to run one of the largest lifestyle brands in the country."

"That's not what I mean," I spit back in frustration. "Why do you not want to do anything about this situation?" I use my hands to indicate the general shape, condition, and location of her head is the very situation to which I'm referring.

"I happen to be *much* more concerned about the tragic situation with that drawer." Her eyes flick to the counter across from her, one drawer beneath it still hanging open. "I'm sorry, but are you trying to put cutlery in a drawer *outside* the sacred triangle?"

I'm dumbfounded. "The sacred whatnow?"

She closes her eyes and takes in a deep, cleansing breath. "Stove, refrigerator, sink. Visualize the location of each, and find the triangle those three key areas make in your mind. Everything you need for the preparation and serving of food should be within that triangle, but in a *mindful* way." The head clicks its tongue. "Think about the purpose of each piece of equipment you own. It should live at home, with its family, and that family should reside in a spot that makes sense during your food prep and service. Speaking of, can you tell me why on earth the toaster is next to the sink? Warming items should live near other warming items, not near items that cleanse and refresh. You're throwing off the whole aura, and digestion can suffer as a result." She glances in the opposite direction. "Move that toaster to the right side of the stove. Then move the produce organizer next to the sink."

I must be in some sort of shock because I do as she asks.

"There. Doesn't everything feel more at home? At peace? The kitchen should always create the feeling of your heart returning home and become a gathering place."

I look at the fluorescent-lit galley kitchen, its laminated cabinets, cheap vinyl flooring, and reproduction granite countertops. "I guess?"

She makes a *tsking* sound of derision. "Open the cabinets so I can see what you've done with them."

It's two hours before I'm finished. The head looks saggier than when I first encountered it, the skin much more gray-blue. Her eyes have lost their shine completely, flat and empty, their blue fading into the same drab shade as the sclera.

"Stop looking at me like that," she snaps. "Show me the primary bedroom." I grip her again by the hair, close to the scalp, noting with displeasure that the blood coating her hair is cold and slightly crunchy to the touch. I let her lead the way like this, out in front of me like a gravedigger's lamp.

"It's small, and there's no natural light," she notes with an air of disdain. "Are the others like this?"

"Uh, it's a one-bedroom."

"A one-bedroom? Where do guests stay?"

I sigh. "I just work here."

"Then let's get to work," she said grimly.

The severed head immediately insisted I move the bed so that the headboard faced south, as apparently facing the north "increases negative vibes, ruins dreamstate, and disrupts liver function." From there, she has me rearrange the closet by both color gradient and length of item, "for ease of locating each piece and matching it to its counterparts, which allows one to start their day relaxed and centered." We then organize the shoes by occasion, "formal event shoes should always be protected and out of sight, then everyday shoes can be kept neatly presented and up front." I learn this "grounds you in the here and now, and keeps your special occasion items hidden, so you can be re-delighted by them each time you discover them again."

I own three pairs of shoes total, so I'll have to take her word for it.

Next up is the bathroom, which had to be rearranged into a "more womblike space in which one can cleanse, evacuate, and care for the body while wrapped in the serene feeling of safety and comfort." I fold and refold the hand towels until I achieve the fan shape that she insists is conducive to the "flow" of the "enclosure" and move all personal care items to the medicine cabinet to prevent guests from having to "deal with the awkward anguish of sharing someone else's sacred womb."

I wondered if my wife felt anguish every time she saw my old toothbrush, its bristles splayed out from my overaggressive brushing. Did she wish she could forget I existed during those moments she was closed inside, needing a moment of personal comfort and solace the other shared spaces didn't offer?

Why was I thinking of this shit?

By the time I had shoved the living room chairs into an arrangement "more conducive to conversation and relaxation," changed the light bulbs to provide "warming, less harsh light" and pushed the round table around the tiny dining area until it created a "welcoming environment for friends and family to gather, nourish, and reconnect," it was growing late and the head was now severely decomposing. I had placed her in a corner of one of the living room's armchairs with a microfiber cleaning cloth beneath to catch anything that might slough off her, and noted with disgust that the cloth was inadequate to sop up the pool of muddy-brown jello that coagulated around the stump.

"Are you… okay?" It was a stupid question to ask. She'd been violently decapitated recently, and I'm sure that was weighing on her.

"Why wouldn't I be?" she growls in a voice that now sounds thick and slow, her tone more venomous before.

"Well," I shift awkwardly from one foot to the other. "I'm nearly done here and have to get home for dinner. I'm not sure what to do with you, if there's someone I should call, like the police or—"

"Do you not think I'm capable of handling my own affairs?" the words are now slushy, with a heavy almost-drunken lisp at the end of sibilant words, "affairs" becoming "affairsh."

"You needed help getting out of the box," I remind her. "I don't think you're in any condition to—"

"You know *nothing* about my condition," she hisses, eyes narrowing. A viscous black liquid is beginning to pool in her left nostril. "I have overcome *far* worse than whatever your meager little brain can imagine."

I raise my eyebrows. "Far worse?" My tone is incredulous. "Lady, someone *cut off your head.*"

She winces as if I've used an inappropriate slur at a fancy dinner party. "Whatever has transpired between my head and my body is absolutely *none* of your business. You're no one, you know nothing about the situation or the circumstances that brought me here. For all you know, I chose to consciously uncouple from my body and packed myself in that box. Lucky for you, otherwise you'd be letting someone live in the remnants of your absolute failure to create a home. Imagine hiring someone who cannot tell the difference between warm and bright light, or the proper place to leave a framed photo to evoke a return to childhood upon waking.

Imagine having to live in that place, suffering from your slovenly ineptitude."

I recoil a bit. "I'm going to ignore that, because you're clearly going through something, but you really should consider being a bit nicer to the dude who helped you."

She laughs, the noise like dried leaves on cold concrete. "You think you helped *me*? You think you're even capable of helping someone like me? You wouldn't last a day in my world, Buster Brown."

"Buster Brown?" I say faintly.

"I was attempting to be polite, something you clearly don't understand. I take it you don't have a ton of contact with women?" There's a new smell emanating, like old meat and chalky cheese, undercut with a cloying sweet scent.

"I'll have you know I have a wife and three daughters waiting at home for me." I don't know why I'm telling her this. I don't know why I feel I should defend myself at all to this decapitated head that is, frankly, being a real asshole right now.

The smile she returns etches itself into my subconscious, to return to memory in my most stressful nightmares. The lips split as the grin widens, pulpy flesh the consistency of cottage cheese bulging from the rifts in the skin. I idly wonder if its lip fillers that do that, or if that's the consistency all our mouths would turn if left out to rot for a week.

"You know who I am," she says slowly, carefully, the words dripping with acid. "But you don't know *what* I am capable of."

My mouth has gone dry, the tang of regurgitated sauerkraut sharp on my tongue. "Are you threatening me?"

The head tipped forward slightly, so she could stare up at me through uneven eyelids, one stuck open wide, and the other fluttering ineffectually against the sagging orb it covered. "I am more than what sits on this cheap reproduction Eames. If you have women at home, I'm already inside them. They are on my website, they are browsing my articles, they pay attention to the way I place my flowers on my credenza, the way I pair my white, fur rug with white, leather chairs. They absorb my thoughts, my feelings. They internalize the inadequacies I point out, the failures, the flaws. They know all the ways they are not living up to the ideal I set. They know they can't have the perfect, white carpet, the unblemished, leather chair, the idyllic home I present. They see all the little errors, the cracks in their lives that keep them from being *me*."

"You know nothing about them." My words are defiant, but my chin is quivering and there's nothing I can do to stop it.

"Oh I do. I know that when they see me on the cover of Vogue, or in an interview in my bright kitchen larger than your entire fucking house, they wish that they were me. They look around at the degradation of their mediocre lives and try to fill the giant gaping hole of inadequacy they feel every time they see my face, compare the slimness of my wrists and ankles to their own processed-food bloated flesh, wish they could achieve the perfect gleaming straightness of my hair, or afford my perfectly starched oxford shirt." The smile quirked oddly at one corner. "And then they ask, why they aren't me? What befell them that makes their lives so puerile, so insufficient?"

The trail of old sweat running between my shoulder blades has gone ice cold. "You're blaming me."

"It's not blame, it's a fact."

I think then of my wife, the disappointed frown when she goes to rearrange the couch cushion after I have hefted myself off of it. Her heavy sigh as she lowers a toilet lid I forgot to close, or a cabinet door I left open. "Fuck off."

"Such an unsurprising response from your deficient mind. One never likes knowing one is the cause of pain in another's life, do they? Your constant lumbering presence, reeking of old sweat and cheap beer, leaving residue on the furniture, fingerprints on the stainless steel appliances she's so proud of. Your daughters cringing when one of their friends gets a look at her oafish, paunchy father lurching around the kitchen in his tighty-whiteys, scratching at his patchy, hairy back with dirty, uneven fingernails, telling themselves they'll never settle for someone like you. Knowing they want and deserve so much more than what you represent: mediocrity."

I try not to react, but my eyes prick with tears. It's a fear that stabs me in the chest every time I see embarrassment on my oldest's face when we're out together in public. Embarrassed of her old man, a dopey working guy who never went to college, and doesn't own a suit that fits him. Always hoping I won't do anything to draw attention to just how average and humiliating I am.

"See? You know it. You know what they feel. You know you'll never be good enough for them. You know they resent you, resent the life you've shackled them to."

A fat tear makes its way down my face, collecting in the stubble I didn't have time to remove this morning.

"But it's okay," the airy tone is back, as if the stale decay of her voice before was all an act. "I help."

I snort. "Oh, I bet you think you do."

"I give them a glimpse of what could be. I move into their soft little heads, rent-free. I make them believe that if they just buy the right coasters, the most expensive hand cream, or a crystal wand to rub under their eyes, that all their problems will disappear."

"My wife doesn't even buy your shit," I snuffle as I wipe away another tear.

"You might not think so, but she does. They *all* do, eventually. That's my power. I *infiltrate*. I convince them that an extra few dollars for organic is the difference between your baby's life and death. I tell them that squatting over a pot of boiling water and potpourri will make them young again. I sell them rose quartz eggs to shove in their vaginas and assholes and they write *glowing* reviews. Half this fucking shithole of a country buys my candles so all your homes are filled with the smells I choose. Do you know what the most popular one is? The one I tell them smells like *my* vagina. I ensure that every day, when you come home from a long day of work and sit down for dinner with your family, your nostrils are filled with the scent of my *cunt*. I occupy your home more intimately than you could ever *dream*. I *own* your family, whether they know it or not. Your inadequacy allowed me to do that, with barely any effort. That makes me a god."

I feel my fists clench, unable to stop the stream of tears that now course down my face.

"Your inadequacy made *me* possible. And do you know what I do with all that power, once I'm in your home and inside your wife, and fed directly into the feed your daughters ravenously consume?"

I hold my breath.

"I remind them of everything you're not. Everything you'll never be."

I grab the head loosely by the hair this time, not caring that she's swinging and spattering clots of old blood and drifts of hair in our wake as I stomp into the kitchen. The knife block (between the stove and fridge, near the cutting board, in a place designed for maximum efficiency and flow) holds a large butcher knife, one of those infomercial specials that claim to cut a can into slices.

"What do you think you're doing?" she asks in a low voice. "You think you can kill me? I'm a fucking cultural zeitgeist. I'm an icon, a legend, I'm the embodiment of everything you fear, you fat fuck—"

Her next words are muffled as I toss her head into the sink.

I flick the switch above into the on position, the sinkerator garbage disposal spinning into life.

I expect her to scream, to beg, to apologize. Instead, the only sounds she makes is a cackle of complete unhinged glee as I use the large knife to brutally chop at the mass in the sink. The laughter grows thicker and more choked, but no less merry until I manage to carve off enough to cause an unpleasant metal grinding noise from the disposal. I resort to my boot to stomp the last chunks into the wide drain, running the water and the disposal until it sounds clear.

It is well past dark when I pull into my driveway. I exit my truck and shakily examine my reflection in the driver's side window, trying to smooth down my wild hair, chunks of pastrami still clinging to my chin and chest.. I pull off my work shirt in the garage, dropping it into the washer in the mud room as I make the transition from garage to home.

There's a note on the fridge, indicating my wife and daughters had run to the store. Dinner is in the microwave for me to reheat. Could I please bring in the mail once I'm home?

In the dark quiet of our neighborhood, the crickets chirping in the grass, I open our mailbox, and inside I find a white box with a logo that now puts more fear into me than anything I've encountered in my miserable life. The label indicates it is an "introductory wellness kit." It's addressed to my wife. I'm too late. The infection has already taken hold.

As I numbly bring the box inside, I notice wafting from it

the unmistakable scent of bergamot and cedar with a tangy undernote. Nauseatingly vaginal.

8

Echidna

MYKLE HANSEN

I watched the D20 tumble, skitter, bounce on the hardwood. It jumped crooked, and tapped against the box of MAIN BEDROOM, and when it did… the box flinched? It jerked, very slightly, backward, like if the die had knocked it aside. But the die was just a little, green, pointy marble and the box was, I'd estimate, at least seventeen pounds.

I thought I heard something then… no I heard something for sure, coming out of that box! A kind of VVVVVV sound, quiet, high-pitched, like an electric pencil sharpener but far away, and a little muffled in that way that cardboard muffles things. And a little buzzy, the way cellophane packing tape rattles when it's loose.

Something was alive in that fucking box. Do we have rules for this? I am a rules-follower, a job-not-get-fired-fromer, let's see… endangered animal, endangered customer property… contraband? We're supposed to report contraband. But, we can't just set it free.

And for a second I imagined that I was in there, squeezed in the dark, trying to breathe, trying to get out, and the walls of the bedroom seemed suddenly closer…

But then I got a grip. Get a grip! I said to myself, and Yessir! I said back. I am a professional mover. I know the four Cs: courtesy, care, consideration, customer focus…

The box moved again. Like if a little fat person inside had taken a running leap against the inside surface, the side marked THIS END UP throbbed, and the box skidded six inches and went VVVVVV! and crinkle-crackled some more. It was a quiet sound, but in the silence of the empty house, it seemed enormous.

This was messed up. And it was Hour Nine, and I was tired, just exhausted from the soles of my feet to the top of my brain, and this didn't make any sense, and what the hell was inside that box, really?

And, was it going to die?

I needed to escalate this. The company has a procedure, a phone number that puts me in touch with an upper-level supervisor at the company, somewhere. I have my desk in an office mostly to impress customers, but my boss isn't there. The whole company is in the cloud, and actually I dial the same number that a customer would dial, the number that's printed on the side of our truck: 800-O-SHIPPY. I just know how to escalate. I can call in assistance, or advice, or some reassurance that the death of some customer's accidentally-suffocated kitten wasn't on me.

Like that would matter to the kitten.

My phone was out in the truck, and I had one last stack of boxes out there too. So I turned toward the bedroom door.

"Ffffl!" mewled the box, or squeaked, or creaked, and it rattled like it had beans inside. Then it kind of shimmied left and right, shuffling in little twists, away from the wall, toward my feet.

"Vvvvv!" it pleaded. "Ffffl!"

The single band of packing tape around the top and bottom of that box was plain two-inch cellophane, the generic shiny stuff that likes cardboard. I had a whole roll of it in the thigh pocket of my parachute pants, in with my box cutter and my very last energy bar. If I did open that box, maybe I could reseal it again afterwards in a way that nobody would notice. But then if it turned out there was something alive inside I could say that it had clawed its way out of the box on its own, or that I had saved its life, or both things, or some other explanation. The point is, yes, I know the rules, the rules are clear: only customers open customer boxes. But they don't make these rules to kill helpless animals. The rules are to protect customer belongings.

Nobody wants their belongings to suffocate and die in a shitty cardboard box.

Then I started to get the feeling again, this feeling that

had been fucking with me all year, the no-air-can't-see-can't-breathe feeling, and the hot prickles on my neck and my scalp… but there was plenty of air, goddammit, and I could breathe, I knew I could breathe, I made myself breathe, sucking in, blowing out, musty air with the scent of dust and cardboard and no people. I was so sick of having these attacks, these… they say it's not asthma. They say I'm fine. Physically.

I am fine! I am healthy. I am a giant, big, strong mover of other peoples' lives.

"There's nothing wrong with me," I told the box.

The box squeaked, once, weakly, like a toy mouse with a broken valve.

"Fuck the customer," I decided out loud, if they had actually stuck their hamster or guinea pig or bunny rabbit in a box. That's just awful.

I got slowly down to my knees, feeling the Hour Nine soreness in every part of my back and my hamstrings and my wrists. Whatever was in there, I didn't want to make it even more scared.

"Okay buddy," I said to the box. "You're gonna be okay."

"V," said the box. It sat just beyond my reach.

"C'mere," I said. But, the box did not move. And I pictured for a moment how stupid this would look to someone who walked in here and saw me like this, talking to a box and expecting it to move like boxes just don't.

I leaned forward and crawled on hands and knees slowly toward the box.

The box scooted away from me, just six inches or so, toward the wall.

"F," it said.

I scooted closer. The box scooted farther. I scooted again and the box slid with a clunk right up against the baseboard and the other stack of boxes. Right where I had been trying to place the little annoying bastard object this whole time.

I wish I could have left it there. But no, I had this other plan. I scooted up to the box, surrounding it with my knees, blocking its escape. I got out my box cutter, and laid a hand gently on the top left corner of the box.

The box was warm from within, and it was trembling. I felt gingerly along the band of smooth cellophane sealing the top and sides, feeling for a loose corner. I could try to peel the tape off, I thought to myself, then lay it back on afterwards exactly where it had torn off, and then I'd tape that layer down with another layer, and nobody would notice a thing. I finally found a little scrap of tape sticking up on the back side. I pinched it between my finger and thumb, and began to peel.

"Lllllllll!" screamed the box, and it actually jumped! I had a hand on it so it didn't get far, but now it was jumping and shuddering and jerking from within and LLLLLLLL!ing and VVVVVVV!ing in panic, in terror, and rattling now like a box of broken china, and I knew I didn't have long, being sneaky was out the window now, so I said "Hang on!" and I pushed out the box-cutter blade with my thumb, just the barest millimeter, just enough to slit the tape, and I slashed straight down the centerline between the flaps.

And then the box… it made just the most horrible awful bad sad sound, and shook and twisted and shuddered like I could not believe. I tried to calm it down, "It's okay, it's okay, it's okay," but I looked at where I'd cut the tape, and there was all this red… this thick, red, ink gunk seeping out through the slit, like a bottle of it had broken. Red was on my hands, and my red fingerprints were all over the box, and the box was screaming…

I was shocked and scared, gasping, dizzy. It looked like blood, really, but I hadn't, had I? The blade was hardly out at all! I had been careful this time, so careful, I was courteous and compassionate and just trying to help! But the box was howling in what had to be pain, the pain and fear of the poor, poor little whatever-it-was inside…

I just had to see, I had to know, I had to get it out of there. I wriggled my fingernails in through the bloody red slot and started to force the blood-softened cardboard aside… but then the red ooze that had been seeping actually spurted, squirted out onto my shirt and my face and in my eye, and a little arc of it across the floor, and then the box spasmed with crazy inner force—

And then it bit me! A hot shock on my left hand between my thumb and knuckle… the side of the box, the cardboard corner of the box, just like, for a moment, opened up I think? It happened so fast I hardly saw it, I didn't believe it or understand it – but I felt it, yes, I felt the shit out of it! It bit me. Fucking owwch.

I clutched my hand and dropped the box, and it tumble-skittered past me and out the bedroom door like it had been jerked by a rope. Out in the hall I heard sliding and VVVVVVV! And then, the sound of it tumbling down the long, winding staircase to the first floor, with shattered customer belongings rattling inside.

I sat there with my blood and, like, fucking box-blood or whatever, all over me, the floor, and some of the other boxes. Now that same mess was getting tracked all over the customer premises that my crew and I had maintained as clean as a church though eight hours of in-and-out cargo traffic.

"Oh god oh god," I muttered, pissed off, and terrified, and just so fucking tired, really. For a moment I was sure I was going to have another attack, and I thought: I'll just give in this time. For a second, I was ready for the world to close in and choke me, for the air to vanish and the woozy darkness and nausea to come. I would just succumb to it, and just die and get fired, and quit and lose, and forget about my own survival or anybody else's…

But the attack didn't come. There was just the throbbing ache in my clenched left hand, the blood dripping out of my fist, and every other soreness of my muscles, bones, and skin as I climbed to my feet and stumbled out to the hallway.

I didn't see the box at the base of the stairs or anywhere else—I mean, I saw a lot of boxes, a couple dozen of them in the living room, stacked neatly against the walls with the Sharpie-scribbled LR mark facing out, and a few more marked FOYER in the foyer, and in the dining room ten DR boxes were organized peacefully on top of the big dining room table with the anti-scratch courtesy sheet wrapping it like a big housewarming present. I wandered around the premises searching for my little frightened animal, but I couldn't find it among all the other holy customer property, belongings, furnishings, heirlooms and accessories. There were little drops of red box-juice on the steps and on the floor, but they didn't make a trail, they just made a mess.

It was hiding, of course. The poor hurt thing. It was hiding from me.

I saw no more sign of it and heard no more peep from it as I went outside, shut the front door behind me and headed to the first aid kit in the van.

I called. I escalated. I waited on hold, and wrapped gauze around my bleeding hand. It was dark out now, 8:15pm, and the lights were shining through the curtains of the house. I thought about running the last three boxes out with the hand truck, I could do most of it one-handed, just dump them in the foyer, lock up and leave… leave behind all that red mess I'd made, and the questions, and the box, the poor little box…

The supervisor picked up the line. He let me know his name was Tony, and that he was regional, he already knew my name was Jason, and that I should just start at the crux.

"You know what the crux is?" he said.

"Yessir, the crux is, um, there's a box in this shipment that contains something alive, some live animal. I found it in the very back of the truck in the last load, it's been inside that box a while, and I got concerned."

"You got concerned. And then what? Did you open this box?"

"No sir. I started to, but then –"

"Stop. No. Do not open a customer box."

"No sir. I didn't."

"I will alert the customer, okay? I'll call the number on file and we'll see what they want to do about this."

"Thank you," I said.

"Hold the line," he said.

Some soul music started to click through the speakerphone. I held my hand up a little closer to the dome light and peeled back the gauze a little. It was more a slice than a bite. Like a paper cut that was deeper than the deepest paper cut possible, but still, suppose it was a paper cut? Suppose the box had just wriggled in just a perfectly wrong way while I was holding it, and cut me, but it didn't actually bite me, because that was impossible? Let's say?

I glanced out at the customer premises again, a big Tudor thing with too many windows, all the curtains drawn, really obviously not lived in at the moment but still kept up, mowed and painted, like a temple. Houses between occupants, they all look a little bit like they're holding their breath.

"Listen," clicked in the supervisor, "we aren't getting through to the customer at the number on file. I know they're supposed to be showing up in the morning, so I'd say, well, did you get it all shipped?"

"Yessir, all shipped," I lied, but it was almost true.

"So go home why dontcha? You're in Hour Nine, and the customer packed their own boxes."

"I think there's an animal in that box, though, is the thing. I think it's suffering in there."

"Aww. Well listen, if they put an animal in a box I'm sure they knew what they were doing. I don't know, there's a lot of animals, some of them might like being in boxes. Either way, it's a customer-packed shipment, it's a customer problem."

"Yessir."

"They can't hold you or Shippy responsible for what happens if they pack carelessly. Is it labeled LIVE ANIMAL or FRAGILE or anything?"

"Just MAIN BEDROOM."

"Oooh, well, seriously that's a like a double no-go there. People's live animal situations in their bedroom situations? I guarantee you that's not our problem. Was the box damaged in any way during moving?"

"Not damaged, no sir, but it got a little stained."

"But not opened, right? Dented?"

"It cut me… I cut myself on it, somehow. I'm afraid I got some blood on it."

"Blood? Blood? Hold the phone! You didn't say anything about injury. Tell me now, where did the injury take place, and when, and were you following safety protocols, and are you still injured? Tell me everything."

"Oh, it's just a cut, no big thing, I got it from the side of the box somehow, and I bled a little bit on the box, and a little bit in the premises, on the floor. It's kinda gross looking is all."

Silence.

"But the real thing is, the problem is, there's still this animal, or something, alive in there and moving around –"

"Is it out? You said you didn't open it."

"I didn't! The box just, it's being moved from inside somehow. It hops, and makes noises, and scoots around on the floor."

Prolonged silence.

"A snake, maybe?" said the supervisor.

"I don't think snakes make noises like that."

"Or an echidna?" he said.

"A what?"

"It's like a miniature porcupine. They're cute. I saw one on Instagram."

"Do they live in boxes?"

"No," he said. "They live in Australia."

"Well, whatever it is, it's running around the customer premises, and it could die or get hurt, or cause, like, damage to the shipment, or I don't know what."

"Well," he sighed, "I gotta say this is a new one."

Super-prolonged awkward silence.

"Listen," said the supervisor in a brand new kind of voice,

"I know this is Hour Nine for you. Tell me first off: are you in need of medical attention?"

"No, I bandaged it, it's not so bad."

"Are you feeling dizzy or lightheaded? Are you… running a fever?"

"I don't think there's a thermostat in the first aid kit here," I said, "but really, I feel fine."

"Okay. Glad to hear it, yep. So, Jason… can you just, go back in there, and clean up the mess, and get that box stacked and shipped, and lock and leave? The customer will handle the rest."

"Yeah, but there's all this blood –"

"Can you use, like, a rag or something?"

"Okay, but that box won't sit still!"

"Can you just tape it down? Stack some other shipment on top of it? Stick it in a closet and shut the door maybe? Seriously, just make that shipment be shipped? And clean it out and lock it up?"

"Well yeah, yessir I can, but what about the echidna?"

"The kid? What kid?"

"The animal in the box! What if it dies?"

"Listen, that is, you know, sweet. I get that you want to be courteous and careful. Really, I salute that. But at the end of the day, which I'll remind you was an hour ago, we are not responsible for this. We are not responsible for the customer's animals unless we packed those animals ourselves. You're not going to get in trouble over this, as long as you can get me that box stacked, and that premises tidy, and that front door buttoned up. Can you do that for me?"

I looked out the window at the house and noticed the yellow atrium light streaming from the open front doorway, casting a long, warm stripe of illumination on the wide steps and the jagged flagstones.

And a small rectangle of stillness perched on the pathway, casting its own long shadow that pointed directly at me.

I sure did think I had closed that door.

Then, I saw that rectangle move.

"Jason? Hey? Can you do that for me?"

"Yessir," I said, "I'll do what I can."

I spent another long, slow hour finishing up and cleaning little red dots off the floor. I didn't even try to put the box back in the house. It followed me all the way back to the truck, and when I picked it up and laid it on the passenger seat, it didn't struggle a bit, though it scooted far away when I tried to stroke it while driving home.

The trip home was slow, too – some nasty wreck on the I-45, I passed right next to it but I shielded my eyes – so it was almost midnight when we finally got back to my apartment. The box was docile at this point, just fffffffing quietly and rumbling a little, like a content cat. It seemed to trust me to pick it up for short periods of time.

I already had a couple other half-full cardboard cartons sitting out on the floor by the sofa in the living-roomy end of the studio. It was some vinyl records I needed to sell and some ex-girlfriend stuff that I still imagined she might come back for. A pile of bills, collection notices, and such. I laid down this box next to those other boxes, thinking it might feel more at home, and it seemed to; it kind of nestled up against them and was mostly quiet while I went to the kitchenette to get a beer.

Under the little light bulb in the fridge, my hand looked pretty bad; bloody, and pale, and wrapped in drippy, red gauze. But it felt good to hold a cold beer in it.

I flopped down on the sofa and let the weight of the whole day drain out into the cushions. I ran my fingers through my hair. I looked at the TV and the clock on the wall. I took a couple of big, deep breaths. I never have any energy left after a day of this job. I just come home and collapse. The sofa had been just as comfy as the bed since Macy moved out.

I sucked down the rest of that delicious cold beer and closed my eyes. I didn't want to think, to remember, to worry, to understand. I was just a stone, come to rest at the bottom of a long, bumpy hill of a job.

I heard cardboard and tape sliding on cheap linoleum. Then I felt a little nudge against my foot.

"Lllll?"

Okay, fine, I needed to clean up my hand and also see what I could do for this box. I rocked forward and scooped it up with my good right hand, steadying the top with my left fist. We crammed together into the bathroom, and I balanced the box on the toilet, where it sat patiently and made no sound. For a moment, it was just a box.

I ran the sort-of-hot water in the tiny sink, carefully

unwound the gauze, and dropped it in the wastebasket, all the time feeling watched by the box – not in a creepy way or anything, but curiously, like a child. I rinsed the gash and had a brief, painful shot at rubbing it with a soapy rag, but that stung too much. I found some more gauze in the medicine cabinet and wrapped up my wound again, then turned around to clean up the box.

You can only get cardboard so wet before it's a problem, but the box at least did not struggle this time. It flinched a little bit when I wiped the tape with peroxide, but when I laid a new strip of tape down over the slit I'd cut, it seemed to sigh and relax. The peroxide did a decent job on the tape, and I knew it was good for preventing infections, but there wasn't much else I could do about the look of things. It was a gory-looking box; the red stuff had soaked too much into the brown stuff. Nobody wasn't going to notice what had happened.

I dried off the box with one of Macy's towels and carried it back to the sofa, stopping by the fridge for another beer. I guzzled it down, then laid myself out lengthwise with the box on my chest. It was big, but not too big. Warm. Purring. Vvvvv.

Some time later, the sun came up and my phone went off. It was the ringtone of my job. I ignored it for a while. Was I late? No, it was Saturday. My day off.

"Ffff?"

The box was now nestled against the sofa on the floor, right next to my head.

The phone rang. I let it ring. It rang seven times and went to voicemail. Then, it rang some more. With my cheek on the cushion, I watched the box scoot around on the floor, scootch up alongside my phone lying there, and then sweep it over to where I could reach it. It perched there expectantly, watching me. Such a good box.

I laid the phone on top of my ear and pressed a button. "Hello?"

"Please hold," said some recording. Then came some awful jazz fusion music, just for a second, and then a click.

"Good morning, Mr. Jason? This is Bill Trudge at Shippy. I work with Tony, who assisted you last night."

"Yeah, hello," I slowly said, "morning, good morning, yessir. Hi."

"Good morning! I'm calling, we're calling to just loop back and check in, on a few, um, items here, on your most recent Shippy shipment, and your escalation from last night. Number one is: how are you doing this morning? Do you feel… injured?"

"I'm okay, I guess. Getting better. Resting." The hand ached, but the color was coming back to it and the gauze wasn't too bloody. "I'm not scheduled today, am I?"

"No light-headedness? Difficulty breathing? Pain behind the eyes?"

"No sir, no, really I'm fine. Just tired."

"Okay great! That's great. Great to hear that. Checking that off."

"Yeah," I yawned, "thanks, do that." I sat up, put the phone on speaker, rubbed my eyes.

"So," I said.

"So", he said, "last night, at the premises. You checked off in the Shippy app that you got the complete shipment shipped, is that correct?"

"Yessir, that's correct."

The box wriggled a little.

"And then you spoke with the customer?"

"Yeah, um, no? We were pre-arrival yesterday, just me and two crew. Customer arrives today, it says so in the manifest. There wasn't anybody home."

"Well, did the customer call you then?"

"Ah, sorry, just to be real clear: I haven't talked with, or had any message with, or spoken to, or heard from, this particular customer at all. We tried to reach them last night – it would have helped a lot, actually – but they did not pick up. So we just got it, you know, done."

"Hmm," he said.

I felt a wave of heat on my skin, a little pinpoint of pain behind my eyes. I looked down at the box, stationed at my feet like a faithful dog, or cat, or echidna, seeming to look up to me. Seeming to trust me. Seeming to love me.

"Well, listen, Jason, here's how it is. Sometimes a customer and a Shippy team member might just remember some events, maybe, differently? It happens. And when it does, we're going to stand by you, of course, to help you succeed, to get Shippy shipments shipped, because that's teamwork.

We're there for you, but we're not actually there, like you are. Our part of the team, at this level, we can't just listen in."

"Okay," I said, feeling a little nauseous now.

"In some other states we can, through the app. But not in your state. So when the team member and the customer give us conflicting narratives, well, the teamwork thing to do is to remember that the customer always comes first. Right?"

I felt my throat tightening up. "Yeah," I croaked.

"Hey listen! Don't worry about it, you're not in trouble. The customer just asked us to send you back in, because they're having some issue with locating some particular item. Which, if you shipped the whole shipment, should be easy to find. Right?"

I was fucked.

"Jason?"

I was so totally fucked. The customer got home, they went straight to the bedroom to find the one box that wasn't there, they probably saw some drop of blood on the floor that I had missed with the cleanup kit, they probably were crazy worried and freaking out now about their poor box animal. I was going to get fired, lose my bond, lose this apartment, lose my grip, go to jail maybe –

"Jason, can you hear me?"

"Yessir, I'm here, yeah. So they want me back there… today? On a Saturday?"

"Yes! Today, Jason. Whenever you're up and ready to be customer-facing. And listen, this isn't above-and-beyond time, this is actual paid hours. Time and a half. So don't forget to app-in when you get there, and app-out as soon as you're done."

"Yessir. Thanks."

"Sure, buddy. We're just doing what we can, on behalf of Shippy, to help out a teammate and comply with all the labor laws in your state! There's a ton of 'em, too. But also, FYI, this customer really seemed to like you. They gave you five stars. Probably they're going to tip you out handsomely. So no big stress."

"Five stars? Really?"

"Written feedback, too. They said you're a very caring person. We really like to hear that from customers. So, good work! And when can you get over there?"

I got over there close to noon. The box had gotten spooked when I said it was time to leave, it clunked all over the apartment knocking stuff over, it had been a slow process coaxing it into the car, but now it rode calmly on the passenger seat of my hatchback, not minding the lap-belt, just ticking like a slow clock. I parked down the block, peering distance from the big Tudor house. I didn't see any cars in the driveway, or out on the curb. The curtains were still closed, and the welcome brochure was still on the doorknob where I'd hung it, along with the lockbox containing the key. No signs of any customers at all, even though they were supposed to meet me there.

The whole drive there I had been rehearsing in the car some kind of super-embarrassing confession or explanation, that I'd been both concerned about and not allowed to actually open this box, and had been unable to contact them about it. That was all true, but when I practiced saying it out loud I could feel my employment slipping out from under me. I'd done something really wrong: taken customer belongings off the premises, back to my private residence. They would call it stealing. Bringing it back was the right thing to do, and I would be every bit as fired for it.

But also, in rehearsing what I would say to these customers as I drove the long I-45 corridor back to their fancy house, I kept coming back to: why the fuck did they put an animal in a box in the first place? Or else, what the hell was this box, really? And also, thanks for the five stars, but that's bullshit, because we never met at all, so what is really going on here? I was mad at these people at the same time I was scared, and mostly I was worried about what would happen to this box after I returned it.

But now, as I leaned on the doorbell and knocked on the door and shouted "Hello?" with no reply and saw no sign of life around any of the neighboring large-lawned homes, I started to wonder if I might just get away with un-doing everything I'd done wrong. Like, it now seemed obvious what I should have done last night. Like I had lied and said I did.

I went back to the car to get the box. It peeked up out the window at me. What was it? Why did I even care so much? I couldn't say. Living creatures are magical, is all. But really, I was no good at living things, never had been. I couldn't even keep a girlfriend. This box had a family, and a big home in a nice neighborhood. And no matter what it was, it wasn't going to die, or else it would have died by now. I had panicked, I had been wrong… but maybe everything could be right again, if I could just get this last bit of shipment shipped.

I got the key out of the lock box and let myself in.

"Hello," I yelled professionally, "It's Jason from Shippy! Anybody home?" I peered around, but nothing had moved an inch from the frankly perfect arrangement my crew had left it in. Every carton still stacked neatly, every furnishing aligned carefully in its labeled zone. We had transported a life, a home, a precious universe from A to B with care, courtesy, consideration, and that other thing. It was beautiful, how we did what we did. It had been such a simple and rewarding job, until yesterday. The work was hard, but my mind was easy, until yesterday. I never realized how much this job meant to me, until just now.

"I have the rest of your shipment here!" I continued to yell to what seemed like nobody. "Sorry about the mix-up! But it's alive and well, and I'm just going to put it with the rest of Main Bedroom now!"

I had worried that the box might protest, that it might even try to bite me again. I had imagined that it feared this place and wouldn't want to come back. I was prepared for a struggle, wearing the heavy leather gloves that we use for moving woodshop equipment. But the box wasn't bothered when I brought it into the house, and now it seemed calm, warm, and happy in my arms as I carried it up the wooden staircase and into the master bedroom. It seemed to be humming itself a little song of VVVs.

"Thanks little guy," I whispered to the surface of the box. "Everything's going to be good now."

"Mmmmmm," said the box.

"I was only trying to help!" I said out loud to anyone listening.

"Vvvvv," said the box.

"It's just," I said, "I grew up on a county farm, and my dad made me take care of the animals, but he never really told me how I was supposed to do it."

"Ffff."

"Dad didn't know either. I think we were always just pretending to know what we were doing. My dog died, and my duck died, and I had a tame skunk that somebody just shot, from a truck, out on the county road when I wasn't looking. And I had to put down a sick goat once. She had tumors all over her. But I didn't do it right at all. I just had this little small-gauge rifle and not enough bullets. It was just awful."

"Lllll."

We were standing there in the master bedroom, me and my box and a dozen other boxes in four neat stacks against the north wall. I kneeled down, placed MAIN BEDROOM gently on the oaken floor – THIS SIDE UP – and stroked the tape on its lid.

"There were other times, too. I didn't know what I was

doing; I was just a kid. I hurt a lot of animals. My dad made me. I'm really sorry."

The boxes considered my confession.

"Living things are magical," I said. "I just want to get them home."

Under the dim light streaming through the closed curtains into the silent bedroom, the four stacks by the wall began to shuffle toward me, gingerly, patiently, in soft, simple motherly motions, while I kneeled there, sobbing, before the little bloodied carton full of customer life. The boxes gathered around, closer, until finally they surrounded me, cradled me, and I heard their gentle shushing through the layers of kraft paper and cellophane.

9

The Sound Of Infinity

CYNTHIA PELAYO

The noise came from outside, I tried to lie to myself.

Or, maybe it was inside?

I'm standing in the bedroom and the windows are open and there's the slow shush of early morning noises all melding into one; cars and people murmuring and a radio playing in the distance.

The noises dull for a moment, and I take a deep breath.

My thoughts come back to here, right here. I was so close to turning off the light, leaving this room, getting back to the truck, getting off work, and getting on with my life. All I wanted to do was finish this job, leave the truck at home, and head out to the observatory later tonight. The Perseid

Meteor shower was scheduled to pass through the night sky, and whatever chance I had to look up at the stars I took.

Once again, the noises pick up, and I know they're not coming from outside, but inside, from that box.

That's how noises operate. They cascade around us. No matter how silent one thinks their environment is, there's always something waiting to shift, or bend, or break, to make itself known, if even a memory, if even an idea.

When I wasn't working, I spent a lot of time thinking about noises and the nighttime sky. I thought I'd play music one day, but I never got there. There were a few shows at a few bars, yes, but never enough to make a living. Instead, this is my life, picking up the contents of people's lives and moving them elsewhere. Life is so strange like that.

Since I couldn't play music for a living, I just wound up studying it, reading about it late into the night, and that's where the searches shifted and morphed, moving beyond this planet and into the sky. I learned about all of the sounds that the universe makes up there, when none of us are noticing.

The universe operates most mysteriously, and there are sounds playing in the cosmos. Blasts and clangs, high-pitch, low-pitch, short wavelengths, long wave-lengths, a spectrum of sound. Galaxies are always playing music for us; we just need to listen to the music. Of course, it's wondrous to look up at the nighttime sky and the dotted landscape of stars above and wonder, but what I wish the most is to have the ability to hear the symphony the universe plays for us. It's playing for us even now. We're just not listening. And so,

I wonder, what does that music sound like? The music of infinity? Are there secrets tucked within its notes? Are there mysteries within each rise and fall of its melody? Can that music sway us any which way? To good, to love, to terror?

There are wonders and horrors above.

I used to love going to the planetarium as a kid, looking at models of planets and space, and I'd always wondered, what occupied all of that space. Big stars, little stars, star dust, monsters? Then at night after work, I'd read online about the universe and that's how I learned about black holes and dead stars, exoplanets, gravitational waves, multi-messenger astronomy, and more. I couldn't play music, but I could learn about the music above being played no one really knew or thought about.

I'm interested in the sound waves above and the story they tell. It's all a great mystery, in ways. Something is happening above, we just can't truly tap into it with the technology and abilities that we currently have. Sometimes I even wonder if maybe we need a great messenger to make us hear what it is being played along the Milky Way, more, beyond.

It's true that unexpected noises startle us so. A strange sound brings with it the possibility of something that wasn't supposed to be there, or something unknown, or something unexplained. Mysterious sounds appear, and they are there for the briefest of moments. And when they do appear—

We listen.

We witness.

We measure.

And maybe it's not so much a measuring, but a calculation that processes inside our brain that begins with 'What was that noise?' And so, we pause whatever movement our muscles were shifting to, and we focus, trying to pinpoint where exactly that noise came from.

I should be on my way out, but the die is on the floor pressuring me to open the box. I hear whatever is inside the box once again shift and move and bang against the walls, and I can't ignore it anymore. I reach for my boxcutter in my back pocket, kneel, and press the blade against the edges. I pull open the flaps of the cardboard box slowly, knowing very well I could lose my job doing this, but I can't ignore that it sounds like there's something alive, trapped in this box.

When I look down at the contents, I'm shocked, because how can this thing be the source of that noise? It's a mask. I sit there, poring over its details. The mask is highly decorative, brightly colored, painted red and black, but grotesque with distorted features. Large eyes, two slits for a nose, horns that adorn its head. I can't imagine anyone wanting to display this or even wear it. I reach for it, to see if maybe there's something beneath it, and it's hot to the touch. I pull back. A wave of nausea washes over my face, down my neck, shoulders, and arms. This thing, it just feels wrong, distorted, and since the second I opened the box, it's as if the air has shifted and there's this low vibration—not something pleasant, but something unnerving—that pulses all around me. I feel my arms trembling and my jaw tightening. Something is happening—some transformation—and I don't know how to look away from this, how to look away from myself even.

I turn to the door, and I know I should leave, but my legs can't seem to move. I'm frozen here, in shock, fear, disgust. All of it.

There are moments when your entire life changes, a fork in the path, and we can sometimes anticipate it. Other times, there is no warning, the shift just happens, and the cosmos collapses on us. I feel the weight of the object in my hands, the smoothness of the material, and I know nothing is ever going to be the same.

Put it on, a tiny voice in my head says.

"I'm not going to put this thing on my face," I say, my voice doesn't sound like my own. My eyes remain focused on the mask. Horns jut out from the top of its head. Its eyes are black holes, and its mouth is open wide and lined with sharp teeth. It's all made of paper mache, I can tell, carefully crafted, but why would anyone want this demonic-looking mask? Can demons sing songs and—play music? I wondered. And what does a demon's symphony sound like? Is it soft and quiet, like a breath?

I know that the sound I heard—just moments before—came from this thing I am holding. It sounded like… an exhale. Soft, and then guttural.

"Hello?" I call out to the house, not sure why. It seems like the right thing to do. Maybe it isn't the mask, I think. Maybe it is something else inside the house that I wasn't aware of, I force myself to believe. I close my eyes and listen, and once again, ever so faintly I hear it: a delicate exhale followed by a deep rumble. I eye the mask. How could it make a noise? I shift the object in my hands this way and that. It's an impossibility that such a thing could make sound. There are no wires. There is no way, no mechanism present, for it to emit sound. It is just a simple mask.

Put it on, I once again hear the voice in my head.

Something compels me to touch the mask once again. I brace to be burned when I touch it, but it's no longer hot. I tap on it lightly, and then I raise the mask just so with one hand. I can feel my fingers shaking as I bring it to my right ear, and there it is, a whooshing sound. It's as if I have brought a seashell up to my ear, and it's as if the sounds I hear are great ocean waves crashing into one another, but I know it is not the sound of the ocean. It is the sound of infinity. I set the mask back down into the box.

I can feel my heartbeat quicken, and my pulse begin to throb. I should be in the truck. I should be on my way home. I should not be here right now.

I look back to the mask, and it feels like it's watching me. I wonder for a second if it just wasn't a mask, but something more, an antenna in a sense that, if worn, could transform me into something else that could hear the music of darkness above? And if I could hear that music, could I force everyone to hear it too?

My hands move back to the mask against my will. I feel like I'm no longer in control of my movements or my body. I pick up the mask with both hands, and I close my eyes again, as if closing my eyes can somehow help stop what is happening. I think I had read that in some article, somewhere. We do these strange things in order to focus better, like when we're driving, and we're looking for an address, and we slow the car, and turn down the music, as if quiet will help us better concentrate on what it is we are looking for. Maybe closing my eyes will make this stop.

Maybe.

I open my eyes and I am still here. I am still holding this monstrous mask. There are things within our brains and our bodies that we don't quite understand. I want to believe that. I want to believe that we do not know all of the things that we want to know.

My hands begin to tremble, and I can feel a thin layer of sweat forming on my palms.

I want to scream, call for help, but I can't. I'm being possessed by this brightly colored mask made of paper mache, that I know now is not just a simple mask. It's something else, something greater, something that I may never understand. Or, maybe that's the true dread, maybe I will come to truly understand all of it soon.

The mask continues looking at me, staring at me, enticing me. I hear that noise again, the scratching and the scraping, and maybe it's coming from inside of my skull. I think of the warbling sounds hundreds of thousands of miles of above, millions of miles even, and how those noises play across forever, and how we just can't hear them. I wondered too if that music above carries with it any messages, guides, or instructions. And, I wondered even more so, how could any human ear tap into the sounds of the galaxy, without a messenger?

Then, my focus returns to the mask.

I follow its lines, the outline of its shape, I take in its size, those sharp teeth and horns, and now I hear something different. It's not the sound of scratching or scraping against cardboard, but something else. It's deep, low, guttural. An animal preparing to attack. I know now it's coming from the mask. I know now all of the sounds came from the mask. It had always been the mask.

"What will happen?" I can finally speak, but nothing answers. My thoughts feel like a meteor shower, like fiery spheres are fanning across my mind, and then, it all slowly begins to make sense, and then, I begin to hear that music that plays in the dark above that I've so longed to hear.

"Maybe they all need to hear what it is I hear? Maybe that's what I'm meant to do, not get the truck back to my house, and not go to the planetarium to see the Perseid Meteor shower, and not carry on like I used to. Maybe I need to force them all to listen to the great beating of the stars above.

I slowly inch the mask closer and closer to my face. I hear the sounds of the ocean. It's like the mask is a seashell playing back the sounds of waves crashing into one another. The mask affixes snugly to my face, and just as I inhale, and take a deep breath, I feel thousands of sharp knives pierce into my skin. I feel the warm rush of blood, the cracking and grinding of bone, and I hear the screams, all of the screams that have ever been uttered in the past, in the present, and all of the screams in the future to come.

I know all sound here and there, above and below, from beginning to end, and now that I am the mask and the mask is me, it's time to finally, finally leave this job and leave this life and make everyone listen to all of the darkness that has ever played.

10

Deceit

JOHN WAYNE COMUNALE

The box was light, much lighter than it should've been considering what I knew to be inside. I thought I'd sensed him, caught a phantom whiff of his scent here or there, but convinced myself it was in my head. It had happened before over the years, thinking he was close, *feeling* his presence looming, but it was always just a product of my paranoia. Or I'd convinced myself of as much. This was different, though. This was definite. I'd been found.

I moved to the kitchen, placed the box on the counter, and took a breath before peeling off the tape and unfolding the flaps. There inside, just as I'd suspected, was Abas. He was in the form of a serpent, cliché yet apropos, coiled within the box. His eyes glinted in the light like jade stones cut by an unforgiving jeweler, all sharp angles, and pointy edges. His forked tongue darted in and out of a mouth that appeared to be smiling, an unsettling visual even with all I've seen.

Abas rose, extending his head and part of his slender, scaled body over the lip of the box, while the rest of him remained wound in a neat pile at the bottom. He'd taken many forms over the years we worked together, and this serpent was one of them.

The scales adorning his tumescent form were gleaming gold and black, as if comprised of precious metal and stone. It could've been, if he wanted, though the functionality of such would be limited. His underbelly gave off a soft, pink glow—another personal touch of Abas, who never played down his vanity. We stared at each other for a moment silently as the first thunderclap of the coming many sounded from outside.

It hadn't been cloudy when I'd started working earlier, and while the rumbling was still a ways off, a storm was on its way. The sun set not only early this time of year but quickly too. It was here, then gone in an instant with no pageantry, no dawdling. In the summer months, the sun hung languidly on the horizon for hours, always threatening to take leave while never seeming to go away completely. Just when I'd decided to break the silence, Abas spoke first.

"Raum, my friend," the snake hissed. "Or should I say, Joseph?"

He was referring to the name stitched on my shirt under a

patch for the moving service at which this version of myself was currently employed. *Three Moving Dudes.* There was a pair of sunglasses embroidered above the title as well. The name was a bit misleading because while there were indeed three 'moving dudes,' I was the only one who did any of the moving. The other two men, brothers who owned the company, spent most of their time getting high, gambling on sports, and telling me what to do. It was a raw deal, but I didn't mind. It gave me time to think.

"Hello Abas," I sighed. "I… I guess you…"

"Finally found you?" The snake interrupted. "Yes, it seems so, but I'm not the only one."

Thunder boomed again, still far off, but getting closer. A flash of lightning seconds later lit the kitchen momentarily, before shadows chased the brightness away.

"It sounds like you're right," I conceded, leaning back against the opposite counter, not daring to break eye-contact. "But you got here first. So, what do we do?"

"You have no idea how long I've been waiting to tell you *exactly* what we're going to do." The snake was snide, an aspect of his tone that bled through regardless of the form he took.

I'd first decided to pair up with Abas because of his conniving trickster ways. He was too smart and too crafty for his own good, and we were both into mischief for the sake of it. He also happened to share my affinity and desire for wealth. Not the kind you earned by working, or mining, or even conquering and pillaging, but through the art of thievery. At least, I refer to it as an art. Abas seemed to share the sentiment when we first started, but things changed.

We'd been used to working independently, as it is with our kind, but for whatever reason, we thought we could make it work. There were sure to be growing pains in our partnered venture, but we left the Void confident we'd figure things out together. We started small, traveling between time and realms of reality to steal from all manner of different species and lifeforms, and we stored the amassed wealth in a vault we'd conjured, then hidden amongst the treacherous outskirts of the Void. Our secret treasure trove filled quickly as we stole more and more to feed our ravenous greed, but still we were left unsatisfied and unsated. We needed more, and to get it, we'd have to set our sights higher. We would have to think bigger.

Our new goal became to steal from all the kings of Hell. It was a formidable undertaking, since they were known to spread their riches across several iterations of reality, but being eternal made the task far less daunting. I thought it was a good idea at the time, we both did, and it couldn't have started off better.

We began with Jamaz, the infernal king of Hellfire, as his hotheadedness and quick temper made him easy to distract with misdirection. Our plan was to have Abas manipulate his perception through trickster-magic, leaving me to employ a particular special skill of my own. I've been called a 'master thief' in that I have a knack for making large amounts of riches disappear from one place and reappear in another, though I feel the title doesn't do proper justice when used to describe my talent.

The skills Abas and I possess are typically used to torment beings outside of the Void, those who live in realms where the likes of us are referred to as demons or devils. Earthly realms where the Void is called 'Hell' because their limited capacity makes it impossible to conceptualize such a place any other way. I don't mind those labels necessarily, except it lumps us together, putting forth the misleading inference that we're all 'on the same side,' so to speak. We've been called *Legion,* as there are an unfathomable number of entities like us, but we are all very much alone. We are on no one's side but our own. Something I should've taken into closer consideration when deciding to partner up Abas. I wasn't *that* naïve, but admit I allowed myself to get caught up in the moment.

Like I said, Jamaz was easy as he was already engaged in another of his many wars using troops he raised from the dead or fashioned from dirt and clay. He wielded them to inflict violence across foreign lands for no reason other than bloodlust. He was already too busy for us to register as a blip on his radar. Maybe if we hadn't started with him, maybe if we'd come up against more of a challenge in the beginning, we would've wised up and abandoned the whole thing. Stealing from the king of Hellfire with such little effort only swelled our already enlarged egos, stuffing us with pride well beyond our appetite, but we were gluttons for the force feeding. We reveled in it, and were soon on to our next target, but that was as far as we got.

Abas and I tested our luck with fire and didn't get burned, so we decided to move on to another elemental ruler. Harthan, who holds power over water in and out of the Void, was next on our list. We didn't count on his capacity for jealousy and wrath, or his unebbing desire for vengeance against those who've wronged him. Call it a lapse in memory or judgement, or a bit of both. Harthan suspected something from the start, unfazed by Abas's attempted trickery and unwilling to fall for the same distractions as Jamaz.

In the end, Abas was able to conjure an illusion which momentarily fooled the king into believing his treasure was safe. We didn't have long, a moment or two at most, and in a blink, I moved his magnitude of riches across existence and into our vault.

He was on us in an instant, much faster than either of us were prepared for, and in the end, we barely escaped, and have been running ever since. Abas was clever, but spineless, and I knew I couldn't trust him, so I went off on my own. I left him behind to fend for himself. Like I said, there is no loyalty amongst the *Legion.*

I knew he'd be looking for me, *they'd* be looking for me, so I never stayed in any one place for long. I've been moving between worlds and realities, disguised as different beings, hoping to shield myself from an inevitability I couldn't outrun forever, but I was trying my damn best. Maybe I'd been lazy or sloppy lately, or maybe I'd fallen into the old cliché of wanting to be caught, but regardless of the reason, my reckoning had come. A few reckonings, from the sound of the approaching storm picking up steam outside. It wouldn't be long now.

The only thing I had going in my favor, the *only* reason I hadn't been ripped to cosmic shreds by Abas upon opening the box, was he still needed me. We had to be together to open the vault, and without one, the other could not gain access. I'd long since abandoned the idea of ever enjoying our plunder, but Abas had decidedly not. Going back to the vault was a surefire way to be instantly detected. We may as well turn ourselves over to the water king willingly since, while able to hide for short periods across other planes, he had the ability to know *exactly* where we were once we were in the Void again. He'd be there seconds after we materialized at the vault, maybe less than a second, nowhere near enough time to open it up, let alone retrieve and flee with the contents. There was something off about the entire interaction that was nagging at me.

"I'm afraid you don't have much of a choice in the matter, nor much time to do anything about it," Abas continued.

Another clap of thunder rumbled from outside on cue, as if signaling the storm's arrival. It was accompanied by an explosion of rain that pelted the big, empty house like fat, watery fists, threatening to pound down the walls. They seemed to be working in tandem with the wind in its attempt to pull the roof off.

"Not *much* of a choice," I asked. "Or no choice at all?"

I tried to sound smug and clever as I scrambled to think up a plan. If there was a way to avoid my unavoidable reckoning for even a few moments more, I was going to figure out how. Abas hissed and uncoiled extending another foot higher from the box, his glowering gemstone eyes flashed brightly from the surge of fury.

"Don't be a fool, Raum," Abas spat. "Or more of one than you've already been. You *think* you have a choice? Fine, here are your choices. You know Harthan approaches. You can feel him, same as me. In a matter of moments, he'll arrive, and you can imagine he won't be happy to see you."

"Us," I said. "He won't be happy to see *us*."

"What of us?" Abas laughed. "I'll be gone. Back through the box and in another time and place altogether. I won't even look like this stupid snake anymore, but you won't have anywhere to go. Not this time. So, you can stay here and wait to be obliterated across galaxies as Harthan unloads unreasonable amounts of pain and fury upon you for eons."

"You make it sound so glamorous," I said.

Abas stared silently in lieu of laughing at my quip, his tongue darting in and out of his now scowling snake mouth. Thunder shook the walls as the storm that was Harthan bore down on the house. Water no longer fell in oversized drops, but now gushed from the sky with the force and fury of a giant open faucet. The king was taking advantage of his power over water, using it to make his eminent presence known.

"Your other choice is simple," Abas continued. "You know

what I want, and you know I need you to get to it. I'll take you back to the void, back to our safe, and once we open it you can go on with your ridiculous game of hiding. For a time, at least. I'll give you a short head start before I tip Harthan off to your whereabouts again."

"Wait, so you get to keep all the treasure, all the riches, *and* you'll still sic Harthan on me? Sounds like I'm toast either way, so why give you access to the vault? I might as well take my licks right here, right now, while you scamper off to safety."

A moment of concern flashed across Abas's snake face. It was brief and nearly imperceptible, but I saw it. It was clear he didn't have the control over the situation he attempted to portray, and he snarled trying to keep the ire from his voice as he continued.

"If you come with me, you have a chance, albeit slim, to slip away again. You won't be able to hide as long as you have been, he will find you now sooner than later, but you'll have the chance to try."

"Have you suddenly become blameless?" I was pacing the linoleum in front of the counter, not taking my eyes off the serpent bobbing from the box on the counter. "You had a part in this, and he wants you too. Why do you think you can tell him how to find me without being evaporated by the king yourself?"

"That's where you're wrong, friend. I've made my peace with the water king. Your location in trade for my being absolved. I don't owe you a head start, but I'm willing to give you one *if* you open the vault with me first."

Thunder exploded from above again like the roaring battle cry of an approaching, kill-happy, barbarian horde. The walls did indeed shake this time, and I could feel the floor vibrate angrily beneath my feet. Abas's serpent head bobbled, and he swung it side to side in nervous expectation. The small bit of fear he let show told me he was bluffing. Jealousy and vengeance are what Harthan is known for, not mercy and forgiveness. Harthan would not excuse Abas from his wrath just because he could point him in my direction. He didn't need help from the likes of Abas, me, or anyone.

He was a king in Hell, royalty from the Void. We could both keep running, keep hiding, but even I'd accepted my luck would run out eventually. As long as Harthan kept looking, it meant he would find us both. He required no aid, no tips, no assistance in locating us or anyone else he might be looking for. Abas was being untruthful, which was expected, but there was something else as well. There was something he was hiding, something he was afraid of.

The sound of a hundred locomotives descended on the house from all sides as a mammoth cyclone containing Harthan arrived. It was as close as I'd been to the infernal king since robbing him.

"What will it be, Raum? Your time has run out."

Abas struggled to keep up his menacing air and sharp tone, but he was rattled and trying to hurry me along. He'd already begun to lower himself into the box, keeping only his head above the opening prepared to escape at the last second.

A tremendous crack came from directly overhead, but it wasn't thunder. The roof was being pried from the house by the hand of King Harthan. I truly was out of time, and while hesitant to go with Abas, I finally conceded. If he was truly taking me to the vault, we'd both be just as vanquished as we would be staying here for another moment, but I was willing to gamble with the small extension of time it would grant.

"Okay, Abas," I said approaching the box. "I'll come with you."

The roof broke loose and flew straight up into a spiraling column of spongy, wet clouds. Rain poured in through the improvised skylight in freezing, wet spikes, as I was sucked through the box by way of Abas's transportive magic.

An instant later, the sound of the storm was gone. I was dry, and standing in the darkness of the void. Or so I thought. I began to get my bearings and realized things weren't right. I was still in the kitchen of the house from which I should've departed. It wasn't raining anymore, and the thunder had been replaced with a silence just as deafening. The roof was intact, and everything else about the big empty house appeared just as it had been before I'd opened Abas's box, which was now conspicuously missing.

"Hello?" I called. "Abas? Where have you taken us?"

The serpent hissed from around the counter, as it slid across the floor in my direction. Its body still shimmered despite the lack of light, and glided with hypnotic smoothness across the bone-white linoleum. The gem-green eyes were fixed upwards into mine. The snake stopped a few feet from me, and its shape began to shift, but I already knew this wasn't Abas. Its scales split apart and dissolved into thick black smoke that poured from the broken body. It danced and billowed upward, taking on an amorphous terrifying form. Eyes and lips of varying sizes belonging to various species fluttered in and out of the dark mist, while a putrid death-stench devoured the fresh air of the room, replacing it with the scent of static disease.

"Raum. It's been too long."

The voice of Harthan was the sound of a million lungs choking on saltwater, a gurgling, haunting, death-rattle made verbal. I didn't know where Abas was, or if he was still here. My assumption was we, or at least *I*, hadn't made it through the box in time. The king had snagged me in his clutches upon arrival, keeping me right where I was.

"Hello Harthan," I said. "I suppose it has, but here we are now. You found us, or me. I imagine finding Abas will be no trouble once you've obliterated me, but if you want your treasure back beforehand, you know you'll need us both."

I don't know why I made the attempt at a last second deal. It wouldn't do much to extend my time or curry favor. If he did indeed take us both to the vault, we'd be blinked from existence as soon as the lock clicked open. However, more time, even the smallest amount, still left a chance of escape. We'd fooled the king once, after all. Self-preservation is a hard thing to quash within oneself, even if you are mostly immortal.

The swirling black fog spun before me in what I took as silent contemplation of my offer. I waited a few beats before deciding to continue.

"Abas was taking me to the vault just before you arrived; he's probably there right now, wondering what happened to me. He wanted to keep it all for himself, your treasure, in exchange for giving me a head start before telling you where I'd gone. I guess the two of you already have some kind of arrangement worked out."

I was nervous and rambling, but I was also trying to take up more time while figuring out my next move, *if* a 'next move' was possible. There was something different about the house now I couldn't pin down. Something was off, wrong. I was trying to figure out if I could use the difference to my benefit when Harthan finally spoke again.

"My treasure?" The atrocious-sounding voice projected out from the swirling muck. "Abas wants to keep *my* treasure?"

"Yes," I answered quickly. "Yes, he does. Always been motivated by greed, that one."

Suddenly, the darkness pushed in around me, eclipsing what I could see of the counter and floor, and I felt another change happening. The shadows receded to reveal my surroundings were now drastically different.

"Do you mean… this treasure?" Harthan's voice sounded from all around me, but the cloud he'd appeared as was gone.

I found myself buried chest deep in gold, with a cache of riches surrounding me on every side, stacked high, well beyond the head of my current form. The piles were dotted with ancient magical artifacts, invaluable cursed objects, and books containing knowledge of magic beyond comprehension. This was only what I could see from my vantage point; a small fraction of what Abas and I had stolen during our shortlived run. I wasn't in the house anymore after all. I didn't know how, but I was inside the vault. The one supposedly impossible to access without Abas and I together, but here I'd been dumped in like everything else we'd stolen.

"I'm an infernal king, Raum," the voice said. "I'm older than time. Did you think you and Abas were the only masters of deception? Did you think yourself above being tricked?"

I went to answer but stopped, having no idea what to say. He was right. The king had tricked me. Being used to dispensing terror, I was not familiar with being on the other side of it, but in this moment, I was truly terrified, and I didn't like the feeling one bit. I struggled to move any part of my lower body, trapped beneath the heavy precious metals, but not even my fingers could budge against the pressure of its crushing weight. Perhaps the most distressing realization was: I couldn't change my form. I was stuck as Joseph, the lone moving dude. The human.

"I got my hands on your friend, Abas, some time ago," he continued. "Unlike yourself, he wasn't lucky enough to escape the original scene of the crime."

"You mean, Abas didn't get away at all?" I couldn't help but interject to ask.

"No." Harthan's voice boomed. "No, he did not. I had hold of him before he could get away, but you; you slipped through my fingers. I crushed him instantly, separating every molecule of his being before spreading them across infinite realities. A fate nearly impossible to come back from, but I must confess; I came to initially regret the outcome of my emotionally charged haste.

"It gave you enough time to start hiding, and for a good while you stayed hidden well enough to elude me. I knew you were smart, and moving around, never staying in any place in any form for long. I was a step behind you longer than I would've liked, but I was distracted with my other current conflicts. Once I focused though, I found you right away. I felt your essence and saw your thoughts. Then, I waited until the time was right."

"So, you're saying the time wasn't right before I worked all day loading that truck? You could've popped out of the first box I picked up and saved me some trouble."

The small amount of spectral-like light in the vault blinked out, leaving me half buried in gold, while the other half drowned in darkness.

"I'm glad for the time it took, though," Harthan continued without acknowledging my quip. "I was able to come up with a more suitable punishment for you. You're stuck in your vault, the one you need Abas's help to open, and you'll remain within until he is able to do just that."

"What, no!" I tried to stifle the exclamation, but the reaction escaped through my lips before I could bite it back. "It'll take… a million forevers before he's able to pull himself together after what you did to him, probably longer."

"Yes," Harthan said. "Yes, it will. And until he does, you'll remain here, trapped in that feeble human form. You can think, you can wail, you can plot your revenge, but you'll be doing it until Abas's return. Of course, there's no way for him to know you're in here."

With that, I felt the presence of Harthan retreat from the vault, leaving me trapped between gold and darkness for what could possibly amount to "until the end of time," if there was indeed an end. I remain optimistic, though. I know Abas's greed will bring him back to the vault eventually. Until then, just as Harthan suggested, I'll be thinking, and I'll be plotting.

11

New

CHRIS MEEKINGS

Legs eleven stared up from the die's face. That had to mean something; it was my lucky number, after all. Fuck it, one in twenty meant I HAD to open the box, right? That was what I was telling myself. It was fate, karma; I was commanded to do it by a higher force.

I was stalling because, well, it was illegal… I think? Hell, I don't know; I'm not a lawyer. Opening someone's moving box? Was that breaking and entering… or something? It was undoubtedly rude—crossing the sacred line between mover and move-ee. Once that brown packing tape was broken and that Rubicon was crossed—next stop, petty theft, the odd dollar here, and spoon there, and then next thing you knew, you were out on your ear, never to be a mover again. Black listed. Persona non-mover.

The person whose stuff this was had trusted me and that should not be lightly thrown aside.

Thunder cracked outside, and rain lashed the apartment windows. Big, thick rivulets of water washed away the outside until there was only me, the box, and my curiosity.

There was more scratching coming from the box. A scrit-scrit-scrit, like nails on the cardboard.

It had to be an animal, right? And that was… well, cruel. Definitely cruel. And cruel overrides rude, I think. I'm pretty sure that was a law… somewhere. Probably not, but it should be.

No one could begrudge trying to save a loving pet trapped in a box. Perhaps the move-ee was looking for them, desperately searching their bare apartment for the lost kitten or guinea pig? I could be a hero, the one who saved Barney the pet hamster, or Atilla the budgie… or something. I don't know; it could be anything in there, and I definitely wasn't gonna take it, whatever it was. No sir-ee. Just a peek, check it wasn't something alive, and then tape back on, box stacked and away we go.

At least, that was the plan then.

I started to peel the brown packing tape from the box, removing it at an agonizingly slow rate. I was still weighing up the illegality of what I was doing. I mean, it was wrong, I knew it was wrong, but it was also sort of justified, right?

If you squint at it from just the right angle, in very poor lighting?

A soft moaning sound came from the box. A definite human noise. And definitely a human moan of pleasure?

So, not a dog, cat, rabbit, hamster, budgie, tortoise, marmoset, very-very small elephant, or whatever else my criminal mind was cooking up to get me to look in the box.

Ok, now it was getting a bit weird. What in the hell was in there? A porn DVD that had somehow been turned on? A battery-operated TV and DVD player that had a porn DVD in it that was miraculously playing? That was pretty desperate as explanations went, and a very weird miracle.

Fuck it.

I ripped the brown tape from the box's lid and pushed the cardboard flaps aside to reveal…

Nothing… nada… zip… bupkis.

What the fuck? There was nothing in the box at all, just straight, plain cardboard sides. I worked myself up to commit the ultimate mover crime of opening someone else's box for this?!?

Bullshit! That thing had weight when I was carrying it; it was heavy.

I reached inside and ran my hands up the cardboard, trying to find the thing that must have been in the box—the thing with weight, the thing that moaned.

There was a giggle and another moan of pleasure!

I pulled my hand back.

"No, don't… don't stop, I liked it," said a soft voice.

I took several steps back as the box started moving and unfolding. First, a leg concertinaed into being, then another. An arm appeared, and a hand origamied to life. And then she stood before me: a full cardboard woman.

She blinked hard, as if she were just stepping into the light after being in darkness for a while, which I guess she had.

"Good afternoon, master," she said, folding in the middle, bowing at me.

I didn't know what to say. I was shocked. This was not a normal thing that happened to me. Women didn't usually pay much attention to me, let alone unfold themselves from boxes at me.

I guess she was naked. It was hard to tell, as everything was cardboard, but I could see no evidence of clothes. Instead, everything seemed to be drawn on her in thick black felt-tip. Her eyes, nose, lips and hair all appeared in chunky dark lines on her head. Her breasts were drawn as two u's on her chest with dots for nipples. At the join of her legs was a rough triangle, which I guessed might be pubic hair.

She had a kind of smell about her like new paper crunched up and lit on fire. I liked it; it had a deep resonance for me, built up over many years of online shopping.

"Ummmm, errrrr… hello?" I said. Being referred to as master kind of weirded me out. I was not used to women calling me anything, let alone master.

She stood there, smiling at me with a bubbly, pleasing expression.

"You're… you're the box?" I asked.

The cardboard girl nodded. "Yes, master."

"Don't call me master," I said. "Ted. My name is Ted."

"Ted," she said, rolling my name around in her mouth until it fit. "I like that name." She smiled at me again, and I felt my cheeks start to flush.

"Thank you. Are you… naked?" I asked.

"Yes," she replied as if it were nothing in the world.

"I should get you some clothes," I said, and I started to scrabble around for anything to offer her.

"If that is what you wish," she said, which was an odd response, but I was too busy scrabbling to think about it.

There wasn't really anything to hand that I could offer her. In desperation, I started to open other boxes, thus compounding my criminal actions. Still, I did have to find her some clothing. The other boxes yielded nothing. Goddamn it! Why did this move-ee have no clothes? Why did they have a girl made of cardboard? That would also have been a good question, but the clothes one came to mind first.

"Ummmm. I'll make you some," I said, tearing at the surrounding boxes. Folding flaps, ripping corners and soon I had a passable set of bra and panties in cardboard brown. "Here," I said, "you can put these on."

The girl took them and slipped into them. I turned my back, respectfully, as she did so. See? I'm not a monster. I'm definitely the good guy in all of this.

"What's your name?" I asked over my shoulder.

"I do not have a name," she replied. "I am new."

"New? That's a nice name." I said, because I don't really

listen. "What's going on, New? Why were you packaged up like that?"

I turned back to face her, as I guessed she must have finished getting dressed. There was a puzzled expression drawn across her face.

"What do you mean?" she asked. "You should know. You ordered me."

I was perplexed, and it showed on my face as plainly as the girl's drawn-on expression.

"I ordered you?"

The girl smiled and nodded. "Yes, Master Ted. I am your mail-order cardboard bride, direct from Amazon." She turned around and pulled down her panties to expose one of her cheeks, which had a big Amazon swoosh arrow on it.

"Aaaaaah," I said, beginning to understand. "I didn't order you."

The cardboard girl still looked confused.

"I'm the moving guy. I just opened the box… errrr… you, so to speak."

Alarm drew across her face. "But, you have to be them," she said. "I've imprinted. The download code has been used. So, you're the one I'm bonded to."

I had a nasty sinking feeling. "I'm sorry, but I'm not the guy who purchased you."

"You don't understand; this cannot be undone. I am yours now. Forever. There is no aftermarket sale or return option."

This was all sorts of fucked up.

"Look, you can't be, for some excellent reasons. One, I

didn't buy you, so you can't be mine. And two, someone owning another person? That's wildly unethical!" I said, as if I were some authority on the ethics of a situation.

"I am yours, Ted," she said, taking my arm and rubbing her cheek on my shoulder. "Forever, and ever, and ever." She giggled as her cardboard flesh sliced my shoulder.

The thunder and rain continued outside, leaving me alone with the cardboard girl. Just me and a girl who said she was mine.

That's some weird brainwashed bullshit right there. I didn't like any of it.

Come on, you moron, this girl was in some sort of trouble… or, maybe, I was. Fuck it, I didn't know. Certainly, one of us was in trouble. Either she was severely brainwashed, and a slave, or I'd opened someone else's property and kinda stolen it. Either way, there was a whole heap of shit coming my way.

Probably the best way out was to go with the 'she is clearly a slave who must be saved' angle and then work on everything from there. Oh, she's actually property? Ok, well, innocent mistake. No harm, no foul? Definitely my best option. Time to 'white knight' it up.

"Look, New, you'd better come with me," I said, blood running down my shoulder.

I wrapped her hand in mine and saw her eyes glisten with happiness at my touch. Man, she was in real deep. Her tiny, cardboard fingers intertwined with mine, and my flesh parted once again. It was painful, but I didn't really mind; she couldn't help it; it was how she was. In the end, don't we all want acceptance for who we are, sharp edges and all? Perhaps that should start here, since I was 'white knighting' anyway.

I led her out of the apartment, down the stairs, and onto the street. The heavy rain came down in thick rods, and the sidewalk was a slick, gun barrel grey.

The cardboard girl squeezed my hand as we stepped out onto the sidewalk.

"No!" she said, terror rising in her voice as I led her away down the street. But I was too preoccupied with my 'white knight' ideal to listen to anything she had to say. I needed to get her away from the monster that had bought her to be a slave, and probably, let's be honest, a sex slave at that. That was the important thing, act like a hero, and maybe I wouldn't get into too much trouble.

I pulled New behind me down the street as she tried to resist. Her hand felt wet in mine, but I thought that was from the blood pouring from between my fingers. The city seemed empty; everyone had fled the thunder and rain, as if it would cause them to…

"Oh, shit," I said as I looked down at the cardboard girl's hand in mine. Her fingers were mush in my balled fist. Her whole wrist and forearm had severed from her and sloppily swung from my hand like some grizzly ball and chain.

Her face was running down her face, her mouth too wide in a silent melting scream. Globs of her sloughed off and fell away into a puddle of mush at my feet.

And then, she was gone, and I was left with nothing but

the memory of the sweet girl who had put her faith in me and a mush of cardboard in my hand.

12

It Wasn't A Box

CHRISTINE MORGAN

I don't know how long I stood there, arguing with myself, coming up with various excuses and rationalizations. The longer I did, though, the more tempted I found myself to chuck my professional standards, just this once, and take a peek.

And, hey, okay, maybe it *would* turn out to be a good thing in the long run, maybe the owners *had* accidentally packed up a pet and were even now driving themselves mad with worry, or it was some electronic gadget running down expensive batteries and even becoming a possible fire hazard if left unchecked... rather than being pissed at me, they'd thank me, hail me as a hero for saving the day!

See what I mean? Excuses. Rationalizations.

Bullshit.

I was curious, dammit. Something was moving in that moving box (har har), and I needed to know what it was, even if it meant breaking my own rules.

Just a peek. Just a quick peek. If it turned out to be nothing, no one would ever need to know.

That rustle. That quivering. That faint, almost plaintive somehow, scratching. Growing weaker and more feeble. As if time was running out, while I dithered and debated.

I knelt beside the box. Just another anonymous cardboard box like all the others, plain and simple. But it quivered again, scootching a half-inch across the floor, as if whatever was inside sensed my presence and pleaded for my help. I heard a scuffling. A scraping. And a muffled vocalization, unidentifiable but enough to convince me it came from a living creature.

A living creature in distress. Scared. Trapped.

I slit the packing tape with my ever-present box cutter, telling myself, even as I did it, that I could always just tape it back up again if needed… I had a roll of the same kind of tape in my kit.

Cautiously, in case whatever had gotten into the box one way or another might seize the opportunity to leap out at the first hint of freedom, I lifted one of the cardboard flaps just a fraction of an inch. And saw…

Crumpled, yellowed newspaper. Wads of it.

But, from somewhere deep in the midst of it, I heard

another scritchy, scraping scuttle. The sound had a hollow quality to it as well, almost an echo.

I poked at the newspapers. Nothing happened. I plucked a couple wads out, then a couple more, and caught a glimpse of a curved surface, ceramic-looking, but dulled and pitted.

More perplexed than ever, I burrowed both hands into the papers and found myself cradling an object about the size and shape of a decorative gourd. A vase or a jar of some sort, not crudely made, but not fancy either. Stoppered with a chunk of cork, sealed in place with brittle clumps of wax.

It was clearly, very, very old. The markings on it—images? letters? symbols?—were faded, chipped, worn to ghosts and shadows. Though I couldn't decipher them, the sight of them only increased my curiosity. Inscription? Label? Warning?

A fragment of a half-forgotten joke ran through my mind—*how much does a Grecian urn?*—and flitted away before I could grasp it.

As I held it, I felt, distinctly and with no room for error, movement. Its weight shifted against my palms. And I heard the scratching, more clearly than ever. Like tiny claws against hard clay. Like fingernails against the underside of a coffin lid.

I shuddered; where *that* morbid thought had come from, I had no idea. Then again, the whole thing was morbid… if there was a living creature caught in this ancient jar, it couldn't last long. Was a miracle, in fact, it had lasted *this* long!

Nothing deserved such a grim fate, not even a rat. To die entombed, in a strange dark place, for no good reason?

Yet, as my fingertips grazed the cork stopper, I hesitated.

Maybe I shouldn't.

Maybe it *was* a rat. Or something worse. A spider, a scorpion.

Lifting the jar, I shook it a bit. Heard a corresponding frantic scrabble from within. And another muffled noise, a cry, as of pitiful desperation. Imploring. Its life, its fate, literally in my hands.

I examined the stopper again. A runnel of wax crumbled away to dust at my touch. The cork rested askew, the seal imperfectly done, as if opened before and then clumsily re-closed.

On closer inspection, I noticed a long-dried smudge of some maroonish substance near the edge. My imagination conjured the image not of a rat, spider, or scorpion but a mouse, a harmless and innocent mouse, soft-furred and whiskered, seeking escape but only getting one pink-fingered little paw out before the cruel barrier slammed into place. Injuring, crushing, maybe severing, in a minuscule splurt of blood. Leaving the paw's poor, wounded owner to huddle helpless in the darkness, waiting only for the miserable reprieve of death.

A lonely, abandoned, forsaken death.

Who would *do* such a thing?

I picked at the wax with my fingernails. Maybe it was too late to save whatever had gotten trapped in the jar, but at least I could offer some final comfort, some freedom, and empathy!

As the cork loosened, a sudden chill ran from the nape of

my neck clear to the soles of my feet. A breathy whisper from nowhere curled into my ear like a tendril of cold smoke.

Nooooooo…

Goosebumps broke out all over my skin.

Nooooooo… the whisper repeated, soulful and feminine and desolate. *It's a triiiick…*

Whatever was in the jar skittered and scrambled with renewed fervor, with frantic urgency.

They tricked me, they used me, they liiiiiiiiied…

I almost dropped the jar, almost hurled it across the room, but my muscles had seized so that all I could do was cling to it, trembling, feeling the creature battering itself against the insides, wild.

Gift her with all things, intoned the mournful whisper. *Beauty and grace, music and song, kindness and love. Gift her with a forbidden treasure she must never, never reveal, never look upon. Then gift her with curiosity and free will, and gift her unto mankind.*

Wait…

Hang on, I knew that story, didn't I?

What's-her-name, from mythology, the chick with the box.

Pandora.

Pandora, right!

The all-gifted, sent as wife to Epimetheus, brother of Prometheus the fire-stealer, presented as an offering to show his transgressions were forgiven, while secretly carrying the evils of the world…

Yeah, I remembered it now. They gave her the box, told her to never open it, and drove her crazy-curious until she did.

It wasn't a box…

No, of course not. They didn't have a lot of boxes back there at the dawn of civilization. They had clay pots, vases, and jars.

What *does* a Grecian urn?

Then, when she did open it, like the gods knew she would, instead of treasures, out spilled a host of everything, large and small, that'd plagued humanity ever since. Illness, greed, leg cramps, hate, insomnia, sudden infant death syndrome, hiccups, envy, acne, misogyny, allergies, cancer… lactose intolerance, stretch marks, and male pattern baldness, why not?

How had the rest of the story gone?

Realizing what she'd done, she'd gone to close the box again—

It wasn't a box…

I looked again at the jar in my hands. So simple. So humble. So innocuous.

She'd gone to close it again, and caught the very last would-be escapee before it could get out. Which happened to be hope, so people could still have hope, even when everything else in their lives was turning to shit.

But…

But that didn't make sense.

Hope wasn't an evil. Was it? So, what was it doing, locked up in a box—

It wasn't a box…

—fine, fine; a jar or urn or whatever, with all the bad stuff?

Nope, didn't add up. Even allowing for the rest of it, with gods and magic and all.

So, what, *really*, was in there?

I shook the jar again. Gently, not looking to do any damage. I listened again to the scuttling and scuffling and scratching, and the plaintive, yearning little cry.

Something sure was.

Something tens of thousands of years old, from the time of Greek mythology? Okay, that seemed downright preposterous on any level.

Still, there *was* something. Something alive, and imprisoned, and suffering.

Maybe something nobody else had ever seen.

Right here, in my hands.

Right here, in this jar.

All I had to do was crack through the rest of the aged, brittle wax, and pop out the cork stopper, and see for myself.

It wanted me to.

Needed me to.

After so long, a solitary eternity of torment.

Just for a moment.

A quick peek and then I could close it up again; no one would be the wiser.

Nooooooo… it wasn't a box, and it was never hope…

What did that mean? It made no sense. It made less and less sense the more I thought about it. There had to be an answer, an explanation. Someone had to find out.

Someone like me?

More wax gave way under my fingers. The cork stopper itself felt spongy and dense, swollen by dampness and time. It lodged into the jar's opening almost well enough to have not needed the wax; I had to work at it to loosen it up.

As I did, whatever was in the jar scurried faster, more urgently. With eagerness. Anticipation.

Hope?

I pried at the stopper, not sure if it would give up its hold first or fall apart into decrepit chunks. It came out intact, a musty-sounding pop releasing a whiff of stale, dank air.

Something else came out as well.

Sprang out, leaped out, flew out, shot out, zipped out. A quick, dark, whirring blur of motion, darting from the jar's opening startlingly fast.

If I had consciously tried to grab it, I would have missed by a mile.

Reflex and instinct, though, took over before conscious thought.

I'd let go of the cork and snagged the blur out of midair before I even knew what I was doing. A real Karate Kid moment, not that I could fully appreciate it at the time.

I couldn't really appreciate or think of anything else at the time, because…

What I grabbed, what I caught in my fist, was…

It was horrible.

Vile. Loathsome. Evil.

Assaulting my senses and sanity alike.

Squirming in my grasp, dry and leathery and scaly as a high-desert lizard, thorned and barbed and spiky as a handful of brambles, freezingly hot and searingly cold, piercing my palm like poisoned cactus needles, stinging the tender undersides of my fingers like furious wasps, voicing a shrill shriek a thousand times worse than nails on a blackboard, hissing and buzzing, writhing with a multitude of segments and limbs and vicious pinchers, stinking of spent gunpowder and ozone and bitter alkalines, somehow simultaneously insectile and reptilian and altogether unnatural, an abomination against reality itself, myriad pinprick magnesium eyes glaring at me with malevolent intelligence and sheer unbridled hate.

I knew, then.

I understood fully.

It wasn't a box, okay, mis-translation over the centuries, an easy enough mistake to make.

It was never hope.

It wasn't hope trapped in the jar. It was never hope. Never-hope. Never have hope. The thief of hope, the killer of hope, the devourer of hope, the renderer-impossible of hope.

It was foreknowledge.

It was the most fiendish of evils, because however much we might think we'd like to be able to predict the future, however many pithy 'forewarned is forearmed' sayings we might bandy about, when you got right down to it, foreknowledge was the worst, cruelest curse of all.

How could there be hope when you already knew?

How could there be comfort in what changes might come, what chance might bring, what the future might hold when the future was set, inviolable, and spelled out plain as day?

What was there to wish for, to dream of, to aspire to?

What was life without surprise, novelty, and wonder? Bleak and rote, decisions already decided, choices meaning nothing because the choices were already made.

If this thing, this monstrosity, this sinister imp I held tight in my hand, had gotten free with its host of brethren all those millennia ago, humanity would have been eternally plagued with foreknowledge, left grim and purposeless, plodding beasts for whom hope itself would not exist.

How fucked-up was *that*? And to think, the gods did it deliberately… a set-up, a gotcha… here's this box (or jar, or apple tree, or whatever) brimming with forbidden secrets… don't ever, ever open it (or eat of it, or whatever)… oh, and by the way, here's a hefty dose of curiosity and free will…

If they (or He, or She, or It, or whatever) really wanted to keep such-and-such big secret forbidden, *why* the hell dangle it out there all tempting-like in the first place? As, what, a test? A test they (or He, or She, or It, or whatever) had already built to fail? Rigged game, sucker's bet, the house always wins!

It squirmed and writhed and stung and pinched, acid and pain and fire and ice, and if my muscles hadn't been clench-locked rigid by shock, I would have flung it away, flung it as far from me as possible.

It wanted me to.

I wanted to. To hurl it from me, to let it go, get rid of it.

And then find a hatchet or chainsaw to hack off my hand at the wrist and divorce my skin and flesh from the memory of its loathsome touch... shove a shotgun under my chin and blow my brains out the back of my skull, or dive from a high roof onto unforgiving pavement to erase every trace awareness of its being from my mind...

If I did, I could save myself. Obliterate myself, but save myself.

While foreknowledge, finally released into the world, could go about its merry way. Go far and wide, spreading its message of irrevocable, unalterable destiny.

But I still...

I still held it, I still had it caught in my grasp.

I saw, amid its too-many struggling limbs, one that had been truncated, ending in a scabbed-over stump, and in a flash of epiphany understood... a fraction of its being, sever-crushed under the cork, had been let loose last time.

Just a fraction, but enough to trigger dire premonitions and inflict episodes of hopeless despair. To torment people with visions of events that could not be altered, the living damnation of inescapable predestiny.

And here I was, me, just some regular person, just a moving guy, with the fate of all humanity clenched wroth and seething in my fist. My arm blistering, cracking, peeling, disintegrating… the corruption spreading, rising… the pain unbelievable…

All because I'd just had to go and give in to curiosity, and open something I knew full well I had no business opening.

It wasn't a box.

It was never hope.

I had dropped the cork, but not the jar. The cork, theoretically, was within reach. If I could somehow force the creature back into its clay prison, stopper the gap, and seal it up again—the wax was a lost cause, but the cork *had* fit snug—maybe, just maybe, it wasn't too late.

I could return the jar to its cardboard resting place, nestled safely among the wads of yellowed newspaper. I could tape the flaps with such surgical precision, no one would ever suspect me of tinkering. I could stack the moving box neatly among its fellows, like I'd been pledged and paid to do in the first place. I could finish up the job, file my paperwork, clock out, go home, have a beer, and doctor my arm as well as the contents of my medicine cabinet and first aid kit would allow. No trip to the ER or Urgent Care, though; what would I tell them? Better to deal with it myself, and get on with the business of forgetting or pretending it never happened.

I could do all that, sure.

At least, I could try.

Would I be successful, though? Or, was it already too late?

And, even if I did, what then? What about the people whose new house this is, who hired my company to move their stuff? Who *are* they? Are they aware of the contents of that particular box? If so—or, especially if no—can they be trusted with it? Can anyone? Should something so powerful just be left lying around, waiting for its opportunity? Can I, can we, can any of us, afford to take that risk?

But then, what else can we do?

Surrender? Turn it loose on an unsuspecting world more than plagued by evils enough already? Take away the last shreds of hope humanity has?

Should it—*could* it?—be destroyed? Or would that require some whole big epic Lord of the Rings type of heroic quest? Have to take the jar back to Mount Olympus, or wherever it was created, and huck it into a volcano?

If not destroyed, could it be locked away somewhere safe and secure forever? Like a doomsday vault, or that warehouse at the end of the Indiana Jones movie where they stash the Ark of the Covenant, one more crate among many?

These are big, serious, major-league important questions. Way above my pay grade. I'm just the guy standing here watching (while feeling his arm disintegrate toward flaking bone) the worst all-time evil ever to threaten humanity wriggling in the eroding cage of his fingers.

I'm the wrong person to be making these kinds of decisions.

Then again, does it really matter?

After all, we already know how this story ends…

13

ISH-IM-LLT אִישִׁים (Messengers)

JOHN BALTISBERGER

The die tumbled across the floor, each edge and point on the icosahedron causing it to juke and bounce erratically, and finally came to rest against the side of the box. It landed on 2. Not the worst roll in the world, but not a great roll. It was also an even, which arbitrarily meant I should leave the box the fuck alone.

Then the box thumped again, hard enough that it caused the die to roll a bit. It landed on 13.

The box wanted to be opened; the universe wanted me to open the box. From one extreme to the next. I didn't actually believe in fate, but it was hard to not let my imagination go wild. I had decided that evens were the no go, and the box had slapped it to odd. On top of that, it was thirteen; maybe it was trying to say that not opening the box would be unlucky! Also, I really, really just wanted to open the box. I was intensely curious, and I was also a little worried that if I left it alone, a beloved family pet would die in the box. That would probably cost me my job, right? *"You killed Fluffenheimer"* would not be a great review.

Reaching down, I picked up the die and stuffed it in my pocket, before also lifting the questionable box and setting it on the bare mattress of the bed. I stood there looking at it for a few minutes; now that I had decided to open it, I was worried that whatever was inside might jump out and attack me. I glanced around for something I could use to open the box from a distance—a ruler, dowel, maybe a curtain rod. Finding nothing, I slipped the box cutter out of my pocket and sliced through the tape.

Fuck it.

I pulled at the cardboard flaps and flayed them open before jumping back, just in case.

Nothing happened.

I stepped forward and peered inside as best as I could. It looked empty. All I could see was deep shadow. It was anticlimactic. But maybe whatever was making the noise and moving around was hidden in shadow? It seemed impossible for the darkness to be so complete in such a small box. I grabbed the bottom corner of the box and moved it around, tilting it this way and that to try to get the light to hit those shadowed corners.

Instead of being illuminated, the shadow seemed to spread, as if I had just sloshed a dark liquid around. The shadow clung to where it had been, but now stained more of the interior of the box. I could feel the frown on my face deepening. I wasn't sure if I was more disappointed that it was empty, or confused by the shadow. I continued to stare down, wondering if maybe I was just going a bit loopy from too many energy drinks and not enough sleep, when a hand shot up from the shadows.

I would like to say that I took a step back and regarded the hand calmly. But I did not. I fell back onto my ass, shrieking like a five-year-old girl who had just seen a spider. The hand, slender and black as ink, clutched the side of the box, and darkness spread from the fingers like a dark wine stain on a brown tablecloth. A second hand emerged from the top of the box and grabbed the far side. The darkness spread from the second hand, just as it had from the first.

I stared at them. Part of my brain was screaming at me to run, to get the fuck up, and get the fuck out, but my body wouldn't listen; my legs stayed splayed out in front of me. The hands flexed, veins popping out as whoever owned them began pulling themself out of the little cardboard box.

A head emerged from the box, bald and covered in the same light-devouring blackness as the hands. I let out a minuscule whimper; I wasn't sure if I was more afraid of the figure that was emerging from the box, or the fact that my legs wouldn't respond to me.

The figure continued to rise, turning its black eyes—deep

as the depths of the ocean—towards me. He—I realized it was a man, as it now stood in the box nude and fully erect—regarded me for several minutes before his lips curled away from blackened teeth.

"Be not afraid." His voice was like the tolling of church bells over a cemetery. Whisps of shadowy darkness followed the words, as though the sound itself drank in the light.

"Fuck that!" I squealed, the sound of its voice finally breaking the spellbound paralyzing fear I felt.

I rolled onto my side and darted, lifting myself up and kicking off the floor to launch myself at the doorway. I hit the door frame and turned to look. The emaciated figure stepped out of the box, and just like with his hands, the darkness bled off his body, creating an ever-spreading shadow where he stood. That was enough for me.

I turned my back on the shadow-man and fled the house. I didn't even bother to close the back of the truck as I wrenched open the door and slid into the driver's seat. I didn't care if shit bounced out the back of the open truck; I just wanted to get the fuck out of there, away from whatever the hell that thing was.

I reached into my pocket for the keys. They were gone. I realized the keys must have fallen out of my pocket when I had pulled out the d20. For a moment, I considered going back for them, but in the rearview mirror, I could see the shadow creeping across the threshold, ever-growing, expanding like a stain on the earth. Like black mold infecting its way across the world in an effort to subsume all things, a seething, scrawling corruption, it spread across the cement and climbed the walls. The spread was slow but uniform, steady, unstoppable. The shadows, by right, shouldn't be able to exist in the sun that scorched the world outside of the spreading darkness.

"Be not afraid." The man's voice rattled the truck as it stepped out of the doorway. From the shadows that swallowed the flowerbed outside the front entryway, I saw another pitch-black hand shoot up and begin pulling a second figure from the shadows.

Nope, not going back for the keys. I was, in fact, very afraid.

I kicked open the door and pulled myself out of the truck, my eyes locked on the two figures. What if there were more? What if there were a bunch of those things inside, all yelling about not being afraid? Was the one in the doorway even the same one who had come out of the box? Or were they emerging and staying put? How far would this shadow thing spread? And why, for the love of all that is holy, was I trying to answer any of these questions instead of calling for help?

Because: I had left my phone in the master bathroom playing music. Somewhere in that darkened three-bedroom house, with its white picket fence, was a phone playing through the late '90s era Britney Spears discography. No phone, no keys. Well, those were dead to me, then. Because I wasn't going back into that house. I turned and ran.

I probably ran about two minutes before the stitch in my side forced me down to a jog, and then a hobbling walk. I was not in good enough physical condition to outrun the end of the world. But I had put enough distance between us that I could no longer see the terrible house containing that terrible box anymore. I sat down on the pavement and buried my head in my hands.

I must be having an episode; schizophrenia did run in the family. My uncle had struggled with mental health, my grandma on my mom's side had killed herself with a smile on her face—something that had haunted Mom for decades—even my brother had been in and out of psychiatric care and rehab facilities his entire life. Maybe it was just my turn. Maybe now my cheese had slipped off the cracker, and I was sitting in the middle of the sidewalk on a street miles away from home, just sobbing for no goddamned reason at all.

It was my greatest fear. What if I was insane and I didn't know it? My uncle and brother never seemed capable of wrapping their minds around their own infirm grasp on reality. It didn't matter that the terror was in their minds; it was real to them. What if that terrible shadow and the thing that crawled out of it was just the same? In my head?

I had almost convinced myself that I was crazy, that it had been an episode. I would check myself in to a clinic, get checked out, get some meds, and then be right as rain. I wouldn't go down the same path of self-destructive mental illness that had taken so much of my family.

"**Be not afraid.**"

It was just a whisper carried on the wind, almost soft

enough that I could chalk it up to imagination. I looked up and back towards the way from which I had run; I could see the shadow. I couldn't understand how it had already spread so far, so fast. And it wasn't just spreading across the ground. From my vantage point, I could see that several houses were shrouded in shadow, despite the sun still being high in the sky. A figure, blacker than the void, stood two blocks away. It was the source of the voice, and it shouted the words as it walked towards the door of a house, the shadow spreading with each footfall.

I could also hear screaming.

I decided it didn't matter if I was insane or not; I was still scared. I wanted to run. But now, I also felt guilty. I had unleashed this thing, this horrible shadow. The woman screaming in that house, the one about to be swallowed by shadows, I had done that to her. I may be a coward in a lot of ways, but I didn't know if I could live with that. I rose and tried to run again, but instead of away from the devouring void, I ran toward it. Maybe I could give whoever was in those houses time to run. I didn't know if I believed that; I didn't know if any of it mattered. But I couldn't live with myself if I didn't try.

When I reached the house, or as close as I could get to it without stepping on the shadow, I saw inside the house a mother, clinging to her two small children, screaming as the blackened figure approached her.

"Hey!" I shouted, trying to get the figure's attention, to distract him from the family. I looked around, grabbed a rock from the ground, and lobbed it as hard as I could at the shadow figure, praying that it wasn't a hallucination and I hadn't just murdered the mailman. It wasn't a bad throw; the rock slammed into the side of the man's head. But instead of being knocked over, he just slowly turned to face me.

"**Be not afraid,**" he said simply.

"Can you say anything else?" I screamed.

It wasn't the best bravado, but it was all I had. His gaze—I assumed he was looking at me, but his eyes were solid black like the eyes of some terrible doll—slid over to me, his head turning with terrible slowness, making his attention feel… inevitable. I stood there waiting for him to move, but he just turned away and took another step towards the mother and her screaming children. Why? Why wouldn't it just leave them alone? I was desperate. I threw myself at the shadow man.

I had hoped to catch him by surprise. I closed the distance between us, hoping that the fact that I was moving would keep darkness from finding me. Despite the suddenness of my lunge, the man was not taken off guard. He turned and faced me as I flew through the air at him. He didn't react other than to look; he didn't try to defend himself as I crashed into and through him.

I staggered to a halt and turned around. The only signs that there had been anything there to begin with were a few whisps of black mist like a mushroom's puffed spores fading in the air. The woman was still screaming, and now she was also pointing at me. At my chest. I looked down.

There, where I should have made impact with the shadow man, was… well… a dark well of void that drank in the light. It obscured the moving company logo and was beginning to spread.

I tried to take a step, but my leg wouldn't respond. A leaden fear gripped my heart as I looked down to see the shadow on the ground slowly creeping up my legs, casting my socks and shoes in the murky darkness that seemed to be the antithesis of light and goodness, a shadow that drank in the light rather than shrank from it. I pulled at my legs. Maybe it was like mud; maybe it would suck in my shoes and I could run before… But my shirt!

I yanked at my legs as hard as I could, simultaneously trying to pull my shirt off over my head. I almost lost my balance and fell. Staying on my feet didn't help me with the shadow, though; it quickly reached my ankles. I could feel it, cold, as if all energy, light, and warmth were devoured into nothing. It was creeping up my body and felt like slowly sinking into an ice-cold bath. I reached down, brushing my hands over my legs, trying to wipe it off. It was as intangible as the man had been, as though there was nothing there but an absence of light. The numbing cold spread across my chest where the shadow had seeped through the fabric and reached me. It was swallowing me whole.

I looked towards the family in the doorway. Why didn't they run? I was going to die—or be carted away in grippy socks—and all they did was stare. I could hear shouting behind me—more people emerging from their homes to see what all the screaming was about. I tried to turn to tell them to run, but I could no longer move my legs or hips; I couldn't catch my breath as the shadows crushed the air out of my lungs. I reached for the woman, begging her to run, to save me, to save her children, to get a gun and kill me before the shadow took me entirely.

It was creeping into my vision, the darkness clouding my sight even as the cold tendrils of it reached into my mouth and began spreading down my throat. I could do nothing; the world was gone, and I floated along in the void between stars that died millions of years ago.

◆◆◆

I saw the void above me, but below, the Earth spun on, oblivious to my presence. I was suddenly aware of the full brunt of history. The world sat there, a milky sapphire in this day and age, but I also saw the primordial orb of fire and broken crusts. I saw the age of towering mushroom forests and saw them retreat from their power as the first ice age came. I watched the dinosaurs roam, heedless of the true masters of the earth, until the comet struck and obliterated life from my orb.

I beheld as catastrophe after catastrophe brought calamity on the sanctity of Earthbound life. Time caught up to me, and I saw the future. It loomed from beyond our universe, a swarm of disease and dark matter. A miasmic cloud of extra-dimensional decomposers would tear the flesh off the bones of the world and leave it a husk forevermore. I watched all things die.

But that was not the most incredible thing I witnessed. I saw the interconnectedness of all things; I watched all things die, but all things live as well. The fungal forests of Earth never disappeared, never lessened. But as spores and branches of reaching mold, they coated the world and protected it. Each living being an incubator for the living planet that could, and would, push back against the voracious microscopic invaders. It had influenced us across time, giving visions and communing through prophets and shroom-powered trips. It was the god worshiped across a thousand cultures, and called a million different names. It was not supernatural but ultra-terrestrial; it was damnation, salvation, entropy, and rebirth; it was one, and we could be one with it and survive.

◆◆◆

I could feel the doomed world around me, a return to Earth.

I felt like I had been standing there, rooted to the spot, for centuries, communing with the mycelium shadows of fungal unreality. But as I opened my eyes again, I knew it had been only seconds. I didn't know what I felt. I was numb. I could no longer cry or scream. But I wasn't tired or in pain either. There was something, an infinite comprehension of the world and my new place in it. I understood what I had to do, now more than ever. For the first time in what could loosely be called my life, I had a purpose. I had a cause.

I looked down at my hands. They were black as pitch, a deep darkness that swallowed light. I took a step forward, shadows spreading from my footsteps to swallow the world. From darkness were we born, and to waylay the chaos of the coming apocalypse, to darkness would we return.

I looked up at the faces of the people who had stopped to watch the shadows devour me. Did they watch with empathy? Did they stand by and stare to sate their own morbid curiosity or sadism? It didn't matter, for now their faces were etched in uncomprehending terror. I could help them. I could save them. I opened my mouth and spoke.

"Be not afraid."

14

A Night To Remember

SUSAN SNYDER

The die click-clacked as it bounced along the floor, making its way toward the box. That wasn't my intention. It seemed to be drawn over like it was caught in a tractor beam. A little bump into the side of the cardboard, and it finally laid still.

Thirteen.

Suddenly, the box shuffled again, shifting itself an inch forward in a little hopping motion and hitting the die.

Fourteen.

Well, alrighty then. I hadn't really considered what action any number would prompt me to do. I was exhausted from the day's labor and confused by the potential of the thing in that box. It seemed like the box didn't *want* thirteen. Heck, the damn thing hopped over to change the number, didn't it? Was it sentient? It had to be a living thing, right?

Walking away wasn't an option. I had a dog at home. Flapjack. I would do anything for Flapjack. No way was I going to leave an animal to suffer, stuck in a suffocating cardboard coffin, lying in its own feces, probably starving and scared.

Taking the box cutter from the front pocket of my denim jeans, dusted with the soot of drywall and tiny bits of cardboard and paint, I had made my choice. Consequences or not, I flicked the blade up and walked toward the mystery box. Sliding the knife across the center tape and through the "Fragile" sticker, there was a sharp prick to my thumb. I had cut myself with the stupid box cutter. But how? If there's one thing movers have down pat, it's how to not cut yourself with a box cutter.

I observed the small incision in my thumb, no bigger than a paper cut. A bead of blood sat for a moment, balanced atop the black letter "F" in "Fragile" but it didn't remain there long. It was quickly absorbed into the box. Just disappeared into it, as if sucked by a straw.

Then I heard it. Music. Not just any music, but a very familiar, tauntingly sexy saxophone signaling the beginning of George Michael's biggest Top 40 ballad. Soft at first, muffled perhaps by the contents of the box.

A walkman? No, who has a walkman nowadays? An iPod? Alexa? I felt slight relief in knowing that all this concern might have been for a stupid music streaming device and not a helpless creature in distress.

The flaps of the box whipped open, causing me to jump back and drop the box cutter on the floor, blade still exposed, causing a nick in the probably very expensive bedroom floorboard.

Shit. Consequences seemed a lot more likely now.

The sax intro got louder and clearer, now that the box was open. More importantly, I could finally see what was in there. It was not someone's cell phone or rogue baby monitor, haunted by the ghosts of pop stars past. It was a large clear plastic bag full of ashes. And I mean a *big* bag of ashes! The thing was stuffed to the gills and took up the space inside the entire box.

Now that the volume of the music was turned up to eleven, I discovered it was not the dulcet tones of Steve Gregory playing the sax, but it was produced by a human voice. It was the voice of a young girl. Had to admit, she was pretty good at mimicking a saxophone. This realization only increased my epic confusion at what the hell was going on.

Then the sax-y karaoke stopped, and the giggling started.

Multiple giggles. They overlapped in tone and pitch. More than one young girl was involved here, and I had no fucking clue where this was coming from. Well, I suppose I did, because it emanated from the box. From the ashes in the box. That was weird, to put it lightly, but it was about to get a whole lot weirder.

"Girls, we got one!"

"Oh, this is gonna be fun!"

"This never happens! We can finally try out our new game!"

Three distinct voices. Three young girl voices. I tried to speak, but I found myself unable to utter a word. In fact, I couldn't even move. Not a muscle. I was stuck there frozen in a stranger's master bedroom with disembodied teeny boppers that live in a bag of ashes.

"Hi there!"

"He can't speak to us, Mikaela!"

"Wait, so it is working? Do we have control of him?"

These first two girls, Mikaela and the other, seemed downright giddy. Then the third girl chimed in.

"Maybe we should introduce ourselves?" I had to admit that would be a nice gesture, given I was being held prisoner and had nary a clue of what "game" these spooky brats were about to play.

Two exasperated sighs and then, "Sure, whatever Ashley." Mikaela let out a snort laugh while the other one emitted a snicker.

"Sir, I apologize in advance for what you are about to endure but…"

"Ashley, are you serious?" came the now familiar squeaky voice of Mikaela. "Brittany, make her stop with that nerd shit!"

Oh, okay. We have Ashley, Mikaela and *Brittany*? I felt like I had been transported to my eighth-grade school dance, where I was getting cornered and bullied by a gaggle of popular chicks. I knew that nightmare scenario quite well, being a bit of a late bloomer. Christ, I still walked around with a 20-sided die in my pocket. Maybe I was still in the process of blooming. In fact, I was pretty sure that stupid sax solo accompanied my harassment during the "A Night to Remember" dance of 1985. This "nerd" type girl, Ashley, might be a voice of reason in this squad, so I didn't allow myself to fall into full panic mode quite yet.

Teenage girls could be reasoned with. Couldn't they?

Ashley continued. "Anyhoo, mister, we are obviously dead, and these are our ashes. You kinda released us into the room with your blood, so…"

"More like *you* kinda released us, Ashley. You made him cut himself."

"Oh, soooo sorry, Brittany! Do you want to keep being super bored, or do you want to have some fun?"

"Ashley's right." Mikaela chimed in. "We are stuck, so we might as well make the most out of it. And let's face it, we *never* get to do this. He always hides us away!"

"Fine, I guess you're right. Plus, we have been talking about this game for so long. Let's see if it really works!"

Clearly, these were ghosts. Unless someone was playing an elaborate prank and a hidden hipster was recording this for YouTube, these were ghosts. Which begged the question, was I having a fatigue induced hallucination? I couldn't move or speak. Maybe this would pass after a bit. Please, please let this pass. Whatever game these specters were about to play, I was not looking forward to it.

I just stood there gazing at the large pile of boxed ashes, awaiting my fate at the hands of phantom teenagers. I could see the box cutter off to the right of my steel-toed work boot and desperately wanted to have it. I doubted it would provide any defense against invisible girls, but it would have been nice to have in my hand. Just in case.

Having gotten the green light to proceed, Ashley was kind enough to explain this game they were so excited to play.

"So, it's like, we change the lyrics to songs but you have to do whatever our songs say."

"We've been working on this for so long and I have a really good one to try out!" Brittany asked the gang, "Should we tell him the theme or let it be a surprise?"

"I think he will understand it pretty quick."

"Mikaela, you go first! See if you can make him do something!"

Make me do something? Would they make me cut myself with that box cutter? Dance around like a monkey? Put on makeup? What the fuck were these girls planning on making me do?

Mikaela squealed. "Ohmygosh, okay!" She cleared her throat and began to sing.

"Sucking on a chili dog, outside the Tasty…"

"STOP!" Ashley blurted. "That is against the rules."

"Whaddya mean?" Mikaela sounded a little hurt by this interruption.

"Yeah, you always do this. You have to *change the lyrics* to fit the theme." Brittany was backing up Ashley on this rule, whatever that meant. "That is NOT the theme, Mikaela!"

"But you didn't let me finish."

"No, dumbass. Let me give it a shot. Oh, that made me think of one!" Brittany squealed with delight, then burst right into a bastardized rendition of Phil Collins and Philip Bailey's duet "Easy Lover," circa 1984.

"He's an eager pooper

He'll shit his pants so you won't have to

Super scooper

Before you know it it's all on your kneeeeeees!"

I didn't have a chance to process what this teen ghost was singing. What I knew was that these girls did, in fact, have full control over me. Most horrific of all was that I was doing what she sang. Just like they said I would.

My bowels let loose like an over-amped soft serve machine. There was no stopping it. Standing there motionless, I shat my pants. The result of this act began to slide down my pant legs, pooling in and around my work boots.

And that's not all.

I dropped to my knees, into this pile of my own waste, and began scooping it up with my hands and dropping it back down. Scooping it up, and letting it drop right back down. Over and over.

This greatly pleased the girls, and the room exploded into a cacophony of squawks, howls, and shrieks.

"That is wicked cool!"

"Brittany, you did it!"

"Okay, okay, who's next?"

"Ashley, you're up!"

"Nah, I want to wait until the end." Ashley sounded strangely pensive, like she was working something out in her head. "You guys keep going."

Mikaela wasted no time getting into her number, set to the chorus of Billy Ocean's "Caribbean Queen."

"I only eat meat

And I can't stop shitting out

When it comes, it comes like mud

I got some on the rug"

I had quickly and fully understood the point of this game by this time and was still reeling from the stench of my own soiled pants and desecrated hands, kneeling in my own feces. I had also begun to comprehend the level of immaturity I was dealing with. These were young girls who, for whatever reason, had their remains packed up in a moving box. My guess was that they were not going to ever grow intellectually. God knows what they went through to get themselves here. I would have felt sympathy for them if I wasn't currently doing what I was being forced to do.

I was not prepared for what I was made to do next. The "only eat meat" part should have given me a hint. We were in the master bedroom, and there wasn't any meat to be found in the immediate surroundings. The homeowners weren't expected until tomorrow, so there sure as hell weren't steaks available in the fridge. I might have had a granola bar left in my back pocket, but that wouldn't really qualify as meat.

Amid the squeals and giggles from the entertained girls, I suddenly stood upright and proceeded to bite deeply into my right forearm, shaking my head violently until a large mass of skin, muscle, and sinew came loose. Bits of fecal matter that had clung to my skin, blood, and viscera spattered out in a several-foot radius around me. All the while, I was defecating uncontrollably. It kept cascading down my legs, widening the pool of fluid at my feet until the edge of it reached the Persian rug that sat still rolled up in the corner of the room, next to the king-size bed.

Then I began to chew and swallow my own forearm. My own meat.

"Wow," Ashley commented after she recovered her breath from the howls of laughter. "That was just… wow."

Mikaela was quite chuffed at her work. "I fucking rock!"

"Mikaela! Watch your language, young lady! You're only thirteen!" Ashley did her best impression of what a wagging-finger mom would say.

"We're *fourteen*, remember?"

Another thunderous eruption of laughter. My chewing, swallowing, and shitting came to an abrupt stop, and I was, once again, frozen in place. The gaping tear in my arm screamed in anguish, but I could say nothing.

Fourteen? I had just a brief moment to try to make heads or tails out of what was happening here. These are fourteen-year-old, vindictive, demon girls who are clearly barring no holds when it comes to torturing me. This game was mean, and they were absolutely loving it.

What had happened to these girls? How long had they been left to ferment in thoughts of their own torture, their own demise? The three of them had spent unknown amounts of time plotting, and giggling, and reinforcing their own desires to enact revenge on any poor slob who happens to come along.

Fucking teenage girls. I was in a lot of trouble.

"Can I go again? Please? *Pleeeeease?*"

Ashley responded with, "Sure, Brittany. I'll wait 'til the end."

"Yay! This is a good one, promise!"

"Shart in the dark

A colon pain

You give love a shit stain

You shat the bed

And you screamed in pain

You give love a shit stain!"

My heart pounded in my chest as I strode over to the bed like an automaton, treading through my own puddle of filth along the way. I had set up this bed frame earlier with two of my coworkers. The mattress and box spring had the plastic covers removed and hauled off when they left. Now here I was, alone, my body taken hostage, crawling atop the brand new pillowtop/memory foam hybrid king-size mattress.

As predicted by this fourteen-year-old moron's parody lyrics, I sharted. And it hurt like a motherfucker. I took off my boots, peeled off my wet, putrid pants, and threw them at the foot of the mattress. Now, just sitting in my soaked brown undies on a recently pristine new bed, I felt an agony unlike anything I'd ever felt before. It started at my diaphragm and rumbled down into my stomach and abdomen. It was what I could imagine a fire-breathing dragon would feel before shooting flames from its maw. Except this was heading in the opposite direction.

The torrent of excrement blasted out of me, splattering the headboard and ivory wall beyond it. I did scream this time. And it did sound pretty similar to what a dragon might bellow when shooting out its hot breath at a hapless knight. Except, as I said before, from the opposite direction.

Applause came from the girls this time, accompanied by another comment from the ringleader-apparent, Ashley.

"Bravo! That was wicked awesome, Brit! And I looooove that song!"

Mikaela wasted no time in delivering her next offering, eager to ride the coattails of Brittany's success.

"Well, since I was *just* humming this song, I might as well roll with it."

"I'm never gonna stop again
All this poop, it's gotten all over
Though you might want to pretend
You'll still shit tarry stoo-oool!"

Although this song didn't pack as much punch in the activity department, a steady stream of viscous, black stool leaked out of me. I could only hope that it was black because Mikaela *sang* that it would be tarry, not because I was hemorrhaging internally.

Ashley expressed some disappointment.

"You did way better with the sax solo."

"Ashley, don't be mean!"

"Well, I mean, he didn't really do anything except shit again. I thought we would push a little harder than that."

It seemed Ashley was not, in reality, the voice of reason. She was a sadist. A nerd sadist. This did not bode well for me.

Mikaela was getting defensive.

"Well then, by all means, Queen Ashley. Why don't you do one for a change!"

In the short pause that followed this challenge, I swore I heard the front door to the house open.

Oh, please, God, let it be a coworker who left his phone behind. Anyone!

As embarrassing as it would be to be seen in my current state, sitting in my underwear and T-shirt, covered in my own crap, with scraps of my right arm hanging from my bottom lip, and a rancid lake of defecation sitting on the wooden floor, it would still be pretty nice to get rescued from this particular situation.

Ashley chuckled. "Get ready for this! Short but sweet."

"Okay, Ashley. Let's hear it."

"Yeah, smarty pants."

She cleared her throat.

"Shit's such a treat and it's time you taste it

There ain't no reason enough to waste it

It's now the time to clean up by yourself

LICK IT UP! LICK IT UP!"

Brittany and Mikaela flat out lost it. They screamed with reckless abandon at the pure genius in Ashley's little ditty.

"It's only right now!" Brittany added in a high falsetto.

Immediately, I slid off the edge of the bed and into the pool of filth awaiting me on the saturated wooden floor. Out came my tongue as I bent forward to lap up my own dung, blood, and whatever pieces of forearm were in the mix.

The ephemeral gang was absolutely hysterical with glee.

Then I heard the floorboards creak. The laughter stopped. I was free to move on my own again. The girls had fled back to their bag of ashes. I felt them leave, felt them release me. But why?

I picked my head up to see who this savior was who entered the bedroom. Who was this amazing creature who came just in the nick of time?

A large man stood in the doorway, surveying what must have been a terrifying sight. It wasn't one of my coworkers. In fact, this guy was in a nice, tailored, three-piece suit, holding a briefcase in one hand. He looked like a run-of-the-mill, slightly obese businessman. Yet his eyes caught my attention. They were practically on fire with rage.

Oh fuck. It's the homeowner.

Here I was in this demented, ghastly scenario with no one else in sight. What must he be thinking? Whether I got out of this alive or not, I sure as hell wouldn't have my job anymore. Shit, I'd probably go to jail.

The man gently placed the briefcase in the hallway and came into the room. His angry eyes scanned the floor, taking in the sights, and probably the smells, of it all. My eyes followed his as I still knelt in my homemade goop. His stare landed on the box cutter. He walked over and picked it up, sloshing right through the mess in his shiny loafers, not seeming to give a rat's ass.

I am in so much fucking trouble. How do I explain this? Oh, sorry, sir. I know you hired me to bring your precious items to your new house with ultimate care, but instead, some teenage, scat-obsessed poltergeists held me captive and tortured me into shitting all over your overpriced master bedroom. And yes, sir, I was about to lick it up.

Much to my surprise, I did not go to jail, nor did I get fired from my job. Sounds like a happy ending, right?

Nope.

That guy picked up the box cutter and walked around behind my still-kneeling and weak body. He grabbed my sweat-drenched hair, lifted me halfway to my feet, and proceeded to slice my throat wide open with my own damn box cutter. The grand finale was when he dropped my dying ass right down into that putrid lake on the wooden floor.

Splat.

"It's only right now!" Mikaela joked when I told her and the other girls about that final act of my life. They missed it. They skedaddled once they realized their dark overlord had come home early. That fucking guy burnt my body in his brother's funeral home and dumped my ashes in with the three girls that he had murdered back in 1986. Right into the same plastic bag, the same cardboard box.

I'm going to be really honest with you, folks. I would much rather be lapping up my own shit than be trapped for all eternity with three very mean and very bored thirteen-year-old girls.

Oh, apologies. Ashley would like me to remind you that they're *fourteen*.

15

A Seabird Where The Seas Converge

LAUREN BOLGER

After the clatter of plastic against wood, silence swelled in my ears.

I stared at the box, waiting for the contents to reveal themselves further. No more scratching, but something in the atmosphere had changed. I felt jumpy… agitated. All around me, a charge prickled.

I shook my head to clear it. This wasn't happening.

A loud whooshing sound surrounded me. Like a car driving past the house, but the sound came from inside the box. I breathed it in. The prickling feeling was gone. The air was cold and wet. Salt stung my nose.

I thought about walking right out that door. I could text

my client, tell them I'd gotten sick. Anything but open a box that belonged to them. Actually, at this point, I wouldn't just be opening the box. I'd be interacting with its contents. Whatever was inside that box responded to my actions. It may not have spoken, but it's communicating with me, all the same.

The curiosity in me was becoming impossible to deny, though. It grew until the decision was clear; my earthly responsibilities paled in comparison to this call to discovery.

Client privacy be damned. Who was I to ignore this? I still could hardly grasp the reality of it, but the importance of it held me in a vise grip.

At this point, the die had landed. The only thing to do was step closer.

Another whoosh of air came from the box, and a roaring sound filled the room to the corners, like a colossal ocean wave. I knelt down, touching the flaps of the box, examining them. Pretty normal.

I ran two fingers underneath. The cardboard felt wet, and swollen. Ready to disintegrate against my skin. When I brought my hand back out, my fingertips were slick with a colorless liquid.

Taking a deep breath, I slipped my hands under the flaps of the box and freed them.

I don't remember looking in, feeling more wind, or the ocean spray prickling my face. All I remember is the feeling of being heaved inside. Of one leg tapping the edge of the box, followed by an abrupt sensation of falling. Down became up. A cold wetness enveloped me, and immediately, my nose and throat burned. I coughed, expelling the water I'd breathed in. Instinctively, I held my breath.

Every part of me stung with cold. Ribs aching, chest burning, I swam up, trying to blink away the blur.

Past the cloud of sediment that surrounded me was a blue background, streaked over and over with endless lines of green, reaching up as high as I could see. Bright stabs of white light broke through everything, illuminating parts and erasing the green and the blue wherever it touched.

Something brushed against my foot, sending my heart pounding.

Just a yellow-green plant, its many slender leaves swaying with the ebb of the water. I was deep in a kelp forest. The water was a fathomless, watery blue, and the endless thin green leaves waved like a billion appendages. A horde of lonely creatures with one consciousness; too old, too different to register my presence. Haunting me with their otherness.

I had to move, now. To reach the surface. I turned everything off except the work. My only directive was up.

Something brushed against my ankle again. My heart fluttered. Terrified, I swooned, then steeled myself, pumping my arms and legs as fast as they would go. My lungs were bursting. I might have been swimming for thirty seconds, but I'll remember it as if hours had passed. When you think you're dying, life becomes elastic, stretching for miles.

I ripped through the surface and pulled for breath, gasping

and coughing up a gallon of seawater. More of it burned my sinuses. My eyes stung. My body was numb with cold.

The sun rode low and bright in the sky. If anything made sense at all, and we were in the same universe, world, hemisphere, whatever, then the sun was setting.

If it was setting, then I was facing West. But how does that help me if I don't know where I am?

I tried to pace myself. To steady my breathing, deepening the length of my shaky inhales and exhales. I should've learned how to meditate or something, I thought. Though I wasn't sure if meditating could really help someone lost at sea. I'd traveled for most of my early twenties, and knew how to get by on land, and where to find odd jobs. I'd never traveled by boat. Never learned anything about surviving something like this.

There was land here. A mountain, maybe one hundred yards away. The base was steep, climbing straight up from the water that skirted it. It looked daunting, but it was better than miles of nothing but ocean. I had a goal, now.

I swam for… not long, really. I tried to take breaks, but treading water wasn't much of a break. I was getting nowhere. I swam until my throat burned. Until the stitch in my side bent me over. My fingers and toes stung from the frigid water. The waves became choppy, until choppy approached violence. The waves threw me, and the undertow sucked me down.

There was nothing to do but struggle pointlessly against the churn of the ocean. I'd opened that box out of curiosity, and despite the fear, I'd hoped for a call to adventure. Soon, exhaustion would pull me all the way down. I shuddered. Desperately, I wished I was at home, safe, on my couch with my dogs.

This was not an adventure. In fact, I'd created my own missing persons case. My girlfriend wouldn't know I was gone until I was long drowned.

Something brushed against my foot again.

Shit. I jerked my foot up and looked at the water, which was far too dark to see past my own fingers. I swam a frantic side-stroke for several minutes, and continued looking around as if it would do me any good. I was afraid to bring my head below the surface again. I pictured a monster, absolutely ridiculous with teeth, its jaws ten times bigger than my head. My heart was in my throat, and I forced my mind as blank as it would go, working on my breathing again. It was just the kelp, I told myself. Just kelp.

Adrenaline pumped through me again. The pain in my middle was muted, and I worked to bring my head higher above the waves. Without the rushing of water in my ears, I could swear I heard singing. In between the roiling waves, I thought I saw a boat approaching.

At first, I could only hear a faint sing-song, I strained to hear over the roar of the ocean. It was a boat. It *had* to be a boat.

I strained some more to hear the words. Something-something "Make it round The Horn." Did he mean Cape Horn? If he did, that rocky headland I was swimming to was

Hornos Island. I'd never visited Chile but I'd always wanted to.

Strangely, it reminded me of a dream I'd been having. A weird sea shanty from another time tossed on violent winds, floating in and out of earshot. A giant white bird with black wings was half in the water, half on shore. Its wing was bent at an odd angle, and it was still. Its eyes shut, orange beak half-open. I tried to drag it further ashore, but it was three times my size. Too heavy. I couldn't find anyone to help.

Was this that same song? The sea shanty?

We'll be all right if we make it round the Horn
And we'll all hang on behind
A drop of Nelson's blood wouldn't do us any harm.
A drop of Nelson's blood wouldn't do us any harm.

"Hey!" I shouted, my voice hoarse, my throat burning from the effort. I waved one arm high in the air, my muscles cramping. I cleared my throat. Pulling in another short, labored breath. "Help!" I shouted again. "I need help!" The attempt got me a mouthful of seawater. I spit out what I could, but it had hit me in the back of the throat.

Slowly, the boat approached. An old medium-sized trawler with a cabin. At least thirty years old. Its hull had been white once, now yellowed. It was covered in brilliantly-colored barnacles of fuchsia, purple, yellow, and cyan. The colors of a coral reef. A huge man with shoulder-length black-blue hair and a long beard stood at the front of the deck, his big arms flexing beneath a white undershirt as he leaned forward, gripping the tarnished silver bulwark. He'd caught sight of me, and he studied me intently. Calculating risk, maybe. Deciding what he was going to do.

When he dropped the inner tube, he smiled, but his cool, stone-gray eyes were serious.

He hoisted me up easily. I clambered weakly over the rail, onto the deck. He crouched near me, giving me distance as I shivered and threw up seawater. The boat rocked without mercy, making it difficult to even kneel without collapsing. When I tried to stand, he stood first, warning me against getting up with a flat palm: *Not yet. Wait.* I couldn't fathom how he was able to stand.

I sat on the deck and waited, appreciating breathing again. The air was heavy with moisture and salt, and the sky was dark, even though I'd seen the sun only minutes before. The rain started down, as the man switched on a bright lamp. It illuminated the rain, and the deck shone wet under a dirty yellow light. The driving rain hammered down. As I caught my breath, I asked if we were at Cape Horn.

"Ah, yes, you know your geography." His voice was loud and rough. "This is, in fact, the Drake Passage, Cape Horn. This is where two oceans meet. And they don't always get along, if you catch my drift." He shouted this over the crashing waves.

"What are you doing out here on such a small boat? And in this weather?"

He helped me up, my arm over his shoulders, and brought me into the cabin. He sat in the captain's chair and I, in the chair next to his. I had to hang onto a grab bar at the side of the cabin.

His voice was quiet, but deep. "This isn't weather anymore. It's just been like this. For a week or more. One thing I'm doing out here is watching. Occasionally, I will influence events, though if anyone asks, you didn't hear me say it."

"What are you, in the importing trade or something?"

"No." He didn't elaborate.

"Aren't you wondering how I ended up out here, in the middle of everything?" I asked.

"I can see you'd like to tell me. I welcome that, if that's what you'd like."

"Actually," I hadn't thought that far ahead. "You wouldn't believe me if I told you, so never mind."

"Let me guess. You traveled with great speed. So quickly, so far, so mysteriously, you had to retrieve your bearings to puzzle out where you were."

"Yeah…" He was describing me being pulled out to sea by the current, right? Why did his description sound so close to what actually happened?

"I'm afraid," the man continued, "now that I've rescued you from certain death, I'll need your assistance."

"With what?"

"There is an animal of sorts that watches over these waters. An albatross. It's been mortally wounded. These kinds of creatures are special. Albatross, especially. They watch over land and sky alike. But this particular one is stationed on land. It remains at Cape Horn, always. It watches the oceans, keeps the turmoil at bay. I'm taking us there, now. I need you to help me help this creature."

What? "Why me?"

"Who's to say why? I suppose you're what I dragged up."

"This isn't something I specialize in. Do you have any veterinarians around here?" What did he mean by stationed, I wondered. Was there a military base? Did the army train birds here or something? That didn't make any sense.

The man laughed. "I have no idea if we have any veterinarians around here."

The ride was rough, but it felt like we were moving fast. The ship was small but powerful, despite its size. I didn't think a trawler could move this quickly. Not a normal one, anyway.

The man kept singing in a low, droning voice that was hard to hear against the waves that roared, battering the little boat. I could tell he sang the same song from earlier.

We'll be all right if we make it round the Horn
And we'll all hang on behind
A drop of Nelson's blood wouldn't do us any harm.
A drop of Nelson's blood wouldn't do us any harm.

I thought about how weird that he chose this song, and that my last name was Nelson. It smelled like metal and old fish in the cabin. I held on as tightly as I could, trying not to throw up.

He helped me off the boat onto a deck. We made our way up wooden steps that scaled the hill, each of us holding lanterns. I moved slowly and kept my head down, shielding my eyes from the rain and watching my footing, but still, I kept slipping and having to regain my balance. There were no handrails, and my heart was in my throat the whole way up. He never seemed to have any issues. I felt sick, cold, tired, but still glad I hadn't drowned. I wondered if my girlfriend was worrying about me yet.

"How much further?" I shouted over the rain pelting the steps.

"Not much!" he shouted back. "Look up, we're almost there!"

The moonlight glowed against a giant, metallic triangle, reaching from the ground to the sky. It was a giant wing, I realized. A huge gray triangle with beautiful gray and blue scalloped shapes, soldered gracefully together, fanning out into smooth curves, in kind of an industrial style. The second triangle-wing had severed, held on by some kind of wiring, swinging dangerously in big swooping gusts of wind.

I kept my distance to avoid being decapitated by the giant sheet of steel. "You need help with this broken statue? I thought you were going to make me put down a dying bird."

"Not put down," he corrected, "Help."

"Ah."

"This statue must be preserved. You don't always do the right thing, but in this case, you've worked miracles on land. This sculpture you created, it has calmed the seas. The Pacific and Atlantic have been warring forever. I had resigned to just leave it like that."

"What? I didn't create any miracle sculpture." *What the fuck is he on about?* I kept his gaze in shifts, eyeing the sculpture every so often to study the guillotine wing.

"I mean the collective 'you'. You humans. Y'all, I think you like to say."

"Us… humans?" I stared at the man. "You're not a human?" What was he implying?

"Ach, you don't need to get too caught up in that comment. We're standing here together, aren't we? I'm communicating with you in your language. Relating to you, instead of bursting from the water, giant and shirtless. What does it matter that I'm Poseidon, god of the sea?"

I was speechless. Stuck on an island with a very weird fucking person. But on the other hand, I just fell in a box and traveled from the United States to Chile.

"Poor thing. You are having a weird day. I'm not going to hurt you, truly. Help me with my task, and then we'll talk about getting you sorted. You don't really have a choice. After all, it's your dream that led me to you."

The sea shanty dream, with the broken bird. "It's true, isn't it?" Cheese on a fucking cracker.

"It is."

"And you just drop this information on me, just like that?"

He laughed softly, exaggerating sheepishness. "Sort of. I admit, I like the reaction I get. But you have to admit, this is all relevant."

"If you're god of the sea, why do you need my help?"

"You have a good back. Good arms. You're sensible. Level-headed. You'll see."

"Why can't you just do this yourself?"

He pointed to the water. "When I'm out there, I can do a lot. When I'm on land, I have the strength of a man. A very, very strong man, of course, right? So, I need two pairs of arms for this. Mine, and yours."

I moved to the back of the statue. One wing was still, and the other had been affixed to a large wooden scaffold. The spot where the wing had cracked off had left a deep "v" that extended all the way into the base.

"All right," I said. "We can do this." I crouched down and lifted the wing off the ground just a little, to get an idea of its weight. Ok. Really fucking heavy. Piano-heavy. Solid hardwood bed heavy. Immense, and flat. In these big headwinds.

Damn.

We lifted the wing together, just enough to get it off the ground. Rotated it until we were right in front of the statue, ready to hoist it back into place.

"You sure we can lift this?" he asked.

No I thought, while nodding yes. "Wait for it."

A huge gust of wind started at my back, gathering speed. "Now!" I shouted. He pulled the wing up, hoisting it until it was upright. I held it from behind, letting my muscles burn until they were spent, and checked the position. "Move it forward!" He did. "Left!" He moved it right. "*Your left goddamnit!* Now *left*-left!" He got it right this time, and I jammed the sharp point of metal into the fissure. Groaning, grinding my teeth, muscles screaming, I kept it like that, waiting for the wind to die.

"How's it look?"

"Ok."

"Then we're cookin'."

"Yep."

We stepped back to check the structure. Make sure the wings looked straight.

Both wings leaned forward, steel groaning, moon lighting them up like the devil himself.

"Oh God!" We hadn't fixed it after all. The wind was tipping them over to crush me. I fell on my ass, scrambling backwards to get enough distance.

Slowly, the wings righted themselves and were completely solid again.

"What just—" I gave up trying to say anything else.

"Maybe it was thanking you," was all he said.

Slowly, we walked back towards the boat. The rain was petering out. I kept checking behind me to see if the wings would move again.

"I guess I'd better get back."

"So quickly? Are you sure? You only have time for one adventure?"

"Yes, just the one. I'm tired, and I have three dogs at home."

"That's a lot of dogs. I understand."

"Thank you."

"In that case, I think there's a box waiting for you in the cabin. That will be your way back."

"That easy, huh?"

"That wasn't easy."

We started towards the boat, walking side by side. Me and this… god-guy. I realized while I was more than ready to go home, I didn't want this to be it. I wanted to make sure he could contact me again. I didn't want to just hope I'd dream about a catastrophe, though.

I reached for my pocket. My business cards were soggy, but maybe still legible.

"Don't waste those on me," he said. "Keep moving those boxes. Next time, you'll know it's me."

16

Not A Lion, Maybe A Bear

CHRISTOPHER HAWKINS

The die bounced once, rolled along the wooden floor, and disappeared beneath the couch. Typical. I bent to go after it, but felt an odd twinge at the base of my spine—not so much a pain but a slide, something shifting out of place, or maybe back into it—and decided that the die could stay where it was. I never should have rolled it in the first place. Like all good gamers, I knew that dice held their own luck, and idle rolls always wasted the best outcomes. Right now, it was out of sight—maybe a hit, maybe a miss, maybe both. Schrödinger bullshit. If I didn't look when I picked it up, maybe it wouldn't count. Maybe it would be the same as if I'd never rolled it at all.

The couch was one of those overstuffed leather jobs with rivets along the armrests; the kind that looked like it would be more at home in a therapist's office than in this old Frank Lloyd Wright knock-off at the end of a country road in the middle of nowhere Wisconsin. Funny that the couch hadn't really registered before, though I must have walked past it at least a dozen times. The furniture guys must have gotten here first, finished their work, and wrapped up early. Furniture guys had it easy. A few big pieces, another guy to help you. The hardest part of the day was figuring out where to go for lunch. Not box guys, though. Box guys, they figured, could work alone. Box guys could lug and lug until their spines started slipping, and no matter how long they did it, there would always be one more box.

Like this box.

Something inside it had moved. I would have sworn to that, would have sworn to it on a stack of boxes full of Bibles. But I was tired, not just tired, but weary, and a weary mind was not to be trusted. That was something my therapist had told me. Never make big decisions when you're tired. I was tired now, and opening this box when it wasn't my box to open was a big decision. It could get me fired. I couldn't afford to get fired. I was one customer complaint away from being out of compliance and losing my crappy apartment, one paycheck away from freezing to death in an alley under a blanket made of cardboard.

No. Shit. Stop anticipating. I could already feel that fight-or-flight thing creeping down through my legs, making my toes tingle. My therapist told me that that feeling was part of our evolution, left over from when we were lesser primates and had to run from lions. But it was a box, not a lion. I didn't have to run. All I had to do was set it down, walk away. The box was marked "Master Bedroom," so I'd put it in the master bedroom. Drop the last few boxes, go home, and take a hot shower. Just forget the whole thing.

The furniture guys had gotten to the bedroom, too. The bed was all set up, a big four-poster like something out of a Renaissance painting. There was a fireplace on the opposite wall, an arty accumulation of jagged limestone that looked like it would make you scream murder if you stubbed your toe on it in the middle of the night. I set the box down on the hearth, thinking that was good enough, thinking that something had just shifted inside while I was carrying it; that was all. And I'd done my job. My boss would be happy. My therapist would be happy. I'd keep my crappy apartment for one more week.

Only, it moved again.

A little wobble from side to side, but it was enough. And I wasn't touching it this time, so I couldn't tell myself any of the excuses that had gotten me this far. It wasn't the contents shifting. It wasn't my joints creaking. It wasn't my imagination.

It had moved. It had done it on its own.

There was that tingle in my legs again. But it wasn't a lion. There were no lions. There were bears, though. Big brown ones, probably right in these woods. And bears could walk right up to the door of your house, break the thing down just by putting a shoulder to it. Bears had claws the size of steak knives, and they were curved like big hooks so they could dig in and just tear and tear and tear.

Stop. Deep breaths. There was no lion. There was no bear. There never had been. It was just my brain telling me stories again. Cool story, brain. Thanks, bro. Don't know what I'd do without you.

I pulled the little box cutter from my pocket. My therapist wouldn't like that I had it at all, but I needed it for the job, and it made a calming little ratcheting sound every time I thumbed it open. Sometimes I'd just open it and close it, open it and close it, over and over again just to hear the sound. I liked it. It was calming, and I caught myself doing it now. Open and closed. Open and closed. Like a heartbeat. There was no lion. There was no bear. There might be something alive in that box, though. A puppy. Maybe a cat. Something that would never think to be worried about a bear. Something worth saving.

That thought was enough for me to zip the cutter across the top and pull the flaps open. The air inside gave a little whoosh when I did it, like an exhalation, like some magic being lost. Or gained. Schrödinger bullshit. Or maybe that was just my imagination, too.

The box was mostly empty, but there was something in the bottom that rattled. The light wasn't good enough for me to see what it was, so I turned the box onto its side and shook the contents out onto the hearth.

Bones. A rib. Two vertebrae. A rounded piece that looked like the knob of a femur. A bit of broken jaw that was missing its teeth.

I held the bits up one by one, turning them in the dim light to make sure I was seeing what I thought I was seeing. There were maybe a dozen pieces in all. When I was done, I saw that I'd arranged them on the flagstones without thinking into a rough approximation of a human body, like they were the beginnings of a jigsaw puzzle.

The weird tingle hit me again, and for a minute I wondered if I should call the police. I went as far as to pull my phone out of my pocket, but quickly changed my mind. There had to be plenty of reasons, non-sinister reasons, why a person might have a collection of bones in a box. Maybe this guy was a doctor. Maybe they weren't even human bones. Just because I'd laid them out like a person didn't mean they came from one. The box didn't belong to me. I could get in trouble just from opening it. I put the phone away. I didn't have any reception out here anyway.

There were only a few boxes left, and I made up my mind to get them moved as quickly as I could and put this place behind me. I left the bones where they were and headed for the door. I only made it as far as the overstuffed couch. There were boxes stacked next to it, and I could see that at least one of them was labeled for the bedroom. Maybe there were bones in that one, too. Maybe if I shook it out, I'd find more pieces to that puzzle on the hearth. Maybe there'd be pieces to a second puzzle, too. And a third. And maybe more, still.

My mind was racing again, making up stories, filling in corners. But they were just stories. That was the first thing I'd learned in therapy, that your brain was always telling you stories. It just chattered away, all the time. And it spoke in your own voice, so whatever it told you, you tended to believe. But it was just noise. You didn't have to listen.

Only, right now, the story it was telling me was that I'd stumbled into something dangerous, like a giant wasp nest, that I'd be okay as long as I took a wide path around it and didn't look back. Just a few more boxes, and I could go. Just a few more boxes, and I'd be clear of this place, and no one would have to know. Not my therapist. Not the court. No one.

Except, I'd opened the box. The owner would know that for sure. They'd see those bones all laid out by the fireplace, and they'd call the moving company, and my boss would see who signed out the truck today, and they'd know it was me.

I could put the bones back. As much as it weirded me out just thinking about touching them again, I could drop them all right back in the box. There was packing tape in the truck, I was pretty sure. I could seal it back up, and maybe no one would notice. Maybe if I did that, the frantic drumming of my heart would start to quiet down a little. Maybe tonight, by the time I was back safe in my little one-room apartment, I'd think back on this and wonder why I'd ever been anxious about it at all.

Before I knew it, one of the other boxes marked for the bedroom was in my hands. I held it out in front of me, almost like a shield, as I passed through the doorway. I tried not to look at the bones; figured that I'd just put the empty box at the edge of the flagstone hearth and sweep them back inside with my arm. But, I did look at the bones. There were more of them now, or at least there seemed to be. Even without counting, I could tell there were more ribs and the long bones of an arm that hadn't been there before. Above the jaw was a broken bit of skull, the smooth curves of what had to be eye sockets, empty but for shadows.

My heart was a goddamn telegraph machine by then, because I knew that it hadn't been me who'd put the new bones there. There had to be someone else here. Not a lion, not a bear, but another person. Someone had seen me cut open the box, someone who was clearly fucking with me.

I turned around and checked behind the door, but there was no one there. The window was closed, and anyway, I was sure I would have heard it if it had opened. There was no closet, so I opened up the wardrobe. It was just an empty space, without clothes or even the hangers to hold them. I dropped to all fours and peered under the bed. There was nothing there, not even a ball of dust.

When I came up again, there were more bones on the hearth. Shinbones laid out in their places. Fingers and toes arrayed like museum specimens. The high curve of the pelvis. The skeleton was so much more complete now, though plenty of bones were still missing. There was no mistaking that they were human bones, that they could only be human bones.

This time I was sure that there had been no one else but me in the room. My heart had slowed by now, but my brain was yammering away in overdrive. If no one else had put the bones there, then what did that mean? They hadn't gotten there on their own. That wasn't a thing that happened. It wasn't possible. It had to be a mistake. I was remembering the bones wrong. I'd put down more than I thought I had. That was a thing that could happen. My therapist had said so. Sometimes the brain spun memories around and smashed them together so it was easier to make sense of them. Sometimes it was just plain wrong, like I was wrong now about how many bones there had been. Cool story, brain. Thanks for the freak out.

I counted the bones again, and this time I made myself look at them, really look at them. Where I had remembered just a partial curve of cranium, there was now an almost fully-formed skull. The jawbone seemed larger, too. It nestled in the notch of one cheek and there were teeth jutting out right where the teeth ought to be. The knob of femur had become whole, and stretched down to meet the lower leg at the knee. The two bones in turn nestled against a knob of ankle.

Don't sing the song, I thought, but I couldn't tell if it was me begging my brain to stop or my brain taunting me to start. Don't sing the song.

Up close, I could see that the bones were singed black in places. Some of the long ones had cracks down their length where the marrow had boiled away. Where the ends were broken, there was only ash, clinging like the tips of cigarettes.

I didn't dare to touch them again, so I poked at a joint with the blade of my box cutter. The whole leg wobbled, and when I got my head down close, I could see the faint wisps of tendon that tied the bones together. With my ear that close, I could hear the sound that they made, like that sound when you've got pop rocks in your mouth, and it feels like your whole head is made of bubble wrap. Like putting your ear to a hive full of wasps.

I ran from the place then, the choice between fight and flight never seeming more clear. I only stopped when I got to the front door and felt the cool of the metal handle beneath my fingers. I paused there, counting by tens, slowing my breathing by force of will alone. My therapist had told me about this too, that sometimes the things your brain told you were more than just words, that your eyes could make up stories the same way the voice did. That's what the meds were for, right? And I'd taken my meds. I'd been good about that. I hadn't missed once, not in a whole month.

I thought about my little one-room apartment, about how much I needed this job. There were only a few boxes left on the truck. I could finish things up without even going back into the bedroom. Just a few more minutes, and I could leave this place and never have to think about it again. And if the owner found the bones laid out on the hearth, if the bones were really there at all, what then? They'd been in one of their boxes. If they wanted to get him in trouble for opening it, they'd have to say what was in it, and would they really want to deal with the kinds of questions that would bring?

Those boxes in the truck were tied up in the little hollow space above the cab, laced in with twine. I got halfway down the driveway before I remembered my box cutter. I'd left it lying on the hearth and I didn't have a spare. My hands were shaking too much, and I knew I'd never be able to pick apart the knots. I'd tied them too tight, anyway.

But more than that, there was a strange urgency in the pit of my stomach, a weird pull that was telling me that I had to go back, if only to see if the bones were really there, that it wasn't just a story that my brain was trying to convince me was true. The feeling grew stronger, as strong as the urge to run had been only moments before. If I could just see, if I could go back and know without question that I had only imagined the way the bones had grown and multiplied, then I could just put it all behind me. I could write it off as just another trick of my surly, broken brain, and the next time I saw my therapist, we could talk about upping my dosage.

I braced myself as I returned to the room, but still came up short at the sight of the fire blazing in the fireplace. More than the bones, that was the thing that made my blood run cold. There hadn't been any firewood there. I was sure of that much. And yet, could I be sure of anything when I was so distracted by the strange box and its stranger contents? I was alone. No one could have started the fire but me. And it was blazing. Mature. The flames were high, and they licked seductively at the limestone chimney as the smoke rose up and up and up.

The skeleton was whole now, still singed black in places,

but intact, with the round cage of ribs tied together with ligaments, with the skull all in one place and grinning up at the ceiling. Ribbons of dark muscle had begun to stretch the length of the long bones, and I could see a lumpy mass in the cradle of the pelvis that could only be charred organs. But it wasn't real. It couldn't be real. This was the distraction that my brain had created for me. This was the illusion, the story it was telling me to keep me from remembering that I had set the fire, that it could only have been me who set the fire, one part of the brain trying to protect itself from the other. That was how brains had evolved in the first place. Bicameral. Adversarial. When ancient men had heard the voice of God it was only the voice of that other-brain, the half that wanted dominion over the other. As the brain evolved, that voice began to quiet, but for some people it was still as loud as shouting and, well, now they had medication for that.

My box cutter lay on the hearth next to the skeleton's outstretched hand. The plastic sheath had melted down onto the stone but the blade still gleamed, its point sharp, as if it had been honed by the flames. I knew that I had to take it with me, that it wouldn't do to leave any evidence of my being here behind. But the skeleton's finger was practically touching it, and the idea of accidentally brushing against the thing made my stomach heave.

As I inched closer, I could see eyes in the hollows of the skull, staring unfocused, and there was something about them that seemed almost familiar. I reached out for the cutter, and as I did, my hand grazed my pants pocket and felt something solid there. It was a box cutter, the perfect twin of the one on the hearth. The same white and orange plastic. The same printing from the moving company on the side. Only this one had never been melted. This one was so perfect that it might have been brand new.

The eyes shifted then in their sockets, and all at once they were focused on me. I staggered back and pressed my palms into my own eyes to try to drive the sight away, and kept pressing and pressing until all I could see was red. It wasn't real. It couldn't be real. I just needed my meds. I'd forgotten them somehow. That was all. I needed my therapist. I needed her to tell me that it was all just a lie that my brain was telling me. I needed her to know that I hadn't meant to relapse, that I hadn't started that fire in the fireplace, not on purpose.

When I took my hands away from my eyes, the skeleton was sitting on the edge of the hearth. Not just a skeleton anymore, its limbs were covered with red striations of muscle that glistened in the firelight. Bits of charred skin clung to its shoulders, split and blackened and oozing. Blood pumped through exposed vessels, its beating heart visible behind the gleaming ladder of its ribs. At its wrists were pieces of singed cloth–all that was left of its burnt clothing–melted against the muscle. In one clenched fist it held that other box cutter, whole again now but still closed, its bony thumb pressed against the opener.

Worse than all of that was the thing's face: Ropes of muscle now connected the jaw to the cheekbones, and the teeth had filled in crooked beneath the fleshy remnant of a nose. There were tufts of burnt hair where its scalp should be. Its eyes, unblinking, stared out at me, tracking my every move. And yet, for all its hideousness, I found myself drawn to it, because there was something familiar in that face, something that my rational mind was not yet ready to see. The thing opened its mouth as if to say something, but it had no tongue to speak.

It stood then, quicker and more sure in its movements than I could have thought possible. Its musculature seemed to be growing before my eyes, stretching and knitting into new connections, the skin sealing itself around them, going from black to an angry red as I watched. It took a step toward me, the box cutter in its fist. My feet moved then without my having to tell them to, that other brain somehow in charge. I had no plan, no goal but to get away. Fighting was impossible. I could only fly.

I made it out to the front room before my feet snagged on each other and sent me sprawling to the floor. I slid like a baseball player, and only then did I realize that I had the box cutter cupped in my fist. I came to rest beside the couch. Beneath it, I could see the die I had rolled. Next to it lay a twin of the same shape and size. My panic subsided long enough for me to scoop them both out. One was the same as it had been when I'd rolled it. The other was melted and split.

I stood, and without even turning around, I could feel him there behind me in the bedroom doorway. I could hear him in my mind, as clear as my own voice, telling me stories, telling me that I'd done it on purpose, that I'd wanted to do it, that I'd even liked it. But it was a lie. I told it so, but all I could hear was that other voice mocking. Cool story, it said. Thanks.

The flames around him were growing now, and I could smell the smoke, like a Cub Scout campfire, like distant burning log cabins. The memory made my heart soar. But he was standing in the doorway, a dark silhouette, an interruption in all that brilliant light. His hair had grown back, and he wore the same clothes I did. The same button-down work shirt. The same dusty work pants. The same confused look on the same confused face.

I stared at him. Or was it only that he was staring at me? I thought of the boxes that were left on the truck, but I couldn't remember if I had been loading them out or bringing them in. The dice clacked together against my palm, and when I opened my hand, they both looked brand new, and both of them showed the same number. I couldn't tell one from the other.

From the bedroom doorway, I stared out at this other me and all at once remembered the box cutter in my hand. He seemed to remember it, too, because he thumbed his blade open and let the dice tumble to the floor. I looked down and found that my blade was open, too. Which of us had done it first, I could not say. The flames were at my back now. I had to get out, and there was only one thing standing in my way.

Together, we fled for the door.

17

Copycats From Outer Space

J9 VAUGHN

...and tumbled into the hall and down the stairs. I dove for it, but it hit one of the stairs at an angle and went flying. I raced down after it, just in time to see it slide under the sofa. Hurrying over, I moved the heavy, wooden coffee table that had taken all three of us to unload earlier. It looked like a giant upside-down half-egg of solid wood and probably cost more than my condo. I managed to slide it enough to lay on the floor and shine my flashlight underneath the recliner sofa, which was just as costly. But it was so low to the ground I couldn't see very far. After trying to find the die by patting my hand around, knowing my arms were probably too short to reach the wall, I finally got up and carefully lifted one side of the heavy sofa away from the wall. I crouched down to shine my flashlight back there. No die. All I saw was an air duct without a cover. I sighed.

"Guess that's it then," I muttered, un-wedging myself from behind the couch. "Guess curiosity really did kill the ca—er, lose the die." I started pushing the couch back against the wall but froze when I heard what sounded like a very large, very fast spider skittering down the stairs and across the floor. I slowly turned to see that a box… No, THE box, was blocking the front door. The top of the box was eye level with me and the bottom of the box was supported by four metallic legs jutting out of the bottom. Then, the box started talking. Or at least, I think it was talking and not just making noises.

"Gäbò HA, Nî-keek!" The words were garbled and muffled by the box, but sounded like whatever was in the box was giving a command.

I threw my arms into the air on instinct, too many negative interactions with cops, before remembering that whatever was in the box couldn't actually see me. I stepped silently to my right, thinking I'd escape through the kitchen door. I didn't really want to know what was in the box, and hey, I could always get more dice. But the front of the box kept turning with me, like it was tracking my movements. I stopped, it stopped. I looked to my right to see how close I was to the opening between the living room and the kitchen. Just a few steps. I ran.

"Wállupœn ka vevükrdęn!"

The shout was followed by what I could only surmise was the cardboard of the box exploding outward as a swarm of flying drone-like creatures, that made kitten chirping sounds, pursued me. I covered my head with my arms as they pelted me with… what felt like kernels of corn? It didn't hurt much, but when they hit my skin just right, they were sharp. They had started low to the ground but were rising, and I couldn't help thinking that those kernels could do some real damage if they got me in the eye. I spun away, shielding my face with my arm, my eyes almost closed. At first, they were all around me. Then they congregated on one side, but as I moved, they would shift to the other side, then another, spinning me like a top. I realized as I was taking staggering steps away from them, I wasn't sure where I was going. Just as I felt like I might topple over from dizziness, they stopped, so I stopped.

I stood where I was, eyes closed with arms still wrapped around my head, for about a minute. I could hear the little drones chirping, but it was quieter, less frequent, and they sounded further away. But there was another sound too. It wasn't loud or chirpy like the drones. It was more of a whooshing sound. When the thrumming of my heart in my ears had settled, I realized that whatever was making that sound was directly in front of me. I slowly opened my eyes and peeked between my elbows. About two feet away from me, a metal, square robot stood on four long, jointed legs. It was a dull gray with four holes on each side of its flat face, like eyes, with a long, straight, and narrow opening below that, like a mouth. A red light shot out of all the eyeholes and hit my own, triggering a migraine. I crumpled to the floor, moaning.

"Oh, come on! I didn't even touch you!" The voice sounded like my big brother, Al.

I snapped my head up and looked all around me. He, of course, wasn't there. Just shards of cardboard box, the big robot, and all the little drones that had drifted down until they were inches off the floor, hovering on every side of me. I looked at the floor and saw they had indeed been pelting me with kernels of corn. I picked one up and held it out to the robot. "Corn?"

The boxy bot nodded. "Popcorn, to be exact."

I flinched as it still sounded like Al.

The bot tilted to one side, reminding me of Al. He always tilted his head before he asked a question. "Why do you do that?"

I sat up straight. "Do what?"

It raised one of the spidery legs and flapped it in the air, like Al used to with his hand when he was confused. "That! You're doing it right now. Cringing, I think, is what it's called?"

"Oh," I breathed. "Um, it's your voice. It sounds like my brother Alvero's voice."

Still using Al's voice, the bot asked, "Is that bad?"

"Well, he's dead, so it's upsetting."

I lowered my head and pressed my palms against my forehead. I could feel tears forming, and I really didn't want to cry, but with this migraine… I could hear the bot whirring again, and the drones were chirping. I covered my ears since the noise was making my migraine worse. Even with my head down and my eyes squeezed shut, I could see the red light coming from the robot.

"Please stop," I whimpered.

Everything stopped. All sounds and the red light. The only thing I could hear was my own ragged breathing. I slowly raised my head and opened my eyes. With only the dim light of the dining room to my left, I could see that all the drones were sitting before me in two almost equal rows of eight, perfectly spaced. Behind them, the bot had also sat down and looked like a giant metal cube; the spidery legs must have tucked up inside it. The word Borg popped into my head, causing me to snicker.

"What is, Borg?" The bot asked, now using my partner Asha's voice.

It was still disconcerting, but at least Asha wasn't dead. I really needed to call Asha. She would be expecting me home about an hour ago, or at least a phone call. I started digging for my phone. One thing I hated about winter, too many damn pockets!

"Is Asha your wife?"

I stopped, looking back at the bot. "Should be, but she's not. We've been together for 20 years. Tomorrow's our anniversary. A Borg is an evil robot alien from the Star Trek universe." I checked my last pocket, an inside coat pocket, and found my phone. I took it out, unlocked it, and started texting Asha. But I got as far as, "I'm running late," and stopped. What could I tell her? I didn't want to worry her, but what if I was in real danger and… one of the drones in the front row zipped straight up into the air, then directly at me. Startled, I jerked back. A metal arm, similar to the appendages the big bot had, but smaller and with pincers at the end, shot out and snatched the phone out of my hand.

"Hey!" I shouted, snatching at the air. "Give that back!"

The drone had already zipped over to the big bot and set the phone on its head. Or rather, *in* its head. As the drone lowered my phone, two flaps lifted and my phone descended into the bot's head. The flaps—doors really—closed. A whirring sound, different from the one before, started softly as the block of bot wobbled from side to side. As the whirring got louder, punctuated by beeps and other sounds, the legs shot out from underneath, and it began careening around the room so hard and fast its footfalls left gouges in the floor. Lights, all colors this time, pulsated out of the bot's eyes. The bot began to whistle like a tea kettle and steam came out the top of it. It began talking in that alien language again, with a few English words thrown in, but so fast my mind could not process any of it.

I leaned over, covering my ears and eyes, waiting for it to stop. It was late, I was tired, and had a migraine. Why was this happening?

Remembering what happened before, I gasped out, "please stop."

Everything stopped. Sounds, lights, vibrations. There was one last THUNK, and a hiss of air escaped.

I slowly lifted my head and opened my eyes. The room was completely dark. Even the light from the other room was off. My migraine brain settled a bit. I slowly stood up and breathed with relief. But with that relief came a flood of terror. I started stumbling backwards to get as far away from the bot and the drones as I could. What was wrong with me? There is a robot and loads of drones, and I'm calmly texting my girlfriend?! My heart felt like it would pound out of my chest. I backed into the recliner and sat with a thud as my breathing got faster and faster and…

"Lina, put your head between your knees!" The bot commanded in Asha's voice. Without thinking, I did it. "Now take a deep breath in, hold, and breathe out. Good!"

A feeling of warmth came over me. No, not just a feeling, actual warmth, as the bot talked me through the breathing exercise a few more times. With my head still between my knees, I opened my eyes and saw a soft, orangish glow.

"That's better. You calm?"

I nodded, realized how that might not read with my head between my knees, and said, "Yes."

"Wonderful. Now, very, very slowly, lift your head. We need to talk."

I lifted my head, only feeling slightly lightheaded, and saw that Asha was sitting cross-legged on the floor in front of me. "What the…?"

"Don't worry, this is just a holographic interpretation of your girlfriend. Seeing us the way we are seems so upsetting for you, and I want to put you at ease."

I shook my head, weirded out, but also entirely impressed. The holograph, or whatever it was, caught her amber eyes. Her hair had silvery gray roots at the base of her purple tight braids, just like it had been the last time I saw her. Even her skin was the right shade of brown with all the scars and blemishes I knew so well. The only thing off was that she was wearing the same tan coveralls I was wearing with my company's logo "It's So Moving" on the left chest pocket, written backwards.

"Sorry about the clothes," Asha said. "I tried to duplicate what was in your mind and on your phone, but I couldn't quite get it, so I copied you. I hope that's okay."

Speechless, I nodded.

"Good. I hope my pets are okay?"

I looked down and saw that all sixteen drones now looked like teeny, tiny kittens. I reached down and wiggled my fingers. A little gray one came trotting over to me with its tail straight up in the air and let me touch it. It felt like a kitten, too! It purred and rubbed against my hand and legs. The other kittens came over to me, purring and meowing softly. I knew it was an illusion, but it was a really good one. Four crawled up my leg. Two laid down on the arm of the sofa, while the other two climbed up to the back and started playing. Three more crawled up, two laying against my left thigh, and the third crawled into my lap, purring softly. The ones left on the floor curled into cute little balls as if going to sleep. The two on the back stopped playing, and each picked a shoulder to lean on and purr.

After a few minutes, I realized that each kitten was the exact likeness of a kitten I had fostered. I looked down at the small tabby in my lap and felt a lump in my throat. It looked exactly like Tyrion, the kitten who died in my arms.

"What is that?" Asha gasped. "You're not supposed to be crying! You love kittens! Wait, close your eyes."

I did. Through my eyelids I could see the red light going down and up again.

"Oh," Asha's voice sighed. "That kitten died. Do you want me to change…"

"No," I replied, shaking my head. "I couldn't bear it. It would be like he died again."

"Curiouser and curiouser," the bot said in the voice of Alice from the Alice in Wonderland cartoon.

I laughed.

"Oh good," Asha's voice again, "you're happy! Let's talk."

"Let's," I agreed. "I have so many questions."

"I'm sure you do. But before we get to them, I must tell you a few things. Rules, if you will."

"Rules?" I asked, absently stroking the kitten drone in my lap.

Asha's image shrugged. "Guidelines? Anyhow, you should know that the—what you keep thinking of as drones, and now kitten drones—are actually my guardians. They will do everything they can to protect me."

I cocked an eyebrow. "With unpopped popcorn?"

She shook her head. "They used that on you because you are not a threat. They were just herding you back to where we needed you to be. No, they have much more lethal ways to protect me."

"Gotcha. I promise not to harm you."

Asha laughed. "No! You misunderstand. You are not a threat. Even before I scanned you, I did not perceive anything threatening about you. No, I am telling you this because you were intending to text Asha and had been thinking about calling the human authorities, or cops, as you think of them. Asha might be okay, but my guardians would maim and possibly kill cops and others to protect me if they needed to. We don't want it to come to that."

I nodded. "I mean, it's not like I can contact anyone anyhow, you've got my phone."

"Which I will absolutely give back to you. I promise. We are not thieves."

"Just stowaways," I smirked.

Asha shook her head, then crinkled her nose. "Not exactly, though I guess that's closest to what we are."

"What are you, exactly?" I asked.

"Loosely translated, we are Intergalactic Robotic Information, Scouting, Gathering, and Recruiting Units of Nebcons in the Tryladok System."

"Wait," I said, visualizing the first letter of each word in my head. "IRIS GRUNTS?"

Asha laughed. "I didn't know if you'd pick up on that so quickly, but good job! We are the eyes of our… I guess you'd call them employers, but that's not quite right. Oh! Masters." Asha's head tilted as her eyes seemed to be scanning what was in her head. "More like owners, I guess? You have some weird ideas about Masters, Mistresses, and Mastresses. That last one! Interesting!" She chuckled, shaking her head. "Also, this laughing thing you humans do is really… I think the word is, satisfying?"

I nodded, smiling. "It is. Okay, let's focus on what's really going on here. Can I now ask more questions, or are there other guidelines I need to know?"

"Shoot. I must say, that is an odd expression. But go ahead."

"Who sent you?"

"Good question. The Eighteenth Moon Tryladokian University sent me. Or rather, Doctor Gamoblyxitooniym, or Ga for short."

"Okay… so you're studying us, the human race? For a doctor?"

"Not exactly. How do I explain this in a way that will make sense?"

Asha steepled her fingers and tapped them against her tightly pursed lips as she thought. I had to remind myself that there was a cube robot underneath this facade since I suddenly had an urge to kiss her.

"Basically, the planet you call Earth is the subject of Doctor Ga's thesis paper for their third doctorate, Primitive Worldlings on the Planet Earth. They sent me to gather more information, first-hand observations, and a witness."

"A witness?"

"Yes. We must bring back one of the Earthanoids to

corroborate the paper before the Tribunal Council of Tryladok."

My eyes widened. "Do you mean me?"

Asha leaned back, her image flickering, showing me glimpses of the boxy bot beneath. The lights inside were swirling, and the box was tilting from side to side. Asha's image faded until it was gone entirely. I noticed that, except for the one asleep in my lap, the kittens were back to looking like drones and had gathered around the bot as it started to spin with each tilt.

I carefully lifted the sleeping drone/kitten off of my lap and set it gently on the couch next to me as I scooted off the couch. With all the attention directed away from me, as the box made louder and louder whirring sounds, I slipped into the kitchen. I didn't dare turn on a light, so I felt along the wall until I came to a door. I was pretty sure it was a pantry door, so I quietly moved past it. I hadn't been able to look around the kitchen the last time I was in there due to the drones pelting me with popcorn, so I wasn't even sure I was going in the right direction, especially with it being so dark.

My hand hit another doorknob. I slowly opened the door, letting in a little light, but it wasn't the cool night air that greeted me. It was the stale smell of a cellar. I was about to shut the door and continue my search when the sounds in the other room stopped.

"Lina," Asha's voice called from the other room.

I carefully felt with my foot and found that the stairs started right at the door. I stepped onto the first stair and closed the door behind me as quietly as I could. I saw there was a railing in the soft glow of light from below. On either side of me were concrete walls, and the floor at the bottom of the wooden staircase was cement. I couldn't see any further into the basement, but I slowly made my way down. I could hear the sound of water dripping from somewhere below, and behind that was a soft whirring that reminded me of how the bot box whirred. I paused on the stairs and strained to hear if the whirring was actually coming from below or if the bot was going into another frenzy. There was a little whirring from above, but what I had been hearing was definitely coming from down here.

Then I heard Asha's voice laughing from the kitchen, "I'm gonna find you!"

I hurried down the rest of the stairs, cringing at every creek. I reached the bottom and could see everything. In the middle of the basement, where the glow was coming from, was a large spherical UFO that looked like it flew off the cover of a tabloid from the 1960s. A ramp slid out from the UFO, stopping just at the foot of the stair where I'm standing. I heard a ka-thunk sound followed by a series of thumps and saw my 20-sided die bouncing down the metal ramp at me. I leaned down to pick it up. It had landed with the 17 facing up.

"Huh," I mused. "That's how old I was when I took my first cross-country road trip."

"Maybe," the robot's voice behind me no longer sounded

like Asha, "it's a sign that you should take your first intergalactic trip!"

I turn around to see the Borg-like box on metallic spider legs blocking my only exit.

"Wait, just wait. Why is your ship down here when you arrived in the moving boxes?"

The robot made a squeaking, spinning sound, then coughed out a metallic laugh. "Oh, that is because we got separated from the ship. One of the drones, the one that's been down here the whole time, managed to track it down. Someone thought it was a toy of the kid who will be living here and shipped it in a box that went ahead of the actual moving. While we can stay small for a long time, the ship needs me to help it. The drone brought it down to the basement so it could expand to its original size without being observed."

"Huh," I said, looking at the bot and the drones. A part of me wanted to push past and run out of the house. But another part wanted to see what would happen. I mean, I'd always wanted to travel and see the stars, right?

I took a deep breath and swallowed my fear. "Okay," I said, my voice shaking. "I'll go with you on three conditions. One, we have to pick up my girlfriend. Or, at least, stop by and give her the opportunity to go with me. Two, you will return me to the exact time and location we left Earth from. And three, I want to bring my cats."

The drones swarmed around me, purring as the box laughed. "Absolutely! Let's go!"

They hustled me onto the ramp and into the ship, where everything was just so bright and silvery that I had to squeeze my eyes shut. I sat in a chair and the drones strapped me in. I could hear the bot box moving around and switching things on. My chair started vibrating and I grasped the arms wondering if I had made a horrible mistake.

"How are we getting out of the basement?" I shouted over all the whirring, and beeping, and high-pitched screaming, followed by deep rumbling sounds coming from all around me. I leaned forward and grasped my head in my hands.

"Same way we got in here!" The bot shouted back. "I will shrink us down."

Everything around me and inside of me swirled into a kaleidoscope of smells and tastes. My entire body felt like a tongue and the things it tasted were not pleasant.

"I'm gonna hurl!" I burped and gagged. When nothing came out, I was relieved since I couldn't figure out where my mouth was. I knew I was still holding my head, but my hands had gone numb, and my head kept expanding and contracting. I felt like I couldn't breathe since I no longer knew where my lungs were.

"Is this how I die?" I thought, my insides feeling like they were on fire.

"Breathe!" The robotic voice commanded. Suddenly, everything inside me fell back into place and I gasped in air. The sounds and lights slowed into lava lamp bubbling lights with only one high-pitched keening sound. It was still a lot, so I clutched what I was pretty sure were my ears. Then everything went dark and silent.

♦♦♦

"You okay, Lina?"

I blinked, realizing I was lying on my side. I rolled over to my back and looked up. My head was on Asha's lap and her face was above mine. She smiled and leaned down to kiss me. We were on a long, red couch and she had a large bowl of popcorn on the cushion next to her. She petted my hair and fed me popcorn. Chewing, I sat up and saw that a window as long as the couch was directly in front of us. The cosmos were swirling past, leaving streaks of color on my retinas.

"Wow, that's beautiful," I breathed. Glancing at Asha's face, I asked her, "How did you get here?"

Asha laughed. "You don't remember flying that small UFO into our living room? You landed it on the coffee table and emerged from it the size of a Barbie doll. Then you excitedly talked me into coming with you, explaining that the, I think you called it a box-bot, had promised that it could bring us back at this exact time as if we never left."

"Oh," I yawned, feeling so very tired.

"Sweety, you've had a very full day." She gently lowered me back into her lap as our gray tabby, Nebula, curled up behind my knees with our black cat, Centaurus. "Why don't you go back to sleep? When you wake, we'll be in another galaxy."

Her eyes shone orange. But when I looked again, her eyes were back to being amber. I closed my eyes and nodded into

248

her lap. As I drifted off, I thought it was just too bad that Asha wasn't able to wear something more comfortable than my overalls.

18

Kaleidoscope

EMMA ALICE JOHNSON

From somewhere outside the darkness that encased her, she heard movement. Something closed in. A muffled voice said, "I'm going to do this, aren't I?" Then, "What's one box anyway?" With that, the darkness ripped open. Light poured in from outside, and the butterfly could see that the tiny black world she'd been born into was no world at all, but a tiny box, and that was far from the worst part of it.

The massive pale creature that had torn open her confines stared down at her, put a hand to its mouth and gasped. "Oh no," it said.

Below and around her, packed tightly in the box, were other butterflies, Painted Ladies like her, with their furry copper bodies and black-tipped orange wings. Most lay unmoving, dead. Some hadn't even made it out of the cocoons they'd been in when stuffed into the box. Their limp bodies hung from cracks in those brown, leaf-like shells. Here and there an antennae twitched or a wing flapped.

The pale creature moved its face closer, reached a hand in, and raked through the butterflies. She flew out of the box, past the giant. Oh, how it felt to fly, to truly fly! She hadn't realized there could be more to life than what she'd experienced in the confines of that dark box. Her wings beat against the air, circling around the giant's head as it wept into the box.

She understood its sadness, looking into that box full of corpses, but she was alive, and so was the giant. Why mourn when their lives were obviously so fragile and finite? There was no time for such indulgences. They could live. They could fly. What more was there?

But as she soared around the crying giant, she realized she had only escaped into another box. This one wasn't as dark as her last, but just as confining with its flat, beige walls. She wanted to fly higher, further. The biggest difference though, was that this box came with an opening into a larger world—an even brighter world.

She flew at it. When she reached it, her body stopped suddenly. A cold, invisible barrier stood between her and everything out there, bright and green and blue. She tried again, flying away and then back at it again, only to be blocked once more. No matter how fast she flew at it, no matter the angle, she could not get past the barrier. She needed to find a way out of this box. Now that she was free, she desired absolute freedom!

She fluttered back to the giant. Perhaps it was big enough to help her escape this box? Perhaps it wanted to escape, too! Perhaps it had been shoved in here when it was a mere cocoon, just like she'd been in that box it held in its strange, pale appendages. She alighted on the giant's shoulder and waved her wings frantically to get its attention.

"What is this?" it asked, still gazing into the box. "Why would anyone do this?"

She didn't understand why the giant was just sitting there, sobbing. What attachment did it have to all the death in that box anyway? Didn't it want to leave here? To fly away? Couldn't the giant see how easy it would be for something of its size to escape? She flapped around its head some more, desperately hoping to get its attention.

"Wait!" the giant exclaimed, standing suddenly. "There are more live ones!"

It turned the box upside down. Dead cocoons and insect corpses poured out onto the glossy wooden floor. But look, there was life there after all! The giant was right. Yes, many had not survived their confines, but now spread out and released from the crushing weight of the death pile, the live butterflies could fly, dozens of them, hundreds of them, a whole cloud that filled up this slightly larger box, swirling back and forth around the giant, who spun around, mouth agape, watching the orange and black wings whipping around.

As the sheer joy of their first escape wore off, she marshalled the kaleidoscope of butterflies together, flew them toward the clear barrier that kept them from the larger world outside and the distant yellow orb whose warmth she could feel even inside here. She demonstrated how, when she flew at it, she stopped suddenly and could go no further. She begged them to fly with her, to combine their strength and break through. The others fluttered around, confused and worried, but she insisted they could escape as long as they worked together.

Convinced, they circled the inside of the beige box as one. After picking up enough momentum, they turned and pummeled the barrier. As one, they were brought to a halt, sliding from the cold, clear barrier down to the floor. They hadn't been strong enough. Now they were trapped again, from one prison to another. She gazed at the bodies that littered the floor around the giant's feet. Perhaps they were better off even, never having known that there was more to the world than the darkness in that box. How long now until she joined them?

"You're trying to get out," the giant said, joining the Painted Ladies at the window. With a power the butterfly could not imagine, it grabbed the bottom of the barrier and lifted it up.

The freshness of the world outside hit her so hard she could barely move, the complete opposite of the dank stagnancy of the dark box where she'd been born. The other butterflies did not experience the same paralysis. They poured through the opening, their wings decorating the world outside, adding their orange and black to the blue and green and yellow. She soon joined the cloud, dancing through the warm air of true, unrestrained freedom. This was life! This was what she'd been meant for, what they'd all been meant for! Not some confining darkness!

Flying was different out here than in the little box or in the slightly bigger box. The air around her wings seemed alive, blowing and moving in its own way, forcing her to react, to twist and turn, and totally relearn what it was to fly, and she loved it.

As she looped joyously around a massive leafy growth that reached from the ground into the air, she glanced back at the box she had come from. In the opening she and the other butterflies had flown through, the giant stood. Water dripped from its eyeballs. It stuck its head out into the open world, but went no further.

She saw now how pale the giant truly was, absolutely colorless. Not a fleck of orange or any other color on its body. Even the cloth draped over it was bland. Was it even from this world? She couldn't imagine something so colorless being part of a world filled with such richness. Perhaps it had been caged in that beige box so long it had turned beige, too.

She flew back to the giant, flapped her wings at it. She encouraged it to join her and the rest of the painted ladies. Couldn't it see the joy they were experiencing? Why wouldn't it join them? Then she realized it didn't have wings. Not only was the giant colorless, it could not fly. It had freed the butterflies from the prison, but could not do the same for itself.

As fast as she could, she flew to catch the other butterflies before they could disperse. She gathered them together, begged them to return to the prison, only for one brief moment, only long enough to make sure they could all experience this freedom. It took a while to organize them, to convince them to pause their frolicking. The giant remained in place the whole time, staring at them through the opening in its beige box.

Finally, she led them back, the whole cloud of them. They seeped back into the prison, wings bouncing off each other. As soon as she crossed through the opening, she experienced a moment of panic. What if she could not escape this box again? What if the giant slammed the barrier down behind them? What if it had been the one imprisoning them all along?

No, she refused to believe that, not with the sad expression it wore, how it brightened upon their return. They swarmed the giant, pushing in close to its fleshy body, catching it with their antennae, their legs, their wings, anything. Then, as one, they lifted it off the ground as if it weighed nothing. The giant shouted joyfully as the cloud of butterflies carried it through the opening and into the sky outside. It stretched out its arms as if they were wings, flapping them along to the beating of the butterflies against the air.

They swooped to the ground and then up again. The giant howled with joy. The cloud of butterflies circled other boxes that dotted the landscape. Her happiness abated briefly upon seeing them, wondering what kind of world this was, filled with prisons within prisons? Who had made them and why? She let the thought pass and gave in to the feel of the breeze on her wings. She would not be put in another box. Never again.

"Wooo!" the giant shouted, the cloud of butterflies dense around it.

One by one, butterflies started to leave the cloud, distracted by this new world, eager to explore all of it. They fluttered away, slowly dispersing, until those that remained began to sink under the weight of the giant. She stayed, of course, clinging to its furry head with her legs.

From below, other giants screamed and pointed. She hadn't noticed before, but there were many of them, just like the one she and her kaleidoscope carried. Those giants panicked as the butterflies and their giant descended, picking up speed on the way. The butterfly wondered why they were so upset? What would happen when the giant touched the ground? Would it be returned to its prison? As much as she would hate for that to happen, she and the other butterflies could not carry the giant forever. It was too big.

"I'm flying!" the giant yelled to the others below. "This is beautiful!"

Still, the other giants did not sound like they recognized the beauty.

She still clung to the giant that had released her, but she was one of very few butterflies that remained. Her wings no longer had much effect. No matter how hard she flapped, the weight of the giant dragged her down toward the ground. The rest of the kaleidoscope dissipated, releasing their grip and flying away, but she clung tight, sinking her black legs deeper into its furry head, strengthening her grip, futilely struggling to remain aloft.

They struck the ground, landing with a thud on a soft, green mat. The giant struck face first. It did not move. It lay flat, its arms still outstretched as if ready to fly again. She poked it with her proboscis. Flew up and back down, bouncing on its head. Other giants gathered around them, screaming and crying.

"Help him!" they cried.

"Is he dead?" they cried.

Was that it, she wondered? Had he died like so many of the butterflies she'd been encased in darkness with? Well, at least he'd flown. At least he'd known the sky, and he'd shown it to her too, and so many others like her. She felt no sadness, only joy.

But then, the giant unexpectedly stirred beneath her. It grunted and rolled over. The butterfly launched from its furry head and watched from above as it turned upward to face the sky, red fluid draining from all parts of it. It didn't scream and cry like the other giants, though. It laughed and shouted. It shoved both its pale fists into the air and cheered, making sounds the butterfly would have made if she only could—sounds of pure unvarnished happiness.

The other giants shuffled away with their big, land-bound bodies. Now that they saw this one was alive, they were no longer interested. The butterfly stayed a while longer, circling around her savior's face, brushing its pale skin with the tips of her wings, wishing some of her color could come off on it. She hoped the giant understood how grateful she was to it for tearing open that prison and setting her free, for showing her this world.

Finally, she took wing and soared into the blue, the heat from the yellow orb in the sky warming her body. She had so much more to see.

19

The Mover's Tribunal

BEN ARZATE

The die rolled across the floor, all the way to the box that had been moving. It stopped just before it hit. I walked over and looked at it. It had rolled a 19. I couldn't think of any better sign that I should go ahead and open the box. I took my box cutter out of my pocket. I carefully ran the blade along the tape on top, hoping I could cover it up after I'd gotten a look inside.

After I pulled the flaps aside, something popped up. It wasn't fast, but I wasn't able to process it until it was standing straight up before me. It seemed so much taller, even though it was at my eye level. I was looking at the face of my father. His rough, aged skin crinkled as he looked back at me with deep disappointment. His arms were folded over the work shirt I'd seen him wear every day growing up. He shook his head. My face felt hot. My guts felt tight.

"I'm so ashamed," he said in his gruff voice. "After all those lessons I gave you. After going in with such a promising start. I can't believe you failed such a simple test."

"Test?" I said.

"Every mover has to go through a test like this," he said. "This was supposed to be a simple one. I had so much faith in you. I was so certain that you would uphold the sacredness of a client's trust. Yet you couldn't. You just opened the box, like it was nothing."

I dropped my head in shame.

"I thought…" I started to say.

"You didn't think! You wouldn't have opened the box if you did!"

I shut my mouth.

My father stepped out of the box. He looked inside it and shook his head. He pointed to it.

"You know what happens now. You can either get in the box, and I can take you myself right now, or you can try to get away and let the Greater Mover's Union find you. And they will find you."

The choice was obvious. I remembered the stories that my father had told me about the Union. No mover accused of crimes against the Union's bylaws had ever gotten away. Not for good, anyway.

I stepped into the box and crouched down. My father

looked down at me and shook his head one more time. He closed the flaps on the box, leaving me in the cramped darkness. I heard the sound of tape as he sealed me inside.

◆◆◆

I wasn't sure how long I was inside the box. I felt it being lifted, jostled, and pushed several times. I was grateful my father let me keep my phone, so I wasn't bored and left in total darkness. I kept the volume down, though, because I felt a deep sense of shame at the idea of someone hearing it through the thin cardboard.

I felt the box being carried, several voices murmuring around me. It was roughly set on the ground as a single booming voice called for order. All the others went silent. Someone cut open the flaps on the box. It took my eyes a moment to adjust to the light coming in. The booming voice told me to rise again, but I already had begun to, legs stiff from crouching so long.

When I stood up, I looked around. I was inside a warehouse. Movers in different uniforms were sitting behind me on boxes. My father was among them. I could tell he was doing his best not to look me in the eye. In front of me, a tall box resembling a lectern stood with an even taller mover behind it. His hands were folded over the box, and he regarded me with the stony indifference of a manager. A gavel lay next to his hands. A mover with arms so thick, his rolled-up sleeves squeezed his biceps tight and deep approached me. He extended a smaller cardboard box to me.

"Please empty your pockets into this," he said.

I put my wallet, keys, and phone in the box, along with my box cutter and pliers.

"Thank you, bailiff," the mover behind the lectern box said in that booming voice.

He turned his eyes to me.

"Defendant," he said to me, "you are accused of violating the mover's code. Specifically, you are accused of violating a client's trust by opening a box that, to your knowledge, was full of their possessions without their consent. Do you plead guilty, or do you wish to dispute the charge?"

I thought for a moment.

"I'll dispute it."

There was murmuring from the gallery. I looked back and saw my father put his head in his hands. I wondered if I should take it back.

"Very well," the judge mover said. "Do you have any witnesses in your favor you wish to call?"

I shook my head.

"Do you wish to testify to defend yourself?"

"Um… yes."

"Very well. A representative from the Union will cross-examine you."

A tall, thin mover in a blue uniform stood up from the gallery. He walked up next to me with his hands behind his back. He cleared his throat.

"First, please raise your right hand," he said.

I did so.

"Do you swear to tell the truth, as you understand it, under an additional penalty of perjury against the Greater Mover's Union should you fail to do so?"

"I do."

He walked circles around me as I stood there in the box, questioning me. It made me feel even smaller than I already felt.

"How long have you been a mover?"

"About nine months."

"Would you say you're new to the profession?"

"Well, yes, but…"

"But?"

"Well, my father was a mover…"

"And he made you familiar with the mover's code, didn't he?"

"Yes."

"How long has he been teaching it to you?"

"Well, pretty much as long as I can remember. He took a lot of pride in it."

I looked back at my father. His head was down still, avoiding looking at me.

"How long have you been aware of how important the trust of the client is?"

"I… I think I've known as far back as I can remember. My father always talked with disdain about movers who stole from their clients, the men who went through the clothes of their women clients and masturbated on their lingerie, and the ones who went through belongings for blackmail material to extort their clients. I think he hated those movers more than clumsy ones who constantly dropped boxes or lazy ones who were constantly late."

I was supposed to be defending myself, but I was doing a horrible job. I wondered if there was a way I could request a lawyer or someone to represent me. I could tell from looking around the warehouse, I wouldn't find anyone on my side here.

"After all that," the representative said, "you still broke the code and opened the box?"

I thought for a moment. I knew I had to choose my next words carefully. I thought back to my childhood. I would sit enthralled when my father would tell me about the things he had moved that day. He told me about carrying dressers up multiple flights of stairs by himself. He told me about navigating huge beds through narrow hallways to get them into bedrooms. He told me about taking exercise equipment into the homes of clients. Even then, it seemed so funny the way other adults had to work for the strength that came naturally to my father as a mover.

I would imitate him in the way every child who admired their father did. I remembered playing in the spare boxes my father would bring home. I'd put my toys, clothes, and things I found around the house in them and move them from one side of my room to the other. I'd pretend I was barking orders about where to put the boxes to other movers.

I'd move a small plastic chair, pretending I was lifting heavy pieces of furniture like my father did every day. I recalled a time when I spent an entire Saturday emptying the action figures and Hot Wheels in my toy box into a few cardboard boxes, only to move them all to the foot of my bed just a couple of feet away, before emptying the boxes back into the toy box.

I think I first started taking his lessons about the mover's code to heart when, at the age of six, I tried to move a box that I'd filled with books from around the house. It was far too heavy for me, but I still did all I could to lift it by myself. I felt an intense pain in my back. I cried so loudly, my mother and father came running.

My father, familiar with such injuries, knew it was only a minor strain. He gave me an ice pack and a lecture. A mover never foolishly tries to lift what he can't carry by himself. He always seeks the help of others when it's needed.

I wondered if this trial was something I could carry on my own, but I still had nobody I could call in to help me. I looked at my father again. He was still averting his eyes.

I thought back to one day when I was watching the news with him. We sat at attention when we saw that a mover was on the news. They had been instrumental in busting a ring of illegal parrot trading because he found several of the birds bound up in a box owned by one of his clients. My father, a man who loved animals, had told me the mover was a hero. A mover was not to violate the client's trust by checking their boxes, but the extenuating circumstances in this case meant it could be forgiven. I now had a precedent on my side.

"It's in the mover's code to never open a client's boxes, so that we can keep their trust," I said. "However, is it not true that when there are extreme circumstances, this can be forgiven?"

"That is true," the representative said. "Are you trying to argue that there were extreme circumstances in this case? What could those possibly be?"

I told the story of the mover who busted the parrot smuggler from my childhood.

"That story has always remained with me, because my father loved animals and so do I. When I saw the box move, I feared there might be an animal inside, suffering from being trapped."

"Did you have any reason to believe this? Any particular sound? Any type of scratching that you recognized?"

"Nothing in particular," I said. "But that story always stuck with me. I believe that's why I opened the box, even in violation of the code."

There was some more murmuring in the gallery. The judge mover called out for order again.

"This was a standard test that you failed," the representative said. "Your father volunteered because he was so certain you would pass. Yet you failed."

"The test itself must be flawed!" I said. "If the code is going to have exceptions, a mover can't be treated as a failure for not passing a test like this. Could that mover who rescued those parrots be considered a failure?"

The representative looked at the judge. I looked around the room. The movers in the gallery were whispering to each other. My father's head was still down, but his chin was cradled in his hand as if he was deep in thought. The judge mover again called for order.

"I want to confer with the representative of the Union," the judge mover said. "Bailiff, please move the defendant to a holding cell while we recess this tribunal."

The muscular mover who took the contents of my pocket came over to me. He led me to a box a little taller than me in a far corner of the warehouse. He opened the flap, long as a door, for me to step inside. It was roughly the size of a confession booth. He sealed the box with a long strip of tape. There was a square hole in the box, which let me look out. I could see the movers in the gallery getting up and walking around. Some remained seated on their boxes, chattering with each other. I sat down on the hard ground with only a thin layer of cardboard as a cushion.

I heard someone approach my box cell. I looked up, and saw the face of my father through the hole. I stood up to meet his eyes. We looked at each other for a moment.

"Listen," he said, "I didn't do this to hurt you. I said I had faith in you. I meant it. I still have faith in you. A single mistake does not define you as a mover, or as a man. I didn't expect you to defend yourself here, but you're showing you really understand the mover's code. You understand the spirit."

"Thank you, Dad."

"I want you to understand, no matter how this tribunal ends, no matter what the judge mover says, I still love you. You'll always be my son. My son, a mover just like his old man, and I'm proud to call you that. No matter what happens."

I felt tears well up in my eyes.

"I love you too, Dad."

We stood smiling at each other for a moment before he walked away.

I heard murmuring and saw everyone starting to return to their seats. The judge mover was coming back. He banged his gavel for order.

"Bailiff, please retrieve the defendant," he said.

The muscular mover approached the box I was held in. He took out a box cutter, cutting the entire length of the tape with one swipe. He opened the flap and led me back to the box in front of the judge mover.

I got back in that box, standing tall and confident.

"I believe we've reached a decision," the judge mover said. "Do you have anything further to say in your defense?"

"I don't."

"Very well," the judge mover said. "After deliberation with the representative of the Greater Mover's Union, we have determined that the test administered to you is, indeed, flawed. It will require a re-evaluation by the executive council of the Union to be updated."

I breathed a sigh of relief.

"However," he said. "In view of there being no mitigating factors in your decision to open the box, but those that you apparently only thought may exist, your judgment was still flawed. As the test was flawed, I will give you only the minimum sentence. You will serve thirty days in the penal warehouse. Upon release, you will be allowed to continue working as a mover and will remain a member of the Mover's Union. After a period of no less than two years, should you commit no more offenses against the Union or the mover's code, your record will be wiped clean."

The judge mover banged his gavel.

The muscular mover approached me again.

"Please bend down into the box," he said. "We'll be shipping you to the penal warehouse now."

I looked back at my father. He nodded to me, letting me know, without even speaking, that he would be waiting for me as soon as my sentence was over. I couldn't deny I was afraid of what awaited me. The penal warehouse was a trade secret; even movers were discouraged from discussing it with each other, so there was very little known about it. Knowing that I would have my father and my job waiting for me when I came back, however, gave me the courage to face what would be coming.

I squatted in that box. The muscular mover pushed the flaps down. He taped it shut. In the darkness of the box, I could hear the movers in the gallery getting up and discussing my tribunal.

Some said that I had gotten off easy. That I had bullshit my way through the trial and deserved to be run out on a rail. Others said they thought my punishment was too harsh. That my defense was intelligent and articulate, and that the results of this tribunal would advance the trade. Others had little to say about the outcome. That they just wanted to go back to work or to go home and relax.

As my box was lifted and carried away from the chatter of my fellow movers, I couldn't help but wonder how history would remember me and this trial.

◆◆◆

In the penal warehouse, I sleep in a box just long enough to lie in, and just tall enough to stand up. For most of the day, I work moving boxes of random sizes from one end of the warehouse to the other. Some are just empty. Some are filled with various objects so heavy, I can barely lift them myself. I'm not allowed to get assistance from the other movers imprisoned with me. My only breaks are when I return to my box cell to sleep or stop to eat a simple meal, usually consisting of a sandwich and a piece of fruit on the side. There's no entertainment. No internet, TV, or music. There's no time provided for it. There's only carrying the boxes, going back and forth and back again. The only thing provided in our box cells is a copy of the mover's code and a copy of the bylaws of the union. I read them before lights out. In the morning, when I again must carry the boxes, I contemplate the mover's code. I think about how to be a better mover. I've only been here two weeks, and I find myself close to breaking. I find myself wanting to fall down to the cold, concrete floor, and refuse to move anymore.

Then I think about the words my father spoke to me before I came here, and they keep me going on.

20

Section 20

ERIC HENDRIXSON

A die can be cast in any number of ways—as a projectile, cast off as litter, tied to a line and cast as a fishing weight. But for the roll to mean something, a value has to have been assigned from the beginning, same as for a word, same as for a man. So he picked up the die without looking at how it landed. Even if he'd scored a natural 20, which was unlikely, it wouldn't have answered anything. The contents of a client's boxes were none of his business. That was moving guy 101.

But still, something was moving inside the box, with a crinkling, scratching sound.

Boredom wasn't usually a problem, since sometimes as the day wore on, the repetition put him in a zen state, a sort of unconscious momentum, where his body kept moving even as his mind blanked out. How can you tell the dancer from the dance? Who can tell the moving man from what he moves? He is in the boxes. He is of the boxes. Still, he was glad that something had finally happened to make this day different from the thousands of other days, and his mind latched onto the novelty. The box jolted, like something was kicking inside.

If he were careful, he could open the box, check inside, and then seal it again without the customer seeing that anything had been disturbed. Most people want their privacy. Opening someone else's boxes without them present is the ultimate sin, but if they didn't notice, it would be like it didn't happen.

To make this work, he needed a razor blade and some packing tape of the same color that the customer had used to seal the box. His cardboard-brown uniform came with a black lifting belt for back support, and the belt had a small sheath on it, so the moving man had a utility knife on him most of the time. There would also be some packing tape in the truck. But when he turned toward the truck and reached for his keys, the tape was already in his left hand. So he knelt on his Home Depot knee pads and held the box steady between his knees.

As he bent over the box, it grew wider, the way a window grows larger as you look through it. He clicked the utility knife open a couple clicks, and as he drew it a few inches across the tape sealing the top of the box, he felt a thin pull at his forehead. Then, he pried the lid up with his fingers, not far enough to crease the cardboard or to be noticed at first glance. He turned his head to peer into the box with his left eye.

He took a small flashlight, normally used to check corners and to look under furniture for those clients who paid extra to have their furniture reassembled. With stealth, like a child sneaking in his parent's closet the week before Christmas, he parted the incision, shone a light into the box, and pressed his cheek against the cardboard to see through the tiny gap.

The box seemed larger on the inside than the outside. Inside, the box looked like the whole world, but really, most things are larger on the inside than the outside, like a closet, an eye, France, the grave. From the outside, it's just another place. The moving man saw a single, dilated pupil in the yellow beam. He started back, then looked again. He blinked at the eye, and the eye blinked back at him.

Maybe there was a mirror in the box, like some stupid zen riddle from a '70s Kung Fu movie, but that wouldn't explain the movement. He blinked twice, once quickly and once slowly, and the eye matched his gaze again. As he focused on the box, he felt sweat pooling on his forehead. It gathered liquid and weight until it fell.

A drop of blood shattered against the cardboard flap. The moving man shot back from the box like a crawdad, his tail scooting back and his hands open in front of him. Bent over the box, his knees spread wider as he looked closer at the box until he was almost in a child's pose, his legs spreading wider and his head lowering.

For this to work, the box had to look unchanged. It was okay to sweat on the boxes, but blood would draw attention. He wiped at the blood with the sleeve of his uniform. But the coveralls were plain brown canvas. He looked around for something more absorbent.

Next to the headboard, there was a pile of cardboard and packing blankets—the kind of thing used as padding for the more fragile but awkward furniture. He grabbed a blanket without getting up, pulled it to him, and wiped at the blood until it was a faint stain on the cardboard.

More blood dripped onto the box, and the moving man wiped his face. It came away warm and wet, and the general tension in his head focused on a center of pain. As he'd cut open the box, a line had opened on his forehead and was bleeding bright but thin blood. As his eyebrows saturated, the blood dripped into his eyes, stinging and blocking his vision.

He wiped the blood off of the box, but more blood fell as he scrubbed at the cardboard. Still another drop fell, and another. The task was impossible as long as he kept bleeding. He scooted back into child pose again, protecting the box with his belly and trying to catch the blood in the blanket. He knew there wouldn't be any bandages in the truck. The first aid kit held empty wrappers, expired acetaminophen, and a stale pack of cigarettes. So much for the company health plan.

The moving man pinched the cut closed between his fingers and sealed it with packing tape. He didn't reach for the tape or go to the truck for the tape; the tape had always been in his left hand. He didn't make a smooth job of it.

When you're patching yourself up, it never looks like professional work. There was a crosshatch pattern of tape across his head, stained tape covered with more tape until it was thick and stiff, but the bleeding was slowing down. He wiped his hands somewhat cleaner against the blankets. They were still sticky and stained red, but there wasn't blood dripping off of them anymore.

He scrubbed his blood off the box with a cleaner blanket, but as he worked it became difficult to tell the bloody blanket from the clean one. The moving man covered the incision he'd made with new tape. Then, since the new tape was stained with blood, he covered that with more tape. Then he covered any stains in the cardboard with tape and any stains in the tape with more tape.

When he stepped back to inspect his work, it was more tape than box, still smeared with what might be, under the circumstances, a relatively acceptable amount of blood. He took one of the empty boxes from next to the headboard and assembled it quickly. He put the box inside of the box and quickly sealed it closed. He decided that nobody would see bloodstains on that box unless they were looking for them or unless the lights were on.

The cut stung, and he pressed the tape tighter against it with his left hand and got up to leave. But at the door, something inside his head moved. Had he sealed the first box all the way? It was fine enough to have put it inside another box, but how could he know that the box he had sealed had remained sealed?

He could remember it, sure, but what use is memory when it looks so much like imagination; when we can't really see the past? He found another collapsed box, leaning against the wall where it had been used as padding for the dresser. There were always plenty of boxes. So he checked the seal on the second box and put it inside another box. Sealing each corner and seam of the box, he placed the second box inside a third box and sealed it tight. That should take care of that.

But each time he reached the door, something inside his chest moved. Could he be sure that the box had stayed closed? He couldn't see it. He couldn't know without unsealing the box. The box could be placed in another box, but how could he be certain that the box was still sealed once he looked away? Were the bloodstains visible?

The thought was like an itch in his head, like a small animal scratching inside, barely noticeable, but impossible to ignore. The boxed box went into another box. Then, just to make sure, he put the box inside another box and sealed it closed. And when there was a sixth, and then a seventh layer of cardboard, he still wasn't certain. Still, the box moved. It rose around him, cardboard walls smooth with the use of a thousand moves. Because he was the moving man, and he'd always moved. He was in the box. He was of the box.

He didn't have to go to the truck or reach for the tape. The tape had always been in his hand, and he sealed every seam in every direction. Walled in cardboard, the moving man held the box as tightly as he could and stopped moving. Opening the box would be the ultimate sin, but he didn't open the box.

The box had opened him, and he didn't want to see or know what was inside.

◆◆◆

A call came from the hallway, "Hey, keys, man!" Then, a head poked into the room. "The keys aren't in the truck. Do you have them?"

The moving man wished he could remember his name. He must have had one. Why did he never bother to get to know anyone? Maybe the man could help him. Maybe he could hear him. He shook the box in his arms and tried to scream the man's name.

The mover looked. Something inside a box moved, but that was impossible. Then he dropped his hand into the pocket of his brown coveralls. It had been a long day. "Shit. In my pocket the whole time," he muttered. "Hey, never mind," he yelled down the hall. "I have them." He shook his head and looked away. He turned the light off, left the room, locked the door, and dumped the last few boxes in the entryway. There was almost nothing left. Ultimately, it wouldn't matter if a few things were in the wrong rooms. Nothing was damaged. The clients would be happy. He locked up, left, and forgot about the day, the place, and the box.

Employees Of The Month

Employees of the moving company carry no cash and cannot be held liable for damages.

———

David Scott Hay makes a mean old fashioned and the best ribs on the block. He is a former award-winning Chicago playwright and screenwriter. As a novelist he is a two-time Kirkus Prize Nominee for *The Fountain* and *[NSFW]*. His new novel *The Butcher of Nazareth* will be released March '25 by Whisk(e)y Tit Books. He is a member and volunteer for the SFWA (mentor) and HWA (juror). When not city hopping to sell books, DSH now lives in a valley between the ocean, the mountains, and the desert with his wife, son, dog, chickens, and a dozen typewriters. www.davidscotthay.com for more whatnot.

———

Garrett Cook is a Wonderland Award winning author and editor of Horror and Bizarro fiction. His latest, *Charcoal* from CLASH books is available now in print and audio book and is being translated into Spanish.

Brian Keene is the author of over fifty books and three-hundred short stories, mostly in the horror, crime, fantasy, and non-fiction genres. When I asked him for a 100 word bio, he directed me to his website and said I could pick 100 words from there at my discretion. Since I've already used about 60 words, here are some others chosen from his site to round this out: zombies, media, properties, film, hosted, popular, the, father, cats, Pennsylvania. I should add that he once said of me: "Michael Allen Rose, much like Joe R Lansdale, is a genre unto himself, and always an enjoyable read." So, there's that.

Laura Lee Bahr is an author, filmmaker, and performer of our scrappy indie multiverse. She is the author of *Haunt* (Winner of Wonderland Book Award 2011), *Long-Form Religious Porn,* and *Angel Meat* (Winner of Wonderland Book Award 2017) all from Fungasm press. She is the writer/director of *Boned* (Gravitasmovies.com) and director and co-writer (with Chris Kelso) of the short *Strange Bird.* She also works on creating dynamic educational content with the New England Primate Conservancy and is a co-recipient (with Ezra Werb) of a National Geographic Educators grant at thebugidea.com… And there's more at lauraleebahr.com

Brian Pinkerton takes everyday, ordinary people and puts them through a living hell. His cruelties include *The Intruders* (Flame Tree Press), *The Nirvana Effect* (Flame Tree Press), *Killer's Diary* (Samhain Publishing), *Anatomy of Evil* (Samhain Publishing), *Rough Cut* (Bad Moon Books), *How I Started the Apocalypse* (Severed Press), *Vengeance* (Leisure Books), and *Abducted* (Leisure Books). Select titles have also been released as audio books and in foreign languages. His short stories have appeared in PULP!, Chicago Blues, Zombie Zoology, and The Horror Zine. His newest book, *The Perfect Stranger*, will be released in November 2024. Brian lives in the Chicago area with his wife and two innocent children. He invites you to visit him at www.brianpinkerton.com.

Matthew Henshaw (he/him) is a writer living in Central IL with his wife and cat. He is the co-editor/creator of the *Nafallen University Course Catalog* from Madness Heart Press, and his stories have appeared in several anthologies and webzines. He is also the creator and head writer of *Olde Wyathscope's Quarterly Concern*, a weird almanac with art by visionary creative Mat Fitzsimmons. Henshaw also composes uneasy listening you find at pentamethdemon.bandcamp.com. When he isn't creating, he wrangles 1s and 0s. For YOU.

Bridget D. Brave writes weird and whimsical horror from the foothills of the St. Francois mountains. She can be found nearly everywhere online @beedeebrave.

Mykle Hansen is. He didn't send me a bio, but I thought it was important that you know he exists. After the deadline, he did send a bio, which reads: Mykle Hansen is odorless, colorless, and tasteless, yet he affects millions of Americans each year. Left untreated he can lead to bicycles, sound, comedy, Portland Oregon, and grievous bodily injury. Stay informed for better outcomes—ask your doctor about Mykle Hansen today!

Cynthia Pelayo is a Bram Stoker Award and International Latino Book Award winning author and poet. She lives in Chicago with her family.

John Wayne Comunale lives in the neon-drenched city of sin, Las Vegas, to prepare himself for the heat in Hell. He is the author of *Death Pacts and Left-Hand Paths*, *Deadline*, *As Seen On T.V.*, *Sinkhole*, *The Cycle* and more. He hosts the weekly storytelling podcast John Wayne Lied to You and fronts the punk rock disaster johnwayneisdead. He currently travels around the country giving truly unique and most excellent performances of the written word. Visit johnwayneisdead.com for more.

Chris Meekings is a writer from Gloucester in the UK. Several of his works have appeared on Bizarro Central's Flash Fiction Friday. His bizarro novellas, *Elephant Vice* (released in 2015 via Eraserhead Press) and *Moon Mayor* (released 2022 by Hybrid Sequence Media) are unquestionably things that he wrote. His novel, *Ravens and Writing Desks*, (released in 2016 by Omnium Gatherum) is also a thing that he wrote. His latest novella, *Cthulhu Fishing Off The Iraq Nebula* (released 2023 by Planet Bizarro), is not only a thing he wrote but is also available on Audible, so it's a thing that he wrote that you can listen to. He is a founding member of the British Bizarro Community who recently released the anthology *The Bumper Book of British Bizarro*. None of his works have appeared on toilet walls. He is currently 58 weasels in a trench coat, just looking for love.

Christine Morgan's work spans a variety of genres and settings, from historical to cosmic, from superheroes to smut, from humor to extreme horror, and often combinations thereof. Despite much praise, winning a Splatterpunk Award, and even collaborating with the legendry Edward Lee, she still has imposter syndrome like whoa. After several recent traumatic and turbulent life upheavals, she currently resides in the high desert with her hermit-recluse dad, where she also reviews, edits, makes weird crafts, and gets bossed around by cats. Links and such can be found at: https://christinemariemorgan.wordpress.com/

John Baltisberger plainly stated, is the greatest khabbalist game designer and body horror author of our age who also happens to leave dried clay wherever he steps. 367 arrests, 0 convictions.

Susan Snyder is a two-time Splatterpunk Award nominated writer of horror fiction and poetry. Her debut poetry collection, *Broken Nails*, was released in 2020 and was nominated for a 2021 Elgin award. Her follow up collection, *Picking Scabs*, was released in 2023. In 2021, *Encyclopedia Sharksploitanica* came out to rave reviews. A comprehensive tongue-in-cheek guide to 85 of the best and worst shark movies known to mankind, this book highlights Susan's love of self-deprecating humor and satire. Her novel collaboration with Splatterpunk award winning writer, Christine Morgan, will arrive in 2024.

Lauren Bolger is the author of Supernatural/Occult Horror novel *Kill Radio*, a 2023 Malarkey Books title. Her short Horror has appeared in In Somnio, a Tenebrous Press Modern Gothic anthology and Tales from the Clergy, an October Nights Press anthology based on songs by the band Ghost. Her next book, titled *The Barre Incidents*, a Cryptid Thriller, is slated for release in 2025 with Malarkey. Lauren is a music-obsessed amateur drummer and spends most of her time with her husband, kids, and their cat, Maggie.

Christopher Hawkins is the award-winning author of *Downpour* and *Suburban Monsters*. He is the former editor of the One Buck Horror anthology series and the co-chair of the Chicagoland chapter of the Horror Writers Association. When he's not writing, he spends his time exploring old cemeteries, lurking in museums, and searching for a decent cup of tea.

J9 Vaughn (they/them) is a queer librarian who lives in a town with more dead than living and may have traveled the cosmos in a past life. Their publications include Ludlow Charlington's Doghouse Anthology, Whigmaleeries & Wives' Tales, and Hair Trigger 2.0 among others. They reside with their bestie/partner, a motley crew of rescue cats, random foster kittens, and an assortment of housemates. You can find them at theincomparablej9.com

Emma Alice Johnson grows wildflowers and writes. She lives on a farm dedicated to conservation of native plants and endangered insects. She has released a number of zines, chapbooks, micro press and art press novellas. Her short fiction has appeared in more than 75 publications. When she isn't planting or writing, she can be found running through the woods with her pet pig, singing to her chickens, lifting weights, watching B-movies, or reading while snuggled with her cat. Learn more at www.freaktension.com.

Ben Arzate lives in Des Moines, IA. He is the author of several books, including the story collection *The Complete Idiot's Guide to Saying Goodbye* from Feel Bad All The Time, the short novel *Saturday Morning Mind Control* from D&T Publishing, and the play collection *PLAYS/hauntologies* from Madness Heart Press. The latest one is the novel *If today the sun should set on all my hopes and cares…* from Unveiling Nightmares. He also assisted fellow Iowa author Rob Ramirez in editing and publishing his debut novel *Doomsday Daytrip* from Swann + Bedlam. Find him online at dripdropdripdropdripdrop.blogspot.com.

Eric Hendrixson is the writer of *Bucket of Face* and the beloved American Classic *Drunk Driving Champion*.

Courtney Rader (designer) is a multifaceted artist who finds inspiration in a plethora of the world's intricate details. Occasionally people are affected by a fey spirit known for creating photos and designs. Her name is Courtney and she can be summoned with an offering of a soy milk latte, a plate of various weird fruit, and the promise of an adventure. Her lens captures meticulously crafted photo sets that breathe life into narratives, while her design work transforms ideas into tangible realities. Go to www.courtneyrader.com please.

Michael Allen Rose (editor) is an award-winning writer, musician, editor, and performance artist based in Chicago, Illinois. His stories have appeared in The Magazine of Bizarro Fiction, Heavy Feather Review, and Tales From The Crust among other periodicals. He has published several books including *Jurassichrist* (Perpetual Motion Machine Publishing) which won the 2021 Wonderland Award for best bizarro novel, and *The Last 5 Minutes of the Human Race* (Madness Heart Press), winner of best collection in bizarro fiction 2022. He is the host of the annual Ultimate Bizarro Showdown at Bizarro Con in Oregon. Michael also releases industrial music under the name Flood Damage. He lives with an awesome cat named Dr. Light, and enjoys good tea. You can find more at www.michaelallenrose.com